PRAISE FOR ANDREW FORREST BAKER

"*The House That Wasn't There* is utterly riveting. A meditation on trauma and loss, Andrew Forrest Baker has created iridescent stars to a constellation that you won't fully connect until the last page. Simultaneously vivid and blurred, this book pulses with heart."

-Jenny Sadre-Orafai, author of *Dear Insiders*

"Intense, intriguing, and philosophical, *The House That Wasn't There* is a modern approach to the gothic that feeds our biggest fears...a prominent metaphor on its own. In all sense, Baker demonstrates that sometimes the haunted ones are the body and the human mind by our inner demons, trauma, and sicknesses."

-*Inkish Kingdoms*

THE HOUSE THAT WASN'T THERE

ANDREW FORREST BAKER

©2022 Andrew Forrest Baker
Cover ©2022 Drew Holden

-First Edition

Publisher's Cataloguing-in-Publication Data

Baker, Andrew Forrest
    The house that wasn't there / written by Andrew Forrest Baker
ISBN: 978-1-953932-13-6

1. Fiction - General I. Title II. Author

Library of Congress Control Number: 2022945140

To Sean, for giving me the key.

To those who found no other way.

To all those left behind.

THE HOUSE WAS COLD, even in the dead of summer, and sat there, halfway up the block like an insolent child who refused to go to his room and planted himself in the hallway——out of place and small, but with a great air about it that echoed down the alleys in the evenings. Can houses have tempers? Its temperament was one of frustration at times, solace at others. It sat there, halfway up the street, begging to be cared for, to rebel. A child mind trapped behind the sweeping grey shutters, the robin egg siding. A container for life. An imagination run wild.

Two words filled Rafe's head. Two. Words. Not echoes. Not repeating. Two simple words growing so large they jockeyed to drown out thought altogether. What and If. The question. The ellipsis. The precipice.

This is where it all started to unravel. Threads like splinters fraying, twisting, jabbing beneath the fingernails. This is when it shifted. On a Tuesday morning. Nothing exciting ever happened on a Tuesday morning before this one. A gentle dew slowly evaporated off the dandelions and crab grass that pushed through the concrete slabs of the sidewalk, a fabricated rainbow that shifted the morning sun prism ever so slightly so that, if the eyes were in just the right spot, revelation was possible. The breeze, too, gentle and provocative, sifting through the baby hairs along the necklines of all the dawn walkers, wafted the frog footed leaves of the ginkgo trees just so to lay bare the house. The house that wasn't there. The house with the temper. Forgotten for decades or centuries——time worked funny there——and, on a Tuesday morning, revealed behind the wrought iron fencing, the two story, grey shuttered, child mind construction forgotten within the brick and mortar, cement and steel that licked the ash laden sky. Discovered and reborn in the late summer of the earliest year of a tantrum.

Rafe's hands clutched at the spiderwebbed metal of the gate. Cold against his palm, it sent a shiver out to linger beneath his capillaries. Fore-

THE HOUSE THAT WASN'T THERE

boding tiptoed across his stomach, a troupe of ballerinas threatening to trade their tutus for fatigues, their promenade for a march. The latch gave easily. Lost air whispered out onto the street and jostled the car alarms to activity for three square blocks. Rafe listened as the lock slipped back into place and the streets returned to silence. His breath was still and imposing and constant. Wind picked up in swirling gestures of starry nights and water lilies along the city sidewalks of an early dawn. And even as the sun peaked its first colossal rooftop, blistering the sky in tangerine and persimmon, Rafe felt an unexpected darkness fall, its density cold and stern on his shoulders, as he tested a knob that couldn't help but turn.

Silence had never been a good listener. There was simply too much going on inside of it. Too many ideas cultivated and left to run half cocked, half formed and limping through the abyss. Silence was said to be so easily broken but only to defer blame from itself. So when Rafe called out to the hollows, when his questioning salute reverberated from the peels in the wallpaper, found its way beneath the once white sheets draped over maple and tweed cushioning, and peered, wide eyed, into every room all at once: silence broke, smiled, and went to say hello.

1

THE HOUSE THAT WAS. T DHERE

"LIGHTS ARE COMING ON, GENTS."

A cascade of groans waved over the chestnut bar top, swirled around the condensation rings of long forgotten lagers and scotch whiskeys, and, invigorated by the fumes lingering still above the pour spouts, leapt up to dim the incremental rise of the overhead bulbs.

"I know, fellas, but I've got quite the walk home myself after cleaning up from you lot. And much less of the rotgut keeping me warm from the gullet."

The patrons at The Maiden Name were a stable crew. They liked their ales frothy and their spirits without mixers, which made for an easy paycheck for me. In the year and a half since I first stepped onto the rubber mats behind the bar, I'd learned to appreciate the idling idiosyncrasies that sat waiting to burst forth from them with each new drop of alcohol. They perched on their barstools, asked for change in ones, and occasionally sang along with the rarely tuned piano that overtook the seldom used dance floor. It took a while for them to warm to new faces and for the innuendo to quell from their orders, but by now I felt accepted, finally one of them.

The Maiden Name was a chimera of eras, cobbled and masoned together throughout time as if it wasn't sure when to end. A bricked lion's mane sometimes patched by the slitted wood panel eyes of a goat and tied together with the venom dripping snake fangs of neon posters from shows and events long past. The bar stretched nearly the length of the room with matching mirror backed shelving against the wall and holiday lights tacked up to give the bottles an eerie yet inviting glow. The bar stools looked like they fell out of the backdoor of a 1940s all nite diner, complete with grease stains and ripped white cotton spewing black vinyl. There were always three or four of them haphazardly placed around the baby grand in the corner just in case anyone wanted to perch nearer the music, but

THE HOUSE THAT WASN'T THERE

Lonnie nervously eyed his tip jar whenever anyone was within snatching range which, in turn, turned his melodies into stilted, music box versions of Top 40 numbers so obnoxious most of the drinkers chose to stay closer to the bar. About a third of the onyx concrete floor had been covered with yellowing linoleum at some point over the years, and the tacked silver aluminum divider meant to keep the flooring down had turned almost black with decades of sweat and grime caked into its lined rivets. Plastic beaded curtains draped across the entrance to the gender neutral bathroom, and an old saloon style swinging door led the way into the bottle and keg storage room behind the bar. Patch jobs were more cost effective than a remodel, so over time all that was left of The Maiden Name were a series of shrines to what had been broken and replaced.

"Sir?" I waved a dish rag in front of the slender, copper skinned man at the far end of the bar. He had come in alone, downed half of his beer, and sat, eyes glazed over, staring at some point beyond the wall before him. "I have to get everybody out of here before I can count down the till."

The man sat unblinking. A tan trilby that perfectly matched his loose fitting trench coat rested adjacent to his tapping pinky finger. His cheeks seemed to flush and then to pale, even as his expression remained dormant. His eyes, though, when I got close enough to see them clearly, were trembling ever so slightly, agitated and pulsing while doing their best to remain unnoticed. Eyes can be tricky that way. More revealing than receiving. I didn't recognize him for a regular as I reached to remove the pint glass held firm in the man's grip. But there was something that told me I should remember him somehow. As if we were kindred spirits. Or he'd bagged my groceries once.

"'You don't have to go home....'" I cheesed.

At the mention of home, the man broke his trance. His fingers, blue and calloused, relaxed, and I swiped the glass quickly. I tossed the unfinished beer into the dump sink in one automatic, well practiced gesture. The froth sizzled around the drain. The old man's fist enveloped my wrist.

"Home can be a funny sight when the wind blows just so." His voice: an exodus of moths from an old trunk, fluttering ecstatically in newfound freedom yet longing to return to the feast within all the same.

I smiled and gently pried my arm free. "That's why you're here, is it? I mean, that's why I'm a bartender to begin with, I guess. Most of us here, wandering the late night circuit, prefer the company of strangers to the comforts of our own four walls. It's the pack mentality embedded in the solitude of the human condition. But, you know, every now and again we have to return to the den to sleep it off."

I let my eyes meet the man's in a knowing, caring pity. I had practiced the look through so many nights with so many men afraid to return to their husbands or their boyfriends or their loneliness. There was a familiarity to them all, a mathematical sadness that crept in vectors around their irises. One I could never quite shake off. But they all responded well to my put on persona of Bartender with a capital "B."

"You aren't hearing——"

Bartending was all about listening. To orders, to sob stories, for slurs in speech that would cut a driver off and call a cab to idle on the street outside. I liked to listen. I was good at it. I had become good at it. Here, at home with Reg, and at my now biweekly meetings.

For me, bartending was also all about temptation: succumbing or overcoming. Three years sober, in view of another challenge, I had taken the job as a test of will. It may not have been the wisest decision, and it was certainly one derided by my sponsor, but my adventurous side needed to see if it could maintain control when faced with the seductive forces of the midnight world. I managed to be victorious, though I did keep a prop bottle filled with apple juice or black tea behind the counter to keep up appearances when the patrons demanded I do a shot with them.

"Hey, Howard. Can I get my pull?"

"Sure thing, Lonnie."

I spun to the register and grabbed cash to payout the pianist.

"Music made under the table always has the sweetest sound," he insisted.

I heard the rasp of the outside echo in as the door pushed open. The old man's silhouette hunched against the frame as he adjusted the trilby on his head. I watched it all in slow motion. The wind outside paused to take him in.

He spoke without turning around: "They'll leave the light on for you."

The door swung shut as Lonnie pocketed his cash and reached for a bottle of gin. He plunked down, always the last one at the bar, and poured himself a healthy splash.

"You know that guy?"

"Just another old coot who's scared of the dark but can't stand the daylight," I said, turning from the door to finish wiping down the glassware. "Along with all the other lost souls who find solace on these barstools."

"Cheers to that!" Lonnie smiled and sucked his cheeks at the bitter bite of juniper. He poured himself another. "And here's to the lost souls left here to serve them."

I smirked and grabbed the bottle of booze to return it to the shelf. I busied myself with my closing duties, but something about the old man kept clawing its way into my vision.

"He did seem familiar, though, didn't he?"

Lonnie shrugged and continued to nurse his drink. He pursed his lips and let them smack with his thoughts like a fish gulping oxygen from water.

"I dunno," he said. "I didn't get a good look at him from the piano bench. But at a glance he reminded me a bit of Reg. Ya know, if he'd packed on forty years at the bottom of a whiskey barrel."

I rolled my eyes. "Alcohol is a preservative, not a dereliction."

"It's both if you're using it right. And thank the fermented gods for that!" Lonnie pushed his cup across the counter and raised his eyebrows. "I know we're closed and all, but give us another shot? I won't even bother paying if it's gonna mess up the till. Wanna do one with me?"

✣

There are parts of the city that never make it onto any maps: cartographic irregularities that have never found a way to manifest atop the paper plane and instead explode or wither in brilliant or forgotten displays all around the planet. Some are bold and obvious, even as folks hurry by them and their supposed normalcy. Others are so hideous or frightening——producing the kind of fear that echoes unacknowledged from within the gut——that they become blank spaces in memory, latitudinal lines left longing for the long way around. These are the lockstep spaces between the dog and the wolf. These are the tiny gasps of air where the mask doesn't quite touch the skin.

Yet, every now and then, they will bare their yellowed fangs, catch the eye of the stationary, nomadic sun, or the reflection of the waning moon finally relinquishing the tides, and they will swell, themselves, with a manic upheaval. The emperor's new clothes. The stepsister's toes. And in those moments, all the vanity and desire that has ever been is manifest, is a manipulated festival of what ifs. Whats and Ifs. See above. As below.

I made it a habit to seek out these spaces. That's what had initially drawn me to The Maiden Name. It's what had drawn me to the city. Anonymity of place could only exist within a population so large each face became a blur. The small town that sired me, with its neighborhood socials and Arbor Day parades, had so few eyes on it that every inch was seen, every pebble was known. The city offered the steely blue stare of too many faces too concerned with themselves to know who butchered their steak, who re-sod the churchyard.

I'd arrived to town nearly a decade and a half prior, wide eyed dreams of the geography diploma that would make me a mapmaker knocking around my frenetic brain. I fancied myself an explorer, much too grand for so small a hometown, always on the run from the minutiae that was. I'd relied on my maps to keep me safe——streetbound in a cardinal direction that was always simply away. Yet when the veins of the city got mixed up, when my maps failed me and the streets shuddered and filled and flushed, and the swell of the river threatened to overtake everything I thought I was, to churn all that I had run from within the tepid waters at my feet, I quit my degree and took to staring past the streetlights to the stars. Constellations were, after all, the plotted points of forgotten place, personified and anthropomorphized into myth, immortalized into street signs for the sailors.

It took me a while to return my gaze to my shoes, though I recognized later that one eye seemed always trained on my navel, but when I did finally find myself grounded, I found Reg; I found The Maiden Name. Besides which, with all the greatest wonders already drawn, I needed different means to discover the world.

The night air was cool, but on it still lingered a bit of the cotton candy humidity of the noontime sun; sticky and sweet smelling and barely there. I made sure the door was locked and the security bar was firmly in place before I turned to face the sidewalks and their 3am rigor. Three had always been the true hour of magic. Midnight was for those who had day jobs. At 3am, there was a stillness, a waiting. The sun busied itself in preparation, cultivating colors and borrowing rights back from the moon, while the witches of the world set to their tasks: paper boys bringing the Word of the Day; delivery men with their spell ingredients: fresh milk and eggs and all those enchanting little bobbles. I enjoyed my walks, absorbing it all, submitting to solace. Though I didn't live far from the bar, I took a new way home each night. It would often take hours as I explored alleyways, tried different blocks, approached the streets from different angles in different orders. I wanted to be alive in the mystical. I needed the stars and streets to align.

As my feet padded the concrete, the porch lights of the early risers began to blink on. I imagined them in their apartments, sluggish and meandering through sense memory alone to prepare for the day, to compose themselves against the traffic of their treks, never even aware of the nocturnal creatures who had managed to survive in their assembled, bold world, schlepping home, returning to rest. Two lights here, then four on the opposite side of the street, counting out the cadence of an irregular time signature: the music of the waking world.

My fatigued, hazel eyes shifted before I turned my head as if drawn by some profundity my synapses had yet to sense. The ginkgo leaves fluttered green to yellow as the bulbs aside each doorway flickered on in the greatest trick of all: something from nothing. As I moved, for a moment, I saw a blackness. Not a darkness, but an empty space between. The skin on my shoulders sucked into my throat, and the hairs on the back of my neck and in the gentle bend of my arms pricked and reached out as if trying to meet the space, to fill it, even as the rest of me instinctively pulled away. It was only there a moment. Had I blinked, I would have missed it.

If only I had blinked.

※

The wood of the stairwell was the grey, splintered drift that washed up on shorelines after heavy storms. Three flights, steep and twisted, angled up along the laurel colored tiles of the walls which stopped at the shoulders on each level and gave way to sooted white drywall that continued the ascension skyward. I could hear my first floor neighbors fumbling around behind their crimson door. A young couple, post-marriage and pre-children, they'd moved into the brownstone a few months prior. They seemed nice enough at the block parties that inevitably popped up during the early warm months as they discussed tax law or the promotions they hoped for at their new, Big City Firms. Molly and Hank, I thought. Something along those lines.

The woman on the second floor seemed always angry. She stomped about to water her ferns and whooped at her television as if it had harmed her in some previous incarnation. Her groceries were brought to her twice weekly, and delivery agents were constantly buzzing my place on accident to gain entry to the building as she'd never scribbled her surname——Wilson——on the call box. Still, when she placed her bulging white plastic trash bags into the hallway, I always smiled as I carried them out to the bins.

I rounded the steps to the third floor, and my key slipped into the lock as I listened for the gurgle of the coffee maker inside. It was a familiar sound that always lulled me into a sense of security. In the six years we had lived together, Reg and I made it a point to share my dinner/Reg's breakfast and Reg's dinner/my breakfast every day that we could. As such, our opposite schedules worked for us. Never once had we run out of mealtime stories. Never had either of us feigned interest.

I pushed the door into a darkened room, surprised that my lover had slept in. He was normally so efficient. One of those one alarm types: never hitting snooze. Flicking on the lights, I slid into the kitchen where the automatic pot was finishing its drip. I pulled two mugs from the cabinet and retrieved the cream and a carton of eggs from the fridge.

"Reg?" I called. "Did you oversleep? Better get up or you'll be late for work."

I listened for the rustle of covers, the creak of the mattress springs. Before any noise met my ears, the sound of shells cracking and two eggs sizzling in the frying pan overwhelmed my senses. I ground pepper over the bubbling white and burnt orange and breathed deeply to take in the aroma of the coffee.

"Reginald Adrian King!" I cooed. "You better get your ass out here."

Reg and I had met on karaoke night at Pale Horse Saloon, a bar just north of midtown where I had been a regular, slinging back the sugary sweetness of fermented corn with such predictability the bartenders kept my stool open for me. Reg had been dragged along one night with the ladies from his office and had sat, begrudgingly, through endless offkey renditions of showtunes, 60s folk numbers, and 80s power ballads with a halfhearted, crooked smile that captivated me immediately. The two of us clicked in an instant, in the way that near opposites could have so much in common. Where I was tall and——though defined——lanky, Reg was short and stocky. My chestnut hair was always a bit shaggy at the temples and around the ears; my chin angled sharply beneath my thin, apple peel lips; my skin, where not covered in brightly colored ink, was fair to the point of translucency. Reg had cool brown skin, natural cinnamon hair, and deep chocolate eyes. He was a day walker but knew how to whisper to the night when it mattered. We challenged and supported one another, and that was all I desired.

I dished the eggs with a firm flip of the spatula and plated them with the coffee mugs on the island countertop that separated the kitchenette from the living room. Sunlight peaked through the curtains, and I became entranced for several moments by the glinting particles of dust dancing in the beams, drifting like wayward children playing at greatness in the spotlight of eternity. They wafted without reason, with no sense of gravity to hold them to learned behaviors. So much of the still world was alive when no one was looking. Of that, I was sure. I enjoyed catching glimpses of the ghosts left in each movement's wake.

I tapped twice on the bedroom door before opening it slowly. The sheets atop the bed were still disheveled from the day before. My stomach churned. Though I often forgot to make the bed myself, Reg always made sure to tuck the covers and fluff the pillows. The table lamp on the tiny oak desk Reg would use when he brought his work home with him was on. The closet door was slightly ajar, but nothing really seemed out of place. I listened for the sounds of water running, but no one was in the bathroom. Reg was not in bed; he was not in the shower. He was gone.

My breath cut my throat. I picked up my phone, but there were no messages. I tried Reg's number, but it rang through to voicemail. I could call the office, but no one would be in yet. I wanted to call the police. They would only ask for forty-eight hours.

I sat on the edge of the mattress and pulled deeply to expand, to calm. Reg was fine. He had simply left earlier than usual. Big day at work. So big, in fact, he'd been too rushed to make the bed, to leave a note. And though out of the ordinary, it was nothing to worry about. Nothing at all. I sat and I breathed and I tried to convince myself I was overreacting. People often have trouble believing the things they tell themselves. I know I did. A remnant of years of rationale and heart sparring just below the consciousness. Escalating quickly into innate distrust. Or perhaps attempting to convince oneself that the previous reaction was the one worth noting.

That the calming voice was the lie, the instinctual response as the brain tried to justify, to cope, to live with seeing what was not there. The deafening absence.

I walked absently to the front of the apartment and plopped down by my dinner. My fork pushed at the yolk, and I watched it brighten to yellow; a rising sun sent to swirl across the plate.

Pictures. The cops would want to see a photograph. I could use the one on my nightstand. Reg looked very handsome in that one. Smiling, but not overly so. Casual. Casual and calm.

I left a message on his voicemail:

"Hey, mister. Guess you left for work a bit earlier than normal today. I missed our morning ritual. Call me when you get a chance. Love you."

Bed. I should just sleep. And Reg would be home when I woke. I pulled the curtains tight to block out the light and let my head meet the pillow. I fluffed the covers or I tucked them between my legs. I pulled them over my head or I kicked my feet out from the bottom. I did everything I was supposed to, but sleep would not come.

I laughed at myself. It was out of character for me to be so worried, so sensitive. But I couldn't shake the thoughts from my body. There was just something that had attached to my chest, tight and resting and waiting for the big reveal. Something was wrong. I instinctively knew it.

❦

No.

❦

The marble of the stairwell was the cool, chiseled stone that somehow found its way from the artist's studio into architecture. Four flights, steep and angled, twisted up along the moss colored tiles of the walls that stopped at the waist on each level and gave way to sooted white drywall that continued the ascension skyward like the lonely green candy cane left behind when everyone had grabbed the reds. I could hear my first floor neighbors fumbling around behind their mahogany door. An odd pair, post-children and pre-retirement, they'd put their place in the brownstone on the market a few months prior in hopes of finding a sum that could send them to a nice yard, a neighborhood association in the suburbs. Holly and Mark, I thought. Or something along those lines.

Mrs. Wilkes, the widow on the second floor, seemed always abuzz with the latest tales of who did, what did, where and how. A reporter's repertoire. A gossip monger never too keen on the why of it all but excited to compose a soap opera from the world around herself. She liked tea——Earl Grey, usually, but sometimes a ripe Darjeeling——and whispered tidbits of varying import by the mailboxes.

"I heard the rabbit died for Polly on the first floor. Just when they thought they were done. Have you met the new girl on four? Did you notice her wrists?"

I smiled and nodded politely at her tales whenever I assisted her in carrying in her groceries. I didn't think she had even once heard my voice.

I rounded the steps to the third floor and smiled as my upstairs neighbor bounded down the stairs beside me. She had moved in a week prior, engrossed in the summer courses for her third year at the university and had thus far refused to speak to anyone she passed. We always shared a knowing nod when we saw each other, though. We felt some internal draw, a knowledge of kinfolk. Ships. Or knights. Passing.

My key slipped into the lock as I listened for the gurgle of the coffee maker inside. It was a familiar sound that always lulled me into a sense of security. In the six years we had lived together, Reg and I made it a point to share my dinner/Reg's breakfast and Reg's dinner/my breakfast as often as we could. As such, our opposite schedules worked for us. Never once had we run out of mealtime stories. Never had either of us feigned interest. I told him tales of the night while he explained the intricacies of day.

I pushed the door into a near dark room, surprised that the man I loved so much had slept in. A soft glow emanated from the salt lamp Reg always left on in the corner of the living room to give the apartment a gentle, golden pink glow. Flicking on the overhead lights, I slid into the kitchen where the automatic pot had just finished its drip. I pulled two mugs from the cabinet and retrieved the pancake batter I'd mixed before work from the fridge.

"Reg?" I called. "Did you oversleep? Better get up or you'll be late for work."

I listened for the rustle of covers, the knock of a headboard against a wall. Before any noise could meet my ears, the sound of the batter sizzling on the skillet overwhelmed me. I dropped fresh blueberries into two of the cakes for myself, chocolate chips in two others for Reg, and breathed deeply to take in the lush, fruity scent of the coffee.

"Reginald Adrian King!" I bellowed in that stern but loving way a mother uses when commanding their child in triplicate. Most mothers, anyway. "You better get your ass out here."

Reg and I found each other nearly a decade prior and despised one another by the end of our first date. I was a fulltime jack of all trades and a parttime dog walker in an attempt to make a dent in the student loans of my unfinished degree. Reg was a flustered, Nervous Nellie wearing a hand me down suit from his father on the way to his first job interview in the Big City. As Reg scampered down the barely familiar streets, I rounded the corner with a Lhasa Apso on a leopard print leash and two Dachshunds nipping at their corded harnesses that clipped Reg at the ankle and sent him tumbling, scuffing his knee and ripping the seam of his jacket pocket in the kerfuffle. We laughed, initially, and decided to meet for a drink sometime. But, by the fifth round of Old Fashioneds and seventh bout of dicey conversation, we parted ways and deleted contacts. The universe had other plans, however, and the magnetic pull of the plains needed to attract the poles.

Myself, graceful and lithe in both body and movement, traveled with the ease of pen across paper, as sure of the grid as I was the curve of the riverbank. Reg was a series of dot dot dots, always starting and stopping, always as if something more was waiting to be discovered beneath his surface. I had chestnut hair that billowed when the wind blew, and I emblazoned my shell with spectrums and designs as if their being——their permanence——was then and always would be relevant. Reg wore the suits his mother wanted to see him in, pursued the positions in the financial district his father deemed important and responsible, and spent what little spare time he had constructing wooden and papier mâché masks that could turn his cool umber skin to fluorescent honeydew, his chocolate eyes to fountains, his dragon fruit lips to action. He was a day walker, concerned with should over want, but after a while, he learned how to whisper to the night when it mattered. The two of us reached a place where we challenged and supported one another, and that was all either of us desired.

THE HOUSE THAT WASN'T THERE

I dished the pancakes with a firm flip of the spatula and placed them with the coffee mugs on the island countertop that separated the kitchenette from the living room. Sunlight peeked through the curtains, and I became entranced for several moments by the glinting reflection of day on the corner of a picture frame above the couch. That compressed plastic and faux copper coating tacked against the expanse of wall flared in a blaze so much more efficient than the moon's, as if it were challenging the godly construct with its factory farm charms. As if it had entered the cave and returned in knowing, in sentience. So much of the still world was alive when no one was looking. Of that, I was certain.

I tapped out the shave and a haircut cadence quietly on the bedroom door before opening it slowly. The bed was made, pillows fluffed, and no sign of a head resting against them. My stomach churned. Reg usually refused to make the bed, except when he was upset, anxious, or his parents were coming to visit. Something wasn't right. I flopped into the chair of the ornate cherry drafting desk I used to manufacture my maps and scanned the room for irregularities. I noticed one of my notebooks flipped open and creased and Reg's hand scrawling out an address I didn't recognize. Odd. 1349 Southport. I would have passed that earlier on my walk home. That area was mostly garment manufacturers and canning facilities, the street itself the duplex housing of the workers. The bosses back then didn't want their workers straying too far from the tasks at hand. What would Reg need——

"Oh, hey, Hun. I didn't hear you come in." Reg stood in the bedroom doorway, the waffle weft of his denim blue towel dripping to the floor. He pulled off his headphones and tossed them to the mattress. "I was psyching myself up for today. A little 80s power anthem to lift me to the rafters."

"Right! Today?" I was jovial. I was excited for him. I was present.

He took a beat and sighed.

"You forgot, didn't you? The interview. For the promotion."

My face betrayed my confusion, and Reg shook his head with that crooked smile he knew could melt any iceberg. He pulled me against him and tipped our bodies to the bed.

"I know you probably blocked it out because the idea of me being gone an entire eight weeks for training is more than your little soul can bear," he kissed me on the cheek, "but there's a very good possibility that"——another kiss, this time on the tip of my nose——"I'm a shoo in for this."——and another, the corner of my lips——"So you"——kiss——"and I"——kiss——"will just have to learn what it's like to make do for ourselves." He spun to his feet and crossed to the closet. "But only for the very littlest of whiles."

I sat up and smiled. The interview. Of course. The promotion. Naturally. I must have blocked it out like Reg said. Something was there——I knew it was——tickling the back of my brain. The interview. It must have just slipped my mind.

"You aren't the least bit worried?" I asked. "They say it only takes three weeks to form or break a habit. What if I get used to a life without you here?"

"I hear it's closer to sixty-six days," Reg called as he slid into a pair of navy tweed trousers, "Besides which, I don't have any reason to worry. I'd much rather know how you're going to make it two months without me. You'd forget how we met if I wasn't here to remind you every day."

"Karaoke night."

"No. You body slammed me with those two ferrets and that grey fuzzy squirrel you had attached to that clothesline."

"Right. Dog walking."

"Are you feeling okay?" Reg placed the back of his hand on my forehead and feigned his best mom/nurse concern.

"Just... Just a long night at work, I guess."

I collapsed to the mattress and yawned. He peered down at me with a sly smile and shook his head in a sudden, joyful frivolity. He was so beautiful, smiling down with the onset of day swirling around his face. I wanted to keep that image with me always.

"My poor baby," he said. "Just get some sleep." He pulled on his jacket and adjusted his tie. "I have to run. Wish me luck. I'll see you for dinner."

"Breakfast. But I've got a meeting tonight."

"Right. Well, after the meeting then. And hopefully with some stellar news and a brand new title." He kissed my cheek once more and tapped the tip of my nose with his finger. "I'll leave the light on for you."

He rushed to the front door, grabbing a chocolate chip pancake on the way and rolling it up to eat on the go. As he fumbled with the doorknob, I smiled at the familiar sound of his hands tripping over the metal. I got to my feet to get ready for bed.

"Oh, babe!" I called. "Don't you need that address?"

THE HOUSE THAT WASN'T THERE

I turned to the desk, but the notebook was closed and realigned with its partners at the upper left corner of the table. I must have instinctively returned it before I stood. Not that it mattered, anyway. Reg was out the door and down the stairs before I could even turn back around.

THE STUDY OF THE MIGRATORY PATTERNS of birds is a fascinating exploration into the learned patterns of primal instinct. Food and sex. Weather patterns and poles. Centuries spent without much mind paid to what is going on below, save for when it disrupts food or flight. Fight or just find a way around. And hollow bones, those marrowless features that can't absorb the oh so funny shocks of temperamental locales, acting like sounding boards to signify Dante's warnings. Spaces so foul, centuries of tradition are changed. Bird by bird, flapping its way up and down the northern continent on the whim of some culinary critic singing praise for the Best Grubs This Side of the Atlantic eons ago suddenly altering its route. So much dread in the bones. So much space to house it. So subtle it can easily go unnoticed beyond the species. The flight around the space within. The hollow. The not there.

And so it sat, for days or decades or centuries, unobserved and solely lodged within its own mode of survival. Intent to stare out, to spot the errant eyelash that flicked in its direction, to make quick work of the predators who would disturb it. The house with a consciousness, capable, as it was, of self reflection. The wood? Or the space? Where did origins begin? The beginning or the remembering? The notion of history is so often unraveled by those who lived through it.

The house was wood and stone, copper piping and aluminum ducts throughout, iron cage at the hearth, muddy footprints in the foyer. All things mined and borrowed from the earth and constructed into shapes deemed hospitable atop it. Each material repurposed and finalized and filled with air, left to pulse and vibrate of its own accord. Brought into being with a note of welcomed departure slipped gently under the mat: a golem in waiting; a god created to exist/to dwell/to possess/to continue. It is of no surprise then that one so imbued with Sense of Worth and Perpetuity could deem itself master of its own domain, the keeper of the very

THE HOUSE THAT WASN'T THERE

secret of itself. It is understandable, then, that it should want to remain undisturbed, less it need to lash out against the infection.

When a bird becomes ill, her flock will often turn against her. Though she may be adept at hiding her sickness at first, carrying on with the flapping and the swooping and the twilling cadence of her song as best she can, the pecking order will eventually prevail. And once she is unable to explain away her symptoms, the signs eventually become these: lethargy, apathy, a slight shrill sharpness to her song. She will perch in stillness, feathers fluffed to make herself larger in an attempt to ward off attackers. She will fail to so much as open her eyes as her friends and mates fly off for warmer climes. She will wait and make herself so large until she is hidden. The syndrome then continues until it does not. Death or departure comes slowly, as if both relish the feeling of her lingering moments, the act, itself, of waiting. Both so sure if the other just makes its move it can deny culpability. Neither wanting the blame.

2

I AWOKE WITH TOO MUCH on my mind, my dreamself still running through the hazy landscape just behind my left eyeball. I knew I was still back there sprinting, and however disturbing the dream may have been, I wanted to see it through, to force an ending, to be met with any outcome that could prevail against the murkiness of the unfinished. The dream, however, had other plans and vanished into hiding from the too lucid state of the midafternoon sun. I relished the roughness as I wiped the pebbled sleep from the corner of my eyes. It scraped across the fleshy rounds of my cheek, and the linger of the cutting sensation made me feel somehow substantive. The wet smears from my tear ducts glistened, stretched, and pulled at my skin in cool, exaggerated throbs. I peered at the caramel stones, tiny and fluid against my fingertips, and attempted to divine the last stitches of my dream within them. Mister Sandman's dream remnants washed away too soon.

The two o'clock sun tripped through the wooden blinds to cast bars across the bedroom. There was an emptiness to the air, and I took in shallow breaths——gasps at its nothingness——before the atmosphere returned to lay heavy on my chest and force me back down to the sheets. The lion on the ceiling——the one browned into the white paint from a leaky pipe discovered and rectified almost nine months prior——licked his lips. Reg had never seen a lion. Not in the ceiling, anyway. He insisted it looked more like a grumpy old woman or a cactus holding a firefly filled jar. One or the other, depending on the day. Cumulus watermarks. I listened to the roar.

"You know we should probably call the landlord about that, right?"

The two of us were spending a rare evening together. Sweat drenched our bodies, hot and heaving atop the covers on an early August night. The aftermath of unity. We panted our moisture into the humid air, joined still at the shoulders, unwilling to pull completely apart, and stared at the newly formed shadows darkening the space above our pillows.

"We should," I agreed. "But aren't you at all interested in what sort of picture will come of it? I mean, we'll probably be stuck staring at whatever it is forever. It should at least be something we like."

"Instead of two jaundiced pustules and an ant bite?"

"I mean, if that's what you're seeing, we should definitely wait. I see a mushroom and a cat paw, but——"

"We can give it a week. And then we call the landlord. Deal?"

"Deal."

I smiled and, for a moment, felt the warmth of Reg's body next to mine. Reg had been right: patching the leaking copper pipe had most likely prevented the costly and potentially painful collapse of our bedroom ceiling. But I had been correct as well. The image that resulted from a few extra days of drip drip dripping was way more pleasant to peer into until we got around to painting. Plus it amounted to a much more enjoyable post-coital game. The memory seemed so clear though the magic of mere seconds ago was lost. All that was left was a gnawing sensation that I had discovered something important within my subconscious thoughts. That some great truth had been revealed but was now adrift in the aether, hoping to circle back around upon my return.

The overhead lights flicked on as I made my way into the bathroom. I turned the knobs in the shower and listened as the pipes groaned in a minor key then crescendoed up to whistle against the consonant beat of the water as it lashed against the porcelain tile. My forehead met the mirror as I leaned against the sink. I placed my phone atop the vanity and let the screen flash the time once more. Four pm. No messages. I turned my eyes to meet their reflection. The golden thread stitched through the grass fields of my irises looked like stars, like dying strands of light feeding off the black holes of my pupils. My tear ducts were swollen and exposed, perched in the corner of my vision, used or unused. Agitated. Stubble peppered my lip, my chin, curved up to my ears and tried its best to separate itself from the errant hairs that were finer and longer and sporadically placed across my cheeks.

Steam filled the air and fogged the mirror. I tested the temperature with my palm upturned before sliding in beneath the downpour. The beads massaged my skin then broke to trickle down my back, to drip between my toes. The water glistened and brightened the ink in the tarot card tattoo at my hip——the one Reg had gotten me for our third anniversary. "I give you my World," he had joked as the needles strummed against skin, puncturing, pulsating, depositing pigment. A nude dancer surrounded by laurels clutched a freshly sprouted branch in each hand, symbolic of new life, a gesture toward the future even as both were clipped from their roots at some point along the journey. The laurels that wreathed her svelte frame were anointed with fuchsia and rusted petals that spilled yellow pollen stars atop their stamens meant to mean Enlightenment. Eternity rested in the rubicund shawls figure eighted at the apex and the nadir of the garland. Each corner of the card held an emblematic ruler: water, earth, air, and fire. The child: the waterbearer, Aquarius, Winter. The eagle: Scorpio, when the leaves Fall to the ground. The bull: Taurus, the sweetened smell of new Spring air. The lion: crowned Leo of the sun, the Summer, the flame.

Altogether the card was said to signify completion——the ecstasy amid the world weary culmination of the journey——the beauty of becoming within the fascination of wanderlust. Reg thought it exemplified me perfectly. I thought it the perfect token of our relationship, of all it meant to me, to both of us. And though I never told Reg, I would laugh inwardly sometimes when looking down upon it, catching the chortle in my lungs with deep and heaving sighs. To me, the card would forever be reversed, flipped upon the celestial, glittered tablecloth of the local mystic from far, far away and alluding always to the journey yet to come. To the forevermore.

I let the soap rinse across the whole of me, dripping from my fingertips or down my legs like a glistening armada no longer resisting the whirlpool, the kraken drain. The pipes sighed as I twisted the knobs to off, and the sudden air pricked my skin with a bracing static charge.

I dressed slowly, pausing every few moments, resting between pant legs to check my phone. I pulled on a coral tank top with a random imprint of unidentifiable birds illustrated for their tropical appearance over scientific accuracy. The image conveyed the message, though, elicited a feeling, a memory. Accuracy could not be bothered to be always present. At times, most times really, the emotion invoked was what was truly necessary.

No messages from Reg.

I watered the houseplants: a snake plant that actually started with a cutting from Reg's mother; a jungle fire croton whose green and white leaves shielded a vermillion underbelly; fluted jade and vining philoden-dron; a plumosa fern that feathered into fine clouds. It was my favorite. I'd started it in a small pot, but, as each new frond stretched out to overcast the others, had moved it into larger and larger vessels. I admired the plant, how it tripped over itself to form such intricate and unique webbing with the pinnae so delicate along the blade. How it sent out new and longer stalks on exploratory missions upward, restarting the process at a higher elevation. It created its own canopy, its own underbrush——a beautifully self contained ecosystem——growing exponentially larger: a universe expanding.

No messages from Reg.

I made the bed. It felt odd, as if the muscle memory of the motions were a distant recollection newly implanted. I smoothed the pillows. I creased the corners. I decided the quilt seemed upside down——top to bottom, not over to under——and reversed it until the stitching appeared to lie correctly, then I tucked the corners once more. I thought about washing the sheets, undoing what I had finished to begin again from scratch.

No messages from Reg.

I traced a line along the bedroom wall——first with my fingertips, then with the felt point of a marker——plotting out the distance between bisecting lines that mimicked imagined neighborhoods. Dead end streets and cul de sacs. Hundreds of souls growing weary with monotony. I referenced the sketches inside my notebooks to highlight a path that shaped the howling snarls of wolves chomping at the skies. An impromptu map careened over the headboard and turned sharply beside the framed photographs of Reg and me posing with expectant smiles; a kingdom forced by mountains and seas, by the weary pull of the horse drawn carriage to create its shape on the path of least resistance.

No messages.

A timid knock at the door shook the stare from my eyes. I flipped the deadbolt and was surprised to see the young woman from upstairs tracing the toe of her running shoes along the faded lettering of the welcome mat Reg and I had purchased our first week in the unit. She tucked a strand of blackbird hair behind her ear and adjusted the large framed glasses perched atop her petite nose as she mumbled her greeting.

"I, um, I just moved in, um, upstairs." She stuttered in her shyness, constantly urging each word from her throat. "My, um, my printer broke.

Well, it's out of, um, toner, and I'm——well, I'm broke. And I, um, have a paper due in a couple, um, days. So, I was, um, wondering..."

"Yeah, I uh——" I picked up her cadence as I smiled at her diminutive frame. There was something about her that I immediately connected with. A reminder of the reticence I had fought so hard to overcome. I felt it more strongly now as she spoke than I had each time we'd passed on the stairs. "I've got work tonight, but I'll be around pretty much all tomorrow afternoon if you want to drop by and use mine."

"That, um, that wouldn't be a problem?"

"Not at all," I assured her. I assured myself. It felt nice, inviting someone in. It felt needed somehow. "Plenty of toner. And paper. And coffee."

"Okay. Thank you."

She turned abruptly to ascend to her apartment.

I checked my phone.

No messages from Reg.

✳

"My name is Howard, and I'm an alcoholic."

I paused for a moment to take in the traditional greetings offered up by my cohorts and fidgeted with the paper coffee cup I gripped between my knees. My feet shifted nervously amongst the pastry crumbs atop the beige tile floor. Every meeting was helpful. Every meeting was a cinematic cliché.

"I am three years, fifty-two days sober, and every time I enter this church basement, I feel like I'm stepping into a confessional booth. 'Forgive me, Father, for I have drank. It's been three years and fifty-two days since my last recession.'"

I scoffed at myself as I took in the dissociative mixture of understanding, pity, and the faces that actually got the joke, as bad as it was.

"I started my relationship with fermentation when I was nine years old. It was back before micro brews and seasonal concoctions had taken over the taps, and my dad thought it was funny to watch my face as I sipped from his cans of hoppy, bitter piss water. As you can probably tell from my vivid description, I hated it. In fact, nearly a half decade went by before I discovered the pleasure of candy coated vodka drinks that would eventually find me face up in the bowed in side of the whiskey bottle. But when I moved here and started college: that's when the real joy began."

I cleared my throat and adjusted in my seat as I peered around the circle. There were enough new faces tonight to hear my origin story. I liked to tell it. It was rehearsed and comfortable. It kept me from getting too close to myself.

"I, uh—— I found myself drinking to manage my workload, to find that spark of creativity I thought I needed to finish that project. I drank to manage my fear of public speaking, which is kind of ironic considering where I am now. I drank to alleviate my fear of coming out to my parents, to meet boys, and——hell——because it felt good. I remember one time I showed up to give a presentation in my History of the Grecian Warriors course with so much of the Dionysian spirit coursing through my bloodstream, I actually toppled over the base of my professor's podium and got this beautifully ridged Roman nose you see before you today. So maybe it was the spirit of Bacchus, and I was in the wrong class."

I let my eyes bounce through the crowd. I saw people filled with hope, with fear, with shame. I imagined my own energy cycling through a myriad of emotions as I intoned the story I'd told a thousand times before, but with so many new faces, so many quieted voices, I felt that I should speak.

"But don't let me fool you. It wasn't all fun and comic nose jobs. I got kicked out of the dorms. I flunked out of my classes. I lost touch with my parents, but that may have been the fag thing more so than the inability to hold my liquor thing. Or maybe it was both. I come from a long line of ruddy cheeked men who think of busted capillaries as badges of honor. I ruined relationships, romantic and platonic, and I kept making excuses that it was okay because I always found a way to land on my feet, even if I was wearing the wrong shoes in the worst part of town."

All eyes were on me now, exploring my face or checking out the soles on my feet for the proper wear of three years and fifty-two days trekking across the arid streetscape.

"I almost ruined my current relationship. He had packed his bags and everything. That was the wake up call I needed. And somehow, I convinced him to stay. I've relapsed twice. And every day is easier. And every day is harder. I wake up most afternoons——I work nights now instead of staying up on benders——and I want more than anything to be farther away from who I was. I want more than anything to divorce myself from that person and be free of that burden. That embarrassment. And then I remember that I can't do that. But I guess more importantly I realize that I shouldn't do that."

I wound up for the big finish.

"He is me. And I will always be him. But I can learn to control myself. And I'm stronger for that. I am a better person today because I can live with my past and choose not to repeat it. Without facing that man in the mirror every single day, I could too easily become him again."

I pulled my lips tight against my teeth and let out a sound that lingered in the space between a tsk and a kiss as I watched the waves begin to form in my coffee cup; the early moon pulling the strings of any source of liquid it could find, its divining rod not hampered by steel or smog or stone. I listened intently as the others spoke, trying my damnedest to be present with them, to show everyone there the same respect they had given me, to take those precious moments to be outside of myself, but my thoughts continued to return to Reg. I still hadn't seen him. I still hadn't heard from him.

As the meeting adjourned, my hand shot into my pocket and fumbled with the buttons on my phone to turn it back on. My foot tapped impatiently as I waited for the screen to cycle through its welcome.

"Hey, Howard." Annie's lilting voice broke my concentration, and my eyes turned to hers just as the phone vibrated in my palm. "It was nice to hear you speak again tonight. But I do have to say, your story is getting a bit rehearsed."

She had been my sponsor since my first days in the basement, back when anonymity felt more like solace than freedom. I had always appreciated the unruly frizz of her carrot hair, the dimple in her chin, and the way her songbird voice made me feel calm and collected, like I could weather the withdrawals.

"I don't want to overstep," she sang, "but you know how important it is for you to share your experiences here. The new ones. The now ones. When you are ready. I just get the feeling that something more is going on. Something has seemed amiss the last several weeks. If you don't feel comfortable sharing with the group, I just want you to know that you can always share with me."

"I know, Annie. It's nothing. It's been kind of a weird day."

"If you've relapsed, you know you can tell me. I know you're still working in that bar."

"I am, and that's its own set of strangeness, but I haven't relapsed. If anything, pretending to be drunk while watching a bunch of actual drunk people helps keep me off the sauce."

I glanced at my phone. One new message. Relief cascaded down my spine, shivered its way into my fingertips as they tapped impatiently against the screen. My cheeks bulged with my best smile as I batted my eyes at Annie.

"Look," she said. Her voice dropped a register into the tone she used when companion made the switch to confidante. She flipped one of the fold out chairs in an effortless swoop, took my hand, phone and all, into her palm and guided me down so we were sitting face to face. "I know Reg has been a large part of your recovery. And that is good. I'm not denying that his presence has been a positive influence and stabilizer for you. But with him gone———"

"Gone?"

My eyelids tightened as I focused in on my sponsor. Everything about her was suddenly, inexplicably suspect. Her cheeks flushed, melding the spotted melon freckles that flecked her face into a tangled mass of embarrassment. Her eyes searched the room, her memory; attempted to ascertain time within space within the context of her conversations. She sighed into her response, defeated somehow.

"You mentioned before that Reg was leaving for a few weeks. Training for a big promotion."

Training. Promotion. Interview.

"I guess I just assumed he was gone."

"Right." I replied, timidly tapping my phone screen. Annie's smile widened, stretched, attempted to reach out to stifle the quick beating of my heart. "I forgot I told you all about that. No, he—— the interview was today."

"For the big promotion?"

"Right. I haven't heard from him yet. Whether he got it or not."

"I'm sure he did," Annie's voice wavered between her singsong style and a staccato monotone. "And where does Reg work again?"

"His office. With Cassandra and Olivia. Both of whom love karaoke, apparently."

"And his office is———?"

"In midtown?"

A sturdy, calloused hand clamped the pink and grey plaid which covered Annie's shoulder. Charles leered down at the two of us. His eyes, the hypnotic grey blue pair that had made him so adept as group leader, both scolded and comforted us with a quick, smiling gaze.

"I'm sorry to interrupt. Annie, can I speak with you for a moment before we lock up?"

"Sure thing, Charles. I was just wrapping up with——"

"Howard. Thank you for sharing tonight. You should check that message you've been dying to hear since the meeting ended." Charles nodded toward the phone and squeezed tight on Annie's shoulder. "I've seen you stealing glances at it since you turned it back on. Annie?"

Annie's smile filled with pity as Charles led her across the room to gather the left over donuts and pour out the remainder of the coffee. She took a defensive stance as the group leader seemed to scold her. Her hands crossed her chest then broke to gesture wildly in exasperated wing flaps before resting again over her stomach. I averted my stare when their eyes turned to meet mine. I collected myself, hit the recall button for my voicemail, and took the stairs two at a time as I exited the church.

❧

The early evening air was brisk, bolstered by the baked in rays of an early summer sun trying too hard to prove its worth against a city made of asphalt, as if it needed to be useful, to show it should once again be worshipped. It knew its sister had somehow claimed its magic, had captured the hearts of the covens still secreted away, and it gladly poured its light across her skin. As night neared in graceful strides——displayed the abyss behind the bulwark——the moon kept her quiet reverie contained behind streetlights and evaporated calefaction; waited her turn, her spotlight.

I found serenity in dusk much more so than I had ever found in a meeting. The vitality of space was palpable. The beauty of the temporal shift, the firmament cleansed of its refraction, created an electric pin drop between submission and defiance that overwhelmed me whenever I stopped to just breathe. It showed me an existence as part of an unwielding acclivity; it gave a purpose for the climb. That bluster of energy made me feel connected to everything. There was true solace in it.

Reg's voice dripped through the phone speaker like sweet molasses. A bit of a southern inflection clung to his words, the lost accent that resurfaced when he wanted to get his way, harps into banjos into believing. Reg's voice tripped through the phone speakers, stung through with static, an out of range radio station stuck with for a favorite song. I listened to the message again as I tried to piece together the story.

"Hi, Love... for a while... so... soon...."

The twilight throbbed in orgasmic rhythms. *Reg got the promotion.* People hurried past, late for a late dinner, early for a nightcap. *Training to begin immediately.* Charles and Annie locked up the doors behind me and waved as they set off in the opposite direction. *At least two months.* The streetlamps flickered into their best impressions of Lyra, every one of them jockeying for the starring role, for Vega. *Minimal cell reception.* For Vegas. *No time to talk.* For Venus.

A FAINT BREEZE SPILLED LIKE GASPS from newly opened doors. Their thick and swollen frames wicked the moisture of the centuries, leaving the space dry and dusty and surprised. A catacomb of relics far too ornate to be fully remembered, much too simple in function to be forgotten. The lives of fallen trees, like soldiers, stained and well trod, supported the childhood ghosts of wicker, floral cushioned sofas, of walnut end tables with dovetail joints and a built in magazine rack, of cherry coat racks and cheval mirrors and coeval dreams in crystal vases. Memories all, covered in slowly yellowing fabric, draped for safety, shrouded in fond commemoration. Paul wanted to cut eyeholes in the sheets, for him to see inside as much as for the furniture to breathe out. He wanted to find what was buried there, to attempt to ascertain why he had come.

The house had always been there, out of the corner of his eye. He had seen it in the periphery during his morning jogs, a pale but glowing blue sparking through the beads of sweat that summersaulted from his eyelashes as he bound down the sidewalk. Its ashen window frames shuddered against the evening rain from just beyond the curved edging of his umbrella as he marched homeward through the summer showers. Windows upside down in raindrops; railings electrified in the heat of the lightning. The house with the wrought iron gate that he had never noticed yet was suddenly so familiar to him when he saw it. The house was so a part of his history that it trickled its way into his memory, implanting itself always into the corner of his eye, right where it had always been. And it pulled him inside. An exploratory voyage. A curiosity called to quell.

Paul passed silently through each room. He found the study with what he knew to be a large oak desk, sturdy and resting beneath a bright white cover. Tall maple bookshelves with dusty and broken spines lined the walls. The remnants of burnt wax clung to silver candlesticks. It did its best to reclaim form, to return to what it was.

THE HOUSE THAT WASN'T THERE

A shuffle sounded in the room beyond.

The kitchen smelled faintly of honey and lavender. A wood burning stove in the corner emanated heat despite the blonde wood chips gone red to black to white in its hearth. A center island butcher block stood ready for fresh kill and sweet meat. In the corner, resting hungrily, waited a small breakfast nook where families past must have sliced fruit into their porridge, discussed the homecoming dance. He heard a faint clatter in the room beyond.

The dining room was elegant. A table for ten set for one. His favorite meal——plump, purple potatoes dusted with hard cheese; a fowl breast seasoned with whole sprigs of rosemary, of thyme; a vinaigrette drizzled frisée topped with dried blueberries and slivered almonds——rested atop ornate bone china trimmed in yellow gold. His mother had made him this meal for his birthday, every year he came home, every year before she died. She had never had much money, but she always took care of him. She understood the importance of life even more so as it slipped away. He sat at the table and breathed in the aroma of the dinner. His mind swam through her plaid aprons, her off centered smile with the lipliner always just slightly askew from the edge of her kiss.

He noticed his hands. His fingers were thinner, somehow longer yet gnarled in on themselves, reaching and gripping simultaneously. They held an uneven pallor as they twisted around the sterling fork, the sharpened knife, ready to dine. Then: there was a rasp which suddenly echoed from the center of his chest. New and discomforting, it had always been there. It seeped its way into his memory, up through the tense muscles of his neck to rattle its cup, full yet in need, inside his head. It had always been there. It would always be there.

3

WEDNESDAY NIGHTS AT THE MAIDEN NAME were a cacophonous display of the hyper ego of male fragility. Muscle bound men who trained to be doctors or hedge fund managers by day bared their chiseled and groomed pecs as they danced upon the bar at four foot intervals to the oontza oontz oontz broadcasted from the digital turntables propped atop Lonnie's covered piano. Men with names like Rip and Chase. Wig wearing men donned extralong eyelashes and painted on cleavage, moved their glossy, reddened lips to the voices of powerful female singers, and tried their damnedest to own the femininity of their tuck. Men with names like Amanda Freeme and Ivana Bang. And boys piled in from the streets to slam back drinks and slip folded dollar bills behind breastplates, into the thick elastic of non-utilitarian jockstraps. It was a violent amusement that eschewed societal norms through the very act of diachronic worship. A different kind of church. An epistemic understanding of the innate divine.

My chin caught my smile from dripping into the ice bin, and I forced the corners of my mouth back toward my ears. I could usually stop the overdrive of my mind——especially on such a busy night——and plaster the grin of a heat stricken wolf across my face. It was a service necessity every good bartender should come equipped with, at least according to Connor. Though it was one the manager himself rarely practiced.

"I'm paying you to smile," Connor playfully snarled through his left molars as he popped the caps from two bottles of tepid light beer and thumped them to the bar. "Or they're tipping you to smile, at least."

"I know!" I let the string lights glisten in the saliva on my teeth. I widened my eyes a bit, hoping the expression seemed genuine.

Connor danced over and our bodies met, shoulder to elbow, as we rattled the liquor, ice, and fruit juice in our shakers. A simple move, and one we'd practiced a hundred times before, that sent the patrons salivating at the skin on skin contact of the guys more attainable than the ones dancing above.

"You all right? You seem a little off your game tonight."

We poured our cocktails into plastic cups and slid them between the dancers' feet.

"Yeah. It's fine. It's just Reg——"

We paused to applaud the newly introduced queen as she shimmied onto the dance floor. Anita Greencard fell straight into a split that sent the crowd whistling and waving twenties at us in hopes of trading them for ones.

"It's nothing," I finished as I counted out singles. "I can keep my game face on."

"If you need a minute——"

"It's cool. I got this."

Connor nodded and danced away to take another order as I turned back to my service mat. Brian, one of the Wednesday night regulars who tipped well but thought he deserved first dibs whenever he needed a refill, leaned fervently across the bar with a stern look in his tilted eyes.

"You need to get that old fart off my jock," he demanded.

An elderly gentleman cupped his wiry fingers around his lips and leaned into whomever would bend to meet his voice. His snow white hair formed a gentle ring around his scalp, paused at his temples, and hopped a half inch into bushy caterpillars above his eyes. He pulsed slightly, his entire body attempting to decide which way it wanted to go, determined to spread beyond himself in every direction at once. More ecstatic than strained. More determined than defeated.

I leaned in and raised my voice, "What's he doing?"

Brian rolled his eyes and let out a dramatic sigh.

"He's been all over me talking about robin's eggs and ghosts and death and shit. It's like, I know you're close to biting it, old timer, but I'm just trying to dance."

Brian was in medical school, following in the footsteps of his father. Practicing his bedside manner. I nodded and poured him a couple shots of cinnamon flavored whiskey to appease him. I motioned to Connor and left my post to deal with the situation.

"Sir?" I called. "A few people are feeling a bit…infringed upon…by your topics of conversation."

The man bit a quiver in his upper lip and nodded as he registered the words. His eyes scanned the room and rested back on my own.

"Death is in the city. He's dressed in blue, and he's stealing babies from their mother's wombs."

I glanced behind him at the line of restless patrons, counting out their cash and looking out toward their friends holding their spots closer to the action of the drag performance. Most nights the bar was mild enough to offer up a little extra conversation to the lonely souls who found their way inside. Wednesdays, though, were a different story. Wednesdays made the other evenings possible. I couldn't pass up the night that paid my rent, let alone risk making Connor mad.

I sucked in my cheeks and let my most casual smile return to my lips. As I leaned in to gently dismiss the man, he let our eyes meet once more and paused. There it was again. That familiar aberrance. That image punctured just behind what I could remember.

"Tell you what:" There was something about the old coot I sympathized with. I couldn't just turn him out onto the street. And besides, he wasn't actually hurting anyone. He just needed to be heard. And who doesn't need to be heard? "It's pretty busy in here tonight, and I've got to keep the drinks flowing. But the performance ends in about two hours. You promise not to bother anybody else, and I'll set you up with a drink and a barstool."

The old man nodded, and I smiled at him again, this time without having to force it. I pulled a stool out from the backroom where we stored them for more floorspace on Hump Day Drag-a-Go-Go and slid it around the far side of the bar for the wiry man to perch upon.

"You gonna be okay here?"

He nodded again, a little more uncertainty in his gesture this time, as if he had forgotten why he was here, as if he wasn't sure what "okay" meant in the first place. He removed his hat and, after wiping up a spill I had missed with a fistful of cocktail napkins, placed it in front of the barstool and pulled himself onto the seat. He folded his hands together in front of him and tapped out a reluctant Morse Code against his knuckles.

"What can I call you, mister?"

"Paul."

"I used to date a Paul."

The old man blinked. His lips twitched, but no sound emerged. He loosened the belt on his trench coat but did not remove it.

"What you drinking, Paul?" I asked. "My Paul used to love an Aviation."

THE HOUSE THAT WASN'T THERE

"That's the one that's light purple, right? Lavender colored and floral?" The old man smiled dreamily and licked his lips.

❧

Memory, the storage and recall of information necessary to influence current and future events (and the understanding thereof), is flawed. Not in a forgetful, amnestic way. In the assumption that Current and Future exist at all. Because of the way in which memory functions, we are constantly living in the past. One brings forth, with concentration or in automatic response, every didactic tidbit his parents, her teachers, their lovers ever implanted into the grey matter of manipulated folds just behind their skulls——bubbling there in ecstatic synaptic pleasure behind assorted access points for millions of senses (though only four are the most commonly recognized when accessed——sight, smell, taste, sound——sense memory, they call it)——planting it firmly in a Present that can never occur. Time jilted. Thought and understanding already a thing of the past once it has been processed. The Now that already happened.

And Future, too, assumed in the now/then and realized as something yet to come when in memory it has already occurred. Daydreams into nightmares. Careful what you wish for. A life in anticipation. The making of a memory through thought before the future has the chance to manifest. A future then exploited by doubt or the circumstance behind the understanding of the past/present into a world one would never want to be a part of, could never remember to recognize as true. Each thought of Now already a thing of the Past; each idea of Tomorrow a premonition processed in the Before and never easily forgotten.

Too, it is flawed in its recall. They went to dinner. He had the duck/salmon/steak. He had the veggies/lamb/submarine sandwich. The waiter was tall/average, and courteous/curt. He wore a red/green/orange tie. The night was uncharacteristically warm for that time of year——remember?——and he kept his jacket hooked to his finger and draped over his shoulder like he was modeling evening wear for one of the anchor stores at the mall. It had rained earlier that day and puddles were everywhere/water still coursed along the edges of the city streets, searching for drainage grates not plugged with fallen leaves and discarded fast food wrappers. He laughed and splashed in the oceans. He sidestepped and skirted the lakes.

The car was white/grey/champagne colored. The car was brand new/well worn/aiming.

Memory.

He wasn't home, but he was there. Locked inside (of himself). Shutters closed and eyes peering out intensely without focus. He was nothing but home, and still we silenced him——othered him——in our lack of interaction. His eyes were blue/brown/green/purple. His lips were trembling.

The details so clear and ever changing.

Only the past can exist in any real (though non-tangible) way. And yet as the past is always present, it is always on the mend. Always just around the bend.

The house, when seen, had means to force abstraction. A loss. A reiteration of event, of space, of knowing. Coupled with a temper, the cloaking became a consumption, a method set to devour, leaving behind a nothingness that had no choice but to be filled. A past perfect participant in the future of all there was. Forgotten or remembered and always replaced.

"I think you can handle it from here."

I looked up from the dish pit at the sound of Connor's voice and nodded. The go go boys had cleared the bar prior to a valiant finale from the queens——glitter and rose petals and death drops——and with their exeunt, most of the patrons had followed. Pursued by a bear. Connor tossed his bar rag into one of the bus bins and began pulling half the tips from the jar by the register.

"Your admirer over there is going to miss curfew at the nursing home," he laughed.

Paul shifted on his stool. He kept his hands locked together on the bar top. His thumbs twisted around one another in a romantic waltz that sparked something within my memory.

"Seriously, though," Connor pocketed his cash and leaned against the three compartment sink, "I'm proud of you for taking an interest in the older generation. They fought so we could have all of this, after all."

I could hear the sarcasm drip into the sanitized water beneath my manager. It clouded there and scrubbed the glasses.

"Things said in jest."

"I'm not being a jerk," Connor insisted, his best attempt at innocence in his eyes. "But if the geezer forgot his little blue pills, you can just wait for rigor mortis to set in."

I shook my head and gave my boss a playful hip check. Connor laughed loudly and made a beeline for the door.

"Just don't let anybody die in here tonight," he called loudly as he turned to back out of the doorway. "Even if it's just a 'little death.'"

I wiped my hands dry as Connor pantomimed oral sex and took his leave. I tucked the rag into the belt loop at my right hip, poured a Scotch for Paul, an apple juice for myself, and met the old man's gaze.

"So how're you feeling, mister?"

Paul swallowed hard. He wrapped his hand around the highball glass I pushed across the counter and tapped his finger against it as he searched his mind for wording. Like his hands knew better what to say than his throat.

"Robin red breast is hiding behind the egg blue shell. There's death in there. It strips off your youth, and you forget. You forget. You forget it all is there. It's here. It's in here."

The cool brown liquid swirled in his glass. Each word sighed out of him in a painful gasp. His eyes watered as he spoke. He looked as if he were betrayed, as if the words did not match the intention behind them.

"Is there someone I can call for you?"

Paul closed his eyes in frustration and downed his drink in one gulp.

"It's going to find you when you find it," he said. "Water the plants. The thirst is real."

He stood from the stool and snatched his hat from the counter. He nodded, sucked in his cheeks, and moved slowly toward the door. I was not sure how to react. Though his words were erratic, he seemed to have his agency intact. Before I could move, a bloodcurdling shriek echoed from the backroom.

I turned around to see Bitch Attent run half dressed through the swinging doors. Her makeup was mostly in place, though her head was only covered by a wig cap instead of the usual teased to the gods black hair, and her sequined dress was hanging onto her hips to reveal the stuffed bustier on her torso. She didn't speak as she grabbed me by the wrist and pulled me toward the back. Her eyes scanned the bar frantically and her

Adam's Apple bobbed rapidly in her throat, both looking for something else to hold onto, both praying to get away. She pulled me into the make-shift dressing room we set up next to the dry storage for the bar every Wednesday night and desperately waved her arms as she tried to coax sound from her throat.

The room was a flurry of motion with one noticeable exception.

Queens snatched at their garments, swiped makeup and pantyhose into purses and duffle bags, and pushed through the delivery door into the alleyway outside.

The room was a flurry of emotion with one noticeable exception.

Go go boys slid into gym shorts and tank tops, tapped white powder into tiny metal tins, and blew remnants from the foldout makeup table aside.

Everyone's eyes were wide. Everyone looked to me for help.

Bitch Attent finally spoke: "That motherfucker is dead!"

I grabbed Blade's wrist and felt for any sign of flowing blood. His eyes were wide; his nose red; the blood already dry.

I sighed and went back to the front to kick everyone out. Paul was already gone, and only a few post-show stragglers were deciding on sleeping arrangements for the evening. I turned off the music. I called the police.

✤

The cops finished up just before 2am. Bitch Attent sobbed crocodile tears as paramedics loaded Blade's body into the back of their ambulance. Her mascara didn't run as she shook her head in exaggerated pain. The curly black hair from the wig she'd taken the time to put back on before the police arrived cascaded across the sequined shoulder pads of the dress she'd changed into. I looked at the dishes still in the sink and decided to leave them for the following day. I ushered Bitch out with the last officer and locked up the doors behind them.

The night air burned in my throat, and I watched the streetlights ricochet through the leaves of the dogwood trees. I blinked slowly, purposefully, and decided to walk north first, to double back in the opposite direction of home, to clear my mind and discover a new path.

I walked for what felt like hours. Each block offered a static view of the city, still and forgotten, as if it were set in metal and stone; cement and steel and marble enshrined as artwork and left to succumb to dust and silt, to wait for an army of archeologists to assemble and examine the hieroglyphs in the graffiti, to study the oils left in the paint from the fingertips of lost lovers on the bedroom walls. At night, I saw the city for what it was truly meant to be: a collection of space (as if space could be collected); a monument to permanence (if anything truly was) amid a life all too short.

I wandered with purpose, a march in my step, my foot striking stone hard enough to ensure its firmness. I plotted each step. I punctuated them with affirmations of solidity. I recorded each doorway, each window. Counted the leaves budding from every branch of every tree. Heel to toe, rounded, and sending an ache through my ankles up to my shins. The night pressed on at a pace more forceful than mine. Moonlight struggled to bathe the streets in a soft glow, spurred on by an electric fear of the dark.

As the clanging sound of church bells chimed thrice, I found myself a few blocks from my apartment on Southport. I'd been marching in the opposite direction, but I'd managed to saunter my way here. Somehow. Drawn on by the swirling remnants of a life retreating. The sun struck the moon; the moon struck the robin egg siding of a house I had not seen before.

No.

The police offered their condolences with a solemn handshake, a dissociative stare, a liveliness in their eyes that seemed more dead than Blade's before I had attempted to push his eyelids together. They opened and closed their notebooks frantically, as if Blade required an immediacy, as if he had somewhere he needed to be. They took their statements from Bitch, from me. A formality, really. The situation was cut and dried. Dried and cut across a mirror.

An overdose. Obviously. No, the use of drugs was not a regular occurrence at The Maiden Name. Yes, we had a strict policy against illegal substances. No, no one knew Blade's real name. But Connor would have it on file. He'd be available to check the employee records the following afternoon. Yes, maybe he had a wallet in his duffel bag. Yes, his name would be on that. No, we'd never really spoken. Yes, he did have a great ass.

They loaded Blade into the back of an ambulance. It took two paramedics to lift the gurney. Bitch hailed a taxi and straightened her wig as she climbed into the backseat. Her cherry nail polish glowed in the flash of the siren lights. The police took pity on me. They offered me a ride home.

"We may have more questions for you tomorrow," she said. The officer in the passenger seat. The woman with the ash blonde hair eyeing me sympathetically in the sideview mirror. "Is the number you gave us the best way to reach you?"

I nodded first, knowing they both eyed me through their mirrors then spoke my answer aloud because it was the polite thing to do. I rolled down the window of the squad car and felt the false wind whip against my cheeks as the wheels careened down the mostly empty streets. Alphanumeric codes vibrated through the police radio as fixed locations whizzed by in blurred obscurity. I knew each nail of each building from my late night walks. My mind supplemented what my eyes could not perceive.

I tried to decipher the monotonous messages from the CB Radio. I imagined myself a codebreaker, determined to discover the location of the enemy. The address readily given; the why and who disguised.

"We've got to take this call," she said. The officer with the ash blonde hair and the slight crook to her upturned nose. "Is it okay if we drop you off here? You'll make it home safely?"

I nodded then spoke my answer aloud. It was the polite thing to do.

I was just a few blocks away from my apartment on Southport. Halfway up the block and facing the slate grey shutters of a house I ceased to remember when I closed my eyes.

No.

The ambulance sped off with no blare to its siren, urgency in its wheels but nothing to be done. The city sighed its heavy breath into the darkness. Gasps clung to the air and found solace in liquid form. A faint drizzle hummed through the streetlights as I headed southward in a haze.

Minutes passed. Each new street appeared mere moments from the turn before. The sidewalks were abuzz with lonely souls finding hands to hold as the bars flipped their neons to the off position and steadied the security locks across their doors. I watched the menagerie of people collected together of their own autonomy, willing participants in the great experiment of modernity, the hearts within the ribcage of steel and stone. Each soul a marvel; each beast a danger. I rounded corners with an exotic sense of wonder, a tourist in a xenophobic land. One eye trained constantly over my shoulder, the other pointed ahead, begging to absorb it all.

I plotted the path in my notebook, new ink drying quickly over the gridded lines on the page.

I could capture place. I had that ability. The greatly built monuments of structure, of path, of settlement. I could showcase them all, but I could never reveal the life that was behind them. I could try. I wanted to try. To show all the individual cells that flowed along each artery. The bacteria that bustled out new life and sped up the deterioration. I wanted to show where they all went when the lights went out.

I padded my way up Southport, only a few blocks away from my bed, and paused to lean against the wrought iron blockade that guarded the house that wasn't there the moment I turned away.

I arrived at my door much earlier than I usually would have and placed my ear against the wood. I listened to the stillness inside, attempted to coax the oceans within to meet me, to find their cyclical cadence. But the shell was hollow; the home was empty. I was alone. No one had turned on the salt lamp. No one had set the coffee maker. The bed would still be made or unmade. The plants would be asleep.

4

"Someone died at the bar last night."

I whispered into the receiver as if it could understand, as if it actually could hear instead of simply transmitting. It was my fourth call in as many hours. The silence was becoming comfortable, more amiable than the robotic sound of Reg parroting his full name before the beep.

"I didn't know him well; he'd just started. It was only his second night performing. But I just kept thinking about how, three years ago, that could have been me. You know? And how you saved me from that. And how appreciative that makes me. What you did for me."

Reg didn't answer, but for a moment, I saw him grin. I saw him nod and purse his lips to highlight the gleam that flashed against the whites of his eyes.

I sat in the darkness and looked for Reg in the shadows, as if willing him there could manifest his specter. I imagined him kicking his feet up onto the coffee table and smiling as I scolded him, batted his curled toes off the furniture. But that had never happened. I saw him lean against the door of the refrigerator as he studied the shelves to pick out an after work snack to tide him over until I was ready and we could have dinner. Breakfast. But I had rarely woken early enough to be alert and showered and witness that. Not when he was around. Not when sleep was peaceful and came more easily. I could see it, though, clearly in all of its exaggerated nuance.

I realized how much of our daily lives together had functioned separately. I saw how much I had missed. Regret tiptoed across my clavicle, slalomed from lung to lung to seize them. A breath skipped in remembrance of the go go boy with the blue sequin and lamé thong. Maybe less so for him than for what he represented. I desired less of what I had to learn and turned my attentions to what I knew.

THE HOUSE THAT WASN'T THERE

Reg had an infectious laugh that wriggled from his diaphragm in spasms that embarrassed him——turned his cheeks bright red——which only pushed more sound from his chest. I adored it. I saw a shy history peek out through each guffaw, the flustered young man who tried to hide himself, who wanted so badly to subdue the woodpecker song in his throat he produced at a paced and asthmatic chortle that twinkled through the hollows of anyone within earshot. A beautiful suppression. An elegant parallel to the man who loved so loudly he felt a constant need to hide within the shadows in order to cease from overwhelming a world itself too repressed.

It was that same desire to veil that had moved his hands to wood and newsprint and paste. His fingers were nimble as he pressed smile lines into masks, carved eyeholes from the paper, and placed quarters there to bribe the passage of time until they could be used. He'd tried his hand at puppets for a while but had ultimately decided they were mere misdirections of frenetic energy sent to artificial limbs when the real energy was in expression. And so all the golems he created were tangled up in a box buried inside the hall closet. The marionettes were simply moveable pawns, acting out the desires of the one atop the strings. Behind a mask he could be himself. Bold and boisterous and beautiful. He preferred the shield to the necromancy.

I shuffled to my feet and held my breath as I pulled open the window blinds. The late afternoon sun beat down in sharp dandelion shards, refracted in the glass pane, and sliced into the bustling street below. Teenagers maneuvered across sidewalk stones with agile fingers skipping across screens. Nannies, mothers, and fathers pushed strollers along in slow, aggressive bursts. A toddler reached her arm out to tap her fingers along the black bars of my building's fencing. Muffled laughter cascaded through my eardrums; a summer of sound waves oh so equipped at finding any opening to continue outward until they ceased, suddenly into absence. My eyes glazed; the street overlapped on itself. I found myself spellbound by the casual complexity of it all, the willingness to push forward.

"Someone died at my bar last night," I called. But the street did not answer. It simply shuddered in its place.

Three crisp raps echoed through the front door. It felt heavier than normal, swollen with the moisture of an evaporated summer as I pulled it inward, letting the harsh, blanched light of the stairwell bleed in. I flicked the switch for the light and waited what felt like hours for her silhouette to form features. Time moved in sporadic bursts within agonizing moments of stillness.

"Did I wake you? Is this a bad time? I can come back."

She turned quickly, and I reached to touch her shoulder with a static electric shock. Elephants rampaged down my arms and paraded through my fingertips. A sudden desire to replace my wallpaper with yellow, to replace my walls with echoes of suns, filled me.

"No. It's fine," I assured her. "I work nights, so this is my morning." I purposefully left out the u. "Come on in."

She adjusted the bag hanging on her shoulder and shuffled across the threshold. Her hands wrapped the olive straps of her laptop case. She stopped beside the kitchen island and shifted her eyes around the room. Her feet pulsed without leaving the floor.

"Did you want some coffee? I could brew us some."

"I don't want to be any trouble."

We spoke in couplets of trained conversation, polite and demure and wary of where to go next. I set the pot to automatic and smiled as the first drips of boiling water zizzed down into the glass, fogging the pot with the gentle dew of a heat soaked morn. I purposefully left out the u.

I urged her to take a seat. She nodded and obeyed. I talked her through signing into my WiFi and which drivers she needed for my printer, but they were installed before I finished my sentence. I poured her coffee into the mug that Reg usually used, and she asked for sugar.

"If it's no burden."

There was a calmness in her deferment, a reluctant acceptance of a place life had yet to offer her. Seeing her there, with her highlighted textbooks and her stickered computer made me feel at ease. I realized how empty my apartment had felt even though it had been mere days of unoccupancy. I left out myself on purpose.

"Tell you what," I said, slipping the cobalt container across the counter but not yet releasing the clasp for the lid, "you can use as much sugar as you'd like, if you tell me a little about yourself. Open up. Get to know your neighbors."

I tried a smile I hoped would offset the queerness of my words. She twisted her lips to match mine and trained her eyes on her keyboard.

"There's not too much to tell," she said. "All the interesting parts are too complex to really delve into; the more mundane too trite for any interest beyond commonality; and all of it cobbled together from the scars and nodes and echoes of a past Mary Shelley herself would worry to stitch together."

She chose her words deliberately and seemed to come alive as more poured out, losing the agitation and stutter that invaded her usual demeanor. I smiled as she spilled three spoonfuls of white granules into her mug.

"Which is to say you're in your junior year as a Psych——no——Lit major, too oppressed by the moribund learning of an overly active dormitory, which prompted your move here midsemester in order to focus on dense tomes in place of six packs."

She watched me with sharp eyes barely visible through her slanted lashes. Her mouth, agape in question, lingered restless behind her coffee cup. I tried to peer back expectantly but couldn't help but laugh.

"Sorry. Mrs. Wilkes downstairs is a bit of a busybody. She trades gossip with the building manager like she's studying to win a game show."

The girl smiled and dropped her mug to the counter. She pushed back from her computer and cocked her head to the side, her lips pursed as if considering me again for the first time.

"You're mostly right except for two things. I'm actually a sociology major with an emphasis on gender studies."

I listened to the hum of the printer as it shifted left to right to left across the ivory pages rotating through. We poured our language through it, but it didn't care. It could ink the words in any order and still not understand. Still refuse to respond. Its rhythm was calming, even as I realized how much I craved conversation. Even a friendly sparring.

"Well, that explains your reluctance to speak," I jabbed. "Too busy studying those around you to bother with engaging in any real way."

A faint laugh tripped out of her throat, and she settled easily into her seat. "It's more so that I'm rarely ever stimulated by what people have to say."

"That's dreary. The antisocial sociologist."

"That's what I call my blog," she laughed. "Besides, books give me all the back talk I need. Otherwise, I'm rather keen on observation."

"I'm Howard."

I extended my hand from my challenging smirk. She guardedly slipped her palm next to mine and wrapped her fingers along the back of my own.

"Gerrie," she said, and I raised my eyebrows. "Gertrude by birth, and I liked it better than Trudy."

"Pleasure."

There was a decade of experience between us, yet an innate connection seemed to spur from our barbed words. She grew more comfortable as we spoke. I could see the loneliness within her——behind the dark eyes and dyed black hair she periodically tucked behind her ears——reach out to make contact with my own, as if the swirling void of either nothingness could somehow fill the space, could possibly find solace. She lowered her eyes and suckled on her lower left lip.

"You live here alone?"

The printer buzzed its electronic symphony from the other room, crescendoing up and echoing through the hallway.

"I live with my partner, Reg." Her pupils swam across the countertop, weaving in and out of the faux marble waves. "He's away for a while. For work."

She smiled sympathetically, something akin to pity in her nod.

"Well, this is, um, my last paper for summer semester," she said, gulping down each word even as it emerged from her throat. "After that, I've got about a month before Fall starts. You know, if you, um, need company or whatever."

"That'd be nice, Gerrie." I reached to touch her hand, and she recoiled slightly. "I work nights, but I've got most afternoons free."

She nodded and tapped her fingers on the counter as the sounds of the printer fell quiet. Her feet shuffled slowly against the hardwood floors as I led her back to the bedroom to retrieve her paper. She took in the street map I had markered onto the wall as I collected the pages from the printer bed. Her eyes traveled the roads, looped through the side streets, and sidestepped the picture frames that rose like skyscrapers along the paths.

"Yeah," I blushed. "I guess I've been a bit restless without Reg here."

She stepped casually onto the bed and tapped out a point on the wall.

"That's us, right?"

"Yeah. You're pretty good with an atlas."

She pushed her finger along the wall.

"Your map is pretty accurate. You know, Josiah Royce gave us the challenge of assuming a map of England, when manufactured to perfect scale on British soil, must also contain the very same map of England, stretching on into infinity."

Her finger traveled the streets briskly, barely looking which way it was going.

"Yes," I said, "and Jorge Luis Borges built upon that, stating those cartological fears that if a map were perfect, containing within it the map, then the rest of us viewing said map could be merely works of fiction. Not really real. Just icons within, looking within. That's why all my maps contain some irregularity."

Her finger paused at a jumbled intersection, instinct and sense memory in conflict. She pursed her lips and looked sternly from the wall.

"Did you just make up a word to sound smart?"

"It sounded good. Practical." I sounded it out by syllable———"kahr-te-oh-loj-i-kuhl"———and smiled.

She rolled her eyes and snatched her papers from my hands.

"You cartographers are all the same. Thinking you have some say in how the rest of us see the world. By the way, the Brits drop the 'e.' Even though we don't use it much this side of the Atlantic, even in mapmaker circles, cartological is a fairly common word over there."

My jaw gaped as I forced my face to cycle through innocence and shock.

"But that's neither here nor there. When what you really need to focus on," she continued, "is figuring out what lies within that imperfection. What's all this?" Her open palm smacked against the black lines crisscrossing without warning between two troubled crossroads. "What's going on in your map within a map within a clusterfuck of non-understanding?"

I cocked my head to the side as she slipped past me into the hallway.

"We can figure that out next time I come down. Coffee tomorrow?"

I followed her back to the living room, laughing as she gathered her things. She gulped down the thick, syrupy remnants in her mug and rolled the forty or so pages of her paper like a newspaper, tapping them against her palm as she stared at me expectantly.

"So, Gerrie, what was the second thing? From before. You said I had two things wrong."

She tucked her papers next to the laptop in her case and tucked her hair behind her ear.

"Your second inaccuracy? The gossipmonger downstairs. Her surname. It's Wilson, not Wilkes."

🐝

I sat on the edge of the mattress, spine straight, legs angled in a starting position like a runner waiting for the gunshot——a strange, inert attention——even as my mind wandered elsewhere, traced along the bands I drew on the walls, willed delineation, lineament from firmament, within the flat footed felt tipped chaos. Gerrie was right. There was a hollowness in the depiction, great and dangerous, and begging to be known. Without understanding, it would remain incomplete. False. Of no warranted use.

The map is not the territory. Its usefulness was in its similarity to the thing it represented. Semantics, true, but that was Alfred Korzybski's specialty when he said it.

Reg always took a similar approach when crafting his masks. Sure, he'd use elaborate colors to shade the lips, he'd draw out the nostrils and chisel the cheekbones, but he insisted the features be human, however exaggerated they became. When the women in his office asked him to produce feline masks for them one Halloween, he'd declined.

"The beauty of it all," he said, "is not to camouflage what's already there but to bring it out in new and unexpected ways."

"But I just want to be a sexy kitty at the karaoke party," she said. Olivia. Or Cassandra. One of the two of them.

He wanted the world around him to feel beautiful in its own skin but understood the confidence required to convey that beauty was often out of reach.

"I don't make masks to hide," he said. "I want them to be focusing points. To allow the person behind the paper and the glue or the wood and the paint to be able to express. To say, 'look, I'm happy' or 'I'm sad' or 'All of this Everything is going on in here' no matter what anybody else thinks they're seeing on the outside."

He was always so beautiful working with his pen knives and his paints.

THE HOUSE THAT WASN'T THERE

"I mean, look at your tattoos," he told me. "You're peacocking your skin with bright and glorious colors. Some people may see them as shields, but they're not. Some people use them as armor, but they're so much more. They're billboards. They're sign posts. They're showing there's this vastness contained within that maybe just needed a platform from which to jump. Those are the masks I want to make. The stage and the performance. Not just the costume."

"But I just want to be a sexy cat," she said. Cassandra. Or Olivia.

His paintbrush traced the gentle arch of a chartreuse top lip. I placed my arms around his shoulders and leaned in to kiss his neck and knew in that moment how much I loved him. I asked if he could paint that feeling onto my face, so it would always be there, and he said I'd already captured it perfectly.

I felt silly, an insecure schoolboy waiting for his call to boost my confidence. I worried I hadn't heard from him. *The interview. The promotion. The training.* That great big jumble of occurrence. I needed to do something about my map.

I wanted to make the walls yellow, anyway. I decided I would paint over it all and begin again.

THE HOUSE GREW COLD when no one was watching. A solitary breath could hum through the hallways for centuries, slither across the wood panels of the floor and sigh beneath any doorways that had shifted through the uneasy settling of its weight against the soil. It shivered. And it waited. And when it became so cold, it began to burn; its tantrum sent shockwaves into the rapidly decaying summer. When no one was watching, the house longed to be a home.

It turned on the television and watched game shows as the vacuum cleaner groaned along the handwoven carpet in the next room over. It preheated the oven and swept the soot of lost seasons from the hearth. It tucked itself in and whispered bedtime stories through windows left slightly ajar. And it waited.

The house adjusted through the decades. And, when it found itself disappearing, imagined souls careening through its halls. They would appreciate its winding paths and relish in the kaleidoscope of views it presented through its storied windowpanes. Tales of arduous adventures where the hero never died and always returned home. Epic romances that led couples through white picket fences and beautifully ornate doorways. It preferred its wrought iron, found it more regal somehow, but knew to allow for fantasy when the occasion required it. Which, in reality, was always.

Sometimes it shuttered itself, and centuries deteriorated in seconds. Minute specks of pollen or dander or fibers, cellular abjurers, ticked downward like sand, and the television clicked on again. Both touched and unmarred: a constant state of dwelling between the event of creation and the act of retribution. Always. Forgotten. Always apparent. Aspirational. Apparitional.

5

ANNIE MASSAGED HER FINGERS along the outside of her coffee, tactually distinguishing between the smooth, cool paper of the white cup and the rough, corrugated ridges of the cardboard sleeve. Her hair pillowed around her face and alit with peculiar flares from the sunlight streaming through the window behind her. A thousand tiny halos. The crimson asps of a gorgon.

"I'm so glad you called," she said as I slid my cappuccino onto the table and dropped the three gallons of paint I'd just purchased at the hardware store to the floor beside my chair.

The man at the paint counter had been particularly nice. He had let me bore him with swatches that were a tint away from what I wanted. His laugh, when he forced it after my "black and white and red all over" embarrassment, ended in a smile that reminded me for a moment of Reg's. He dished a dollop of each color onto the lid before he hammered them closed, so I could tell them apart when I made it home. He threw in a roller and a tray for free.

"Thanks for meeting me here," I smiled. "These are a bit too cumbersome to head far uptown with."

"Doing a bit of redecorating?"

"In a sense." I took my seat and blew a gentle dip into the micro foam atop my drink. "It's for a project I unwittingly started yesterday."

"I think that's fantastic!" Annie's voice whistled an octave higher than normal, ecstatic with odd relief. The brochure of her position spilled out: "Pursuing hobbies can lead to remarkable focus and resilience in remaining sober."

I let the warm mixture of milk and espresso slink across my tongue. Sweet and bitter, it warmed me from within. Her voice returned to normal.

"But that's not what you called me here to talk about," she said. "I'm assuming you're ready to discuss what happened."

"I am." I stuttered to produce the correct words. "I mean, I haven't been tempted, but something like this could easily lead to a relapse, and I——"

"Need an ear to ensure you don't head down the wrong path."

I nodded and sunk my chin into my chest. I pulled my neck from side to side and felt the tension in my muscles expand and release. The street outside the coffee shop teemed with insects and buckthorn leaves barely witnessed by the busy pedestrians navigating through the rush hour hubbub. Beelining with purpose. Wandering all the same.

Annie reached across the table to cup my hand.

"Something like this can be a very traumatic experience. Trust me, I know firsthand how painful it can be to talk about, let alone endure."

"It was just so sudden and unexpected." Her eyes urged me onward. "I mean, one minute he's gyrating in a g-string on top of the bar, and the next he's just... But it's not like I knew him that well or anything."

"It can often feel that way when someone is gone," she sighed. "Even with those we were closest to."

"Well, it was only the second time I'd seen him in my life."

Annie's brow furrowed as she cocked her head to the side.

"What are you——?"

"Blade. The go go boy who died at my bar last night. What did you think I was——?"

"That. I'm sorry. Please continue." Her palms out gesture invited me to pour my words, like sugar crystals, across the table.

I sank back into my chair and crossed my arms over my stomach. My fingertips played idly at the pockets on my jeans, slipping in and out of their fraying edges like a snake's tongue licking across my phone to the left, my wallet to the right. A steady wind careened between the buildings.

"So even though I didn't really know Blade——gods, that feels stupid. I don't even know his real name. I'm just going to call him Joe. So even though I barely knew Joe, seeing him hunched across that makeup table sort of sucked all the air out of my chest. And I know that it's totally narcissistic of me, but all I could think was, 'Hail Mary, that could have been me.' Which is just awful. And then the thought of thinking that made me feel even worse."

"Howard." Annie's lips squeezed together as she spoke my name, the fleshy rounds disappearing with the consonants. "It is common and natural to hold a bit of survivor's guilt when we are faced with death. The thing you need to realize and remember"——she hit each syllable of the word with staccato force——"is it was not your fault."

"Of course I know that."

"Exactly! You weren't even there."

"Well, I was out front tending bar."

"Right."

"Right." I paused as she swallowed hard. "It could have been 'Hell, Mary' now that I think about it," I said, a failed attempt to lighten the mood.

Annie's eyes pleaded with mine across the table as if she required my assurance that I was going to be all right, as if she needed me to nod for her to know she'd done her job. Her mouth moved in slow motion, urging me to complete the sentence she tried to form. She looked ready to burst.

"Death," she finally said, "is a difficult task for the living. Try as we might to understand it, to accept it, it always catches us off guard. It confronts us with an indifference that seems cruel and gives us no way in but through. We try to cope through fantasy, through language. We prepare ourselves for it by having work *suffocate* us, by *drowning* in debt, by *choking* through unpleasantries. But every time we see it, it's shocking."

"Like an electrocution," I winked, and my face fell.

"See? Death is everywhere in our language. And then we use euphemisms when confronted with the actual act. Our pets went to play on the farm our grandfather bought where our uncle keeps kicking over that goddamn milking bucket. Language teaches directness through metaphor, action in riddles."

As she spoke, her phone buzzed against the laminate tabletop, and she quickly hit the button to silence the call. A few moments later, it lit up once more, jigging across the table toward her cup. Charles—Group Leader lit up the screen.

"I should get this. I'm sorry."

She answered the phone in a hushed tone and dropped her shoulders into a receptive position, intent on listening. My stare glazed and moved beyond her frame to the door. The dual bells that hung from the cross bar and rang with each opening or closing seemed in ever expectant hyper focus. Then I saw the tan trench coat and brimmed hat. Both were weather worn and smeared with grime, and when he smiled in a gesture of humility toward the patrons of the coffee shop, his teeth blended with the fabric. He removed his hat to reveal a sparse ringlet of ashen hair and clutched the headpiece with both hands against his sternum. He moved apprehensively through each table. I searched my pockets for spare change or small bills.

Annie mumbled an "I understand" into the phone, and the screen flashed and went black. She bit her lip and took a moment to replace the phone on the table.

"I'm sorry about that. Where were we?"

"Talking about the Death of Language. Or the Language of Death. You got any change on you?"

She dug in her bag and pulled out a handful of coins, mostly silver, while I waved the panhandler over. His eyes were a dynamic shade of honey accentuated by decades of caked on dirt. His lips moved timidly before he spoke, practicing, attempting to coax the words from his larynx.

"I do appreciate any help you could offer me."

He spoke with an exaggerated southern drawl, a character ripped from the stage midscene during a Tennessee Williams play, too enthralled in the barbaric notion of gentility to forgo dishonest pleasantries. He sought kindness from strangers. He stove off death by renouncing security.

I poured my bills and Annie's change into his out turned hat. His fingers flipped through the metal as he counted his bounty. Annie watched me suspiciously but kept her words to herself.

"What's your name?" I asked, cupping his wrist for a moment before he recoiled.

"I had a name once, but it's gone," he said. His eyes clouded over as they searched the high beams of the ceiling. "Lost it back there in that place. All the work and the toil and the whiskey stretching out into a sunset that couldn't have been. Glorious and indoors, it was. Right inside and waiting. It's waiting for you."

His head shook slightly as he refocused his attention on the coins in his hat.

"You have my sincerest gratitudes," he said with a half hobbled bow as he walked to greet the other customers before the barista on duty could ask him to leave. She was already filling a free to go cup with her dark roasted bribe.

Annie cleared her throat and tapped her manicured nails against the table. Her hair caught the afternoon sun once more, burned orange to red to blue.

"You know he'll probably just spend that on booze, right?"

"Better him than me," I snapped back. "There've been guys like him all over town lately. I keep seeing that get up everywhere. There's something about each of them that reminds me of something just out of reach. Like a familiarity with someone I haven't met yet."

"Howard, look," she sighed, anger immediately yielding to pity, "I'm worried about you. You've experienced a great deal of trauma that you don't seem to actually be processing."

"I told you," I insisted, "I barely even knew the guy. I was worried about the repercussions for myself, but, honestly, after sitting here with you, I know I'm not going to turn to the bottle any more than your charity will extend beyond yourself unless forced."

My words bit without my permission. She couldn't hide her shocked expression. She couldn't hide her hurt.

I sighed through an apology and leaned back in my chair. I watched as the street laughed and frolicked in the full afternoon sun. My coffee was almost gone.

"I really should get going," I said. "I need to get in early to clean up. Blade's final bow kind of put a damper on the dishes I needed to wash."

I rose to my feet and downed the last few sips of java.

"How did you know about him dying, anyway?" I asked. "I don't remember mentioning it in my message."

Annie fumbled with her cup for a moment and turned to me with a blank expression. She spoke like we had not been speaking, as if she were giving up. The forced Story of How as obvious as it was noncommittal.

"It must have been in the paper or something. I recognized the name of the bar as the place you work. So I guess I just assumed."

I nodded and tossed my empty cup into the garbage bin. She let me hold the door for her as we walked out into the pulsating heat of summer.

"It was in the paper already? And it mentioned the bar by name?" I shook my head. "Connor will be pissed."

❧

People are constantly engaged in battle. Preening in their warpaint and armor. Chainmail and barbs in a clustered formation, bumbling through maneuvers without coordinating plays. Making up the rules they forget as they move on to the next scrimmage. Soldiers searching out leaders, jockeying for position, tripping over their fallen brethren. Buddha with his mandates. Machiavelli with his means.

Connor with his rulings.

Campaigns lost and won on the killing room floor. Each step becomes a tactical rampage with only history left to determine the crusaders from the terrorists. History, though, takes its sweet time in arriving. Even within the three minute attention spans of the goldfish on the newsreel. Each struggle surmounting the one before. Sensory overload. Sensory deprivation.

Lonnie was at his piano when I walked into The Maiden Name. He kept his face tilted toward the keys, but his eyes followed me as I joined Connor behind the bar. He gave me a subtle nod as I filled the sinks with sanitizer and rinse water to push through the dishes I'd left the night before.

"Sorry for the mess," I said, attempting to portray the awkward combination of reverence and pity deemed appropriate for such a situation.

"I get it," Connor replied, never looking up from the papers he was shuffling through. "We just need to get it all sorted before the meeting."

"Meeting?"

A business becomes a war room with each malady, however large or small. Keith forgets to replace the trashcan liner. Sue gives out the wrong change. Blade overdoses and croaks next to the back stock of CO2 cartridges. Lines are drawn; new strategies are put into place. A reactionary assault in hopes of being proactive for next time. And then Brenda's till comes up short, and it starts all over again.

The barstools filled with somber faces atop apathetic demeanors. Connor cleared his throat in uncomfortable condolences for those who knew Blade née Warren well. He offered his edicts with the gravelly gravitas of the gods, wildfires within parted seas, commandments so chiseled onto stone.

"Death is bad for business," he said.

For a moment, it seemed clear that death *was* our business. That the libations we peddled were medicines imbibed to quell the fear of its proximity. That we made our money off of convincing folks they were still alive enough to try to numb it all.

"We can't let it happen here again," he said. As if he could control it. As if we'd tried for it to begin with.

I watched the feigned sorrow switch to indignation, a righteous anger burning as Connor explained the new policies. Employees would lay off the sauce while on duty. Even if a customer wanted to buy them a shot. Even if they needed it to perform. Employees would report all non-sanctioned substances or face retribution. And employees included the freelance performers. He spoke with the finality of unearned confidence. Because punishment was greater than death, it could overcome departure.

Connor's cocksure defiance gnawed at something in my memory as the queens and dancers groaned their departing disapproval. Lonnie saddled up to the bar and helped himself to a tug of gin.

"Can you believe this shit?" he declared between gulps.

Connor stared at him from the table he'd perched at to check off the meeting points from his notes.

"What?" Lonnie asked, lifting his glass. "I ain't on the clock yet. This swill is fair game if the cash in my pocket is as good as this guy's."

Lonnie readied himself for the fray as I turned my attention to the first patron of the day. His dark skin was taut over his skeleton, pulled back with age and shrinking faster than his bones could deteriorate. An arch of grey white hair circled the sides of his head, and he fidgeted with his tan hat as he stood a few paces from the bar.

"You believe this shit? Assigning fault to a bottle like the man who picked it up ain't got nothing to carry the blame but the glass."

"Lonnie, settle down," Connor scolded from his table, barely looking up.

Though he would claim differently, as was the custom, Lonnie's anger was not displaced. He was more concerned with his own loss than the loss of life. The cause and the effect amassed to affect, solitary yet still leading the cause in the charge.

"Some dumb shit makes a choice that don't hurt nobody but himself, and this guy's in here trying to take it out on me. Does that seem right to you, Howie?"

I eyed the fake bottle of booze I kept on my line while I considered the damage I'd nearly caused myself. My thoughts drifted to Reg's face the night he told me I had to make a choice between our life together and the bowed in side of the bottle. One of the nights. The days had been different.

We'd been celebrating. We were always celebrating. There was perpetually so much to celebrate. Toni or Abbi or Tori from his office had gotten engaged or gotten divorced or gotten knocked up. There were empty orchestras and cakes and fizzy bottles of consolatory imbibes. It was all so chaotically simple. All so statically extravagant. All of us there were dedicated to a sole idea, to the merriment of the beyond. That is the power of the spirit. Not the specter that remains, but the ghost that's still alive in the moment of anticipation. Whatever the moment, the theoretical beginning or anti-climactic end, it's experienced in expectancy of a fantastical future just beyond the precipice of the tallest building on the horizon, so close and ever shifting. We knew something better was coming, better even than this.

So we celebrated. We relished. We savored and left it behind for the next new thing. My heart caught in my chest just like all those clichéd pop songs say as I looked across the crowd and caught the glint of Reg's smile there. It stabbed through my sternum and froze everything. Sharp and subtle and serene. I knew then I wanted to spend every further anticipation with that man. I wanted everything left to come. I reached the space beyond love then and couldn't wait to discover what was beyond that. I floated. I danced. Our energy enraged the power grid to black out, and I rambled through the spotlight of the harvest moon as she guided me to the basement apartment we'd shared back then. I belted out notes I'd never hit before. I slalomed through the faerie rings of wildflowers that had sprung through the mulch. I watched Reg illuminate the sky, reflecting the centuries of fire. Prometheus finally pardoned in that man's bright flame.

And then I awoke half dressed, drenched in my own sick, and halfway inside a bathtub I didn't recognize. A dull morning light filled the room, seeping in through the weft of floral curtains, overcast and attempting to turn the scene to black and white. I collected my pants more easily than my composure and braced myself against the sink and someone else's reflection in the glass. My hair was matted to one side of my head, the other side a nest of static waves. Gold and pink glitter smeared across my cheek like promises made too quickly. My lips faded to match the sallow circles beneath my eyes. I tried to swallow, to wet my throat, to whet my consciousness.

THE HOUSE THAT WASN'T THERE

The bathroom gave way to a small bedroom: beige carpet covered in discarded clothing, a mattress and box spring on the floor in the corner, a dresser with two of the drawers left open. All signs of a life lived too much for the stage to bother with the dressing room. Two men were tangled together with a paisley printed sheet twined between their mangled bodies. They were beautiful, clutching at contact even in slumber, clawing through dreamscapes at connection, hips taut and turned toward places thought alone could not reach. Another man slouched across a rolling desk chair that was backed into the corner of the room. An unbuttoned dress shirt was draped over him like a blanket, his sleeping fingers instinctively gnawed on the cuffs.

And I didn't recognize any of them.

A few more men slept in overlapping lumps on the sofa in the living room. Beer and whiskey bottles, mostly empty, littered the end tables and patchwork rug, merged in the dim light sifting through closed blinds, attempted their best stained glass. A gallant knight, haloed, lumbering up the hill, spear readied and tipped with the light of the day.

I mapped my way home, and Reg, in a pink rage, tore the sheet from my notebook, shredded the page, denied me my return, and offered me a choice: the whiskey or his heart.

"Please choose me," he said. "Because even though it'd suck to lose you now, I know if you keep doing what you're doing, it's the losing you later that will destroy me."

So I gave him my choice. But it wasn't until weeks later that I actually made it.

I spent my days congratulating myself on being so strong, patting my own back for withstanding the evil devil water, thick and wet with its cool temptation, a swirling sea capturing boats bit by bit. I spent my nights pacing in front of the convenience store telling myself I shouldn't go in. And Reg held my hand and told me he had a faith in me that I knew he'd made up because there was nothing left inside to hold onto. I hadn't noticed when every part of me had emptied. I was doing well, though. So one night I congratulated myself.

"Relapse is a part of my recovery." I parroted the line from every pamphlet, every addict hell bent on not bending themselves.

Reg had so much disappointment in his eyes. It poured out of him in cascading avalanches of guilt, pooling around my feet to make an island of me, thick and wet with its cool temptation, its devil water, begging me to dive straight in. I kept my eyes trained on the floor, and still I saw it. It remained even as he packed his bag, swirled as he paused before he shut himself on the other side of the door.

No.

That's not when that happened.

That didn't happen.

I made my choice. And I stuck to it. And Reg loved me for it like I loved him. And he was so, so beautiful.

❦

"What about you, old man?" Lonnie spun on his stool, more and more riled with each sip that passed his tongue. "You think that if you die just from living your old ass life, I should stop aging myself because it might kill me one day?"

"It's not the same thing, and you know it," Connor said calmly from his papers. "Now I suggest you wander home before you embarrass yourself. Or offend any more of our customers."

"Oh, I'm not offended none," the old man assured us. His voice creaked like a plow across the gravelly strains of his vocal cords. "I guess a little bit of that death he's over there hawking is exactly why I'm here."

"Well, step right up," I smiled. "I got it by the glassful."

Lonnie huffed and made a show of tossing a few bills to the counter as the old man took his seat. I watched as he placed his hat carefully on the empty stool beside him and folded his arms across the bar with a slow, delicate ease. There was that familiarity again. It swept over me like a dream of home where everything fit, in the moment, but expanded awkwardly through memory.

"Let me just put on some music," I said, and turned to the sound system. "You got any preferences, mister——? I'm sorry, I don't know your name."

"Most people don't call me much of anything anymore," he said, a whimsical gleam in his eye. "But go on and call me Mr. King."

"All right, Mr. King. Anything you're wanting to hear?"

He leaned onto the bar eagerly, excited by the options, by the ability to have an opinion. He seemed lonely, lost beneath the descent of the path.

THE HOUSE THAT WASN'T THERE

"You got any Cole Porter?"

"Yes, sir," I smiled. "My partner loves his music."

"Oh, I love his music," Mr. King smiled and hummed a few bars to himself as he swayed in his seat. "Ragtime, jazz, and blues. You can pop on pretty much anything from 1890 to 1940, and I'll want to sing along."

I smiled. He had a casual grace about him that warmed me, a learned expression hard bought from decades of reception.

"What are you having? It's on me."

"Actually, if you don't mind,"——he hummed along to the tune of the song——"I'd just appreciate the company."

I placed a glass of water in front of him and watched his mouth form circles around the lyrics spilling through the speakers. He smiled when he saw me looking and cocked his head slightly to the side, the way Reg would do when he was amused by me.

"You know," I said, "'King' is also my partner's surname. Probably not any relation, though."

"Oh, we're all related." He started every new bit of speech with "oh." A master of song. A pop balladeer. "Every single one of us on this planet got built out of the same stock. Every single one of us is kin."

His fingers seemed agitated as he gripped his glass, but the rest of him found rest.

"Though not all of us was built the right way from the start." He smiled a perfect, crooked smile. "But we find ways of getting there."

He took a shaky sip of his water; the clear liquid hurricaned around the rim.

"All of us find a way to make it home," he said. "It's inevitable. Pops up on us. No way to escape it."

His smile returned as he slipped back into the music. Connor slid behind the bar and whispered as he passed, "What's with you and all these old men?" he teased. "It's like you're playing with death on purpose. I'm beginning to think you're really just trying to get out of cleaning up after your shifts."

"You caught me," I laughed. I laughed like I wanted to be caught.

6

"I LOVE WHAT YOU'VE DONE WITH THE PLACE."
Gerrie surveyed the living room in sarcastic astonishment. I'd spent the morning treating my furniture like building blocks, gleefully constructing a new Tower of Babel, longing for communication, dying to get it right. To make room for everything from the bedroom, the living room was first turned upside down. Pillows seemed just at home on floors as chairs did turned over on themselves. I accidentally broke a vase that had been longing for stems since Reg left town. Then I jammed the corner of my desk against the door frame as I attempted to slide it down the hallway, and a sharp, tiny edge of corrugated wood splintered to the floor. The rough edges of both pieces fit together like a puzzle, slipping into place easily enough but never quite connecting. The divided banks of a river. Memories frayed in the violence.

I removed the bedding from the mattress and flipped it to its side so I could shove it to the space where the coffee table had been. The quilted fabric smelled like Reg as I heaved it forward. His sweat and his rut and his dreams all embedded deep down into the foam and the straw and the cotton encased within. I breathed deeply to take his musk into my lungs, to fill myself with him. His message did say he'd be busy. That was why he hadn't called. The bed frame was dismantled into a jumbled mess on the floor; the headboard leaned against the hallway wall.

Painter's tarps covered the dresser I'd dragged to the center of the bedroom, and my new friend Gerrie placed her coffee mug beside the gallon cans of slightly different shades of yellow paint and the extra roller my new friend Cent had thrown in for free. My imperfect map bled slightly through the first coat like a treasure map on aged paper. One more coat and I could try again. Figure out where I'd gone wrong.

"'Sunrise Daffodil?'" She read the description on the can I'd chosen to go with. "Isn't 'yellow yellow' a little redundant?"

"The guy at the hardware store helped me pick it out. I was feeling my Gilman feminist narrative mood."

"It's captivating." Gerrie smirked at her own pun and hopped up to let her feet dangle from the chest of drawers. "At my old place, I put up reams of butcher paper on the walls. I could make notes or doodle without consequence. And it was much easier to rip down the initials of a past lover than to have to paint over the little heart with the arrow."

"I'm not that smart," I conceded.

"No. Apparently not," she laughed. "Though there is something to be said about the act of covering versus removing. Or the fragility of permanence in a consumable world."

"That the philosophical part of your sociology degree talking?"

"It's the 'fuck my ex' part of my leftover teen angst talking," she quipped. "When it comes to love, I throw all that philosophy crap out the window."

"The third defenestration of Prague."

"Oh, we've got banter."

Gerrie dropped from her perch and grabbed a roller, spinning the cotton in her hand before running it through the pan of burnt flower paint. She touched the wall in a swift, sharp x pattern, crisscrossing diamonds that grew smaller and fuller to block out what had been.

"How do you think Reg will react when he gets back?"

I watched her paint and considered her question silently. Since moving in together, we'd made it a point to come to all house related decisions as a pair. We were building a home, and that took input from all parties involved. Sure, one of us would see a trinket that we liked, and it'd find a new home on a bookshelf. Or a potted plant would catch in one of our irises to then bloom in the light of an opened window. And once I'd surprised him with a new alarm clock I knew he'd had his eye on. But most things, even the shower curtain liner, were discussed and weighed before they found their way into the apartment.

"I guess I hadn't really thought about that." A sullen timbre filled my throat, and I did my best to shake it from my vocal cords. "But I can always paint it again."

"Non-permanent permanence." She sighed and stepped back from the wall. Her canvas was coated. A solid patch of sunlight with the tendrils of my map escaping the edges of her creation. She placed her roller in the pan and reached outward to crack her knuckles. "Your plan is to re-do your map, right?"

"Yeah. To clear up the bits I got wrong before."

I grabbed my roller and began working in the cross pattern I'd seen her do, building off to the right of her sun. She followed suit on the left as she laughed.

"I never really considered a map to be a relationship," she said, "but I guess they've got that in common. Every new attempt at plotting the course teaches you a thing or two you utilize next time. And with every new attempt, you're just wishing against the past that you get it right this time."

"And every time it's easier and it's harder. People. They're always changing things. Tearing down parks to replace them with buildings; re-routing the flow of the streams; catching your eye and changing your opinions. Did you know there's more than one kind of shower curtain liner? Reg does." Gerrie looked at me questioningly, so I continued. "You think you've got it right and all of a sudden someone moves in and your entire worldview is fucked."

"True. But sometimes fucked is better. Sometimes we need our perception to shift. Like you said, people are always changing things."

I stepped back from the wall and dipped my roller back into the pan.

"You sound like my ex," I said. "He was always saying, 'what if we thought about it this way' or 'what if we tried it like that.' He questioned every single thing he encountered."

"And I'm sure you're better for it. I bet a part of you learned to dig deeper than the surface from him. To break the tension without being overly skeptical. You took what you could and threw the rest out the window."

"You've really got a thing for glass, huh?"

"Hell yeah!" she exclaimed. "The window is always a viable option."

"I guess you're right, though. I mean, I probably wouldn't have connected it at the time, and I haven't thought about him in years, but Rafe is probably the reason I question everything today. I used to just blame him for making me distrust myself, but I suppose there is merit in thinking things through."

"I think it's about understanding," Gerrie said, never taking her eyes from the wall. "What I mean is, the way we look at things, the way we remember events, changes how we approach them moving forward. Fuck the fucking fuck out of a bunch of Nazis, but understanding how the world got to that point, questioning what if this had been different or that had happened another way can prevent it all from recurring."

"At least that's what all our history teachers tried to tell us."

"And they were mostly right. Though it's just as important to think about who is telling the history, who has decided the moral of the story. The victors dictate the narrative. The folks left behind in the folds of what was have so little control. At least for a time."

✢

Time. Time becomes distorted by living. Living becomes distorted by time. There is a distinction. Slow or fast. Now or then. All create spatial implications that have no real relevance on the tick tick tocking of the clock. Fast or slow, then or now, can all occur in simultaneity when provoked. When provoked, knowledge can jostle a different understanding, a new remembrance. A fonder appreciation. A shifted means of judgment. Life is then reevaluated. The sum of its parts. The moments that moved so slowly, even as the clock ticked forward, they remained frozen in a simple gesture that repeated over decades of doubt, longing, resentment, fear, solace, love.

The living become distorted *in time*. The living becoming distorted *in* Time. The stress of language is important. The stress on language is important. And suddenly/always it becomes too easy to dictate a course the forward march——of course!——was pushing all along. Pursuing/chasing/leading/letting be.

Do beings require time to exist?

For the time being, they do. For the time in which time had been named. Yet, before the naming of things, before the advent of the concept of naming, things persevered. They ticked forward. They ticked backward. They tic'd. And still, they did not have a name. And still, they moved through something amorphous and hollow in every memory, filled with attributes that came some years later in locales that became some years before.

There's poetry there.

I did not create these words. I simply connected them. Pulled them together from the echoes of wonder left behind in time to be found in another moment.

Or.

I created these words. And their orgiastic pursuit spewed out to tarnish the past, to influence the future. To rest, finally, in a somber understanding of two months, of two minutes, of three years sober, of chips, of coats of paint.

Yellow is a garish color on a bedroom wall in an uptown apartment. Yellow is a halo, is the sun, is worshipped.

My mother thought yellow was beautiful. She had an apron that ripped and frayed each time she passed the dining room table, moving from the smoke stained linoleum to the laminate hardwood floors, that shone as brightly as a stained glass window during the sunrise service. She wore it often. She wore it always. As if it could shine her very self across the vastness of small town life, she wears it often.

Language attempts to solidify time. Tenses tense at the concept of fluidity. Verbs require action and try to place it in the past. Everything has already happened, and the sunset will light the sky in erotic hues again tomorrow, rich and sultry and ever new in their recurrence.

Reg had been gone for three days. Reg had been gone for three days but had left one message——garbled and disjointed by the airwaves as they attempted to feed his voice through a recording on my phone. I missed him as much as I missed him when he was right next to me, and Gerrie and I painted the bedroom Sunrise Daffodil. Yellow. Painting a few minutes into centuries that sped by so quickly. And yet the clock itself—— the measurement never changed.

The guy at the hardware store helped me pick it out. Even after I'd explained to him what it was for. He told me his name was Vincent, and I'd asked him what it was now, and he said his friends called him Cent the last time they called him anything. He was kind, and when he smiled, his teeth didn't meet one another in the expected locations. He'd asked me if I needed help but spoke with an eagerness that implied a need for contact, for connection more so than a paycheck. He listened to my story as if time didn't matter, as if there were no other customers, as if he weren't waiting to clock out. We knew we were minor characters in one another's lives, a period in the middle of a sentence that spanned a much longer course of action. He listened to me bemoan the absence of Reg, and, as the dyes rocked rapidly to mix with the base paint inside the can, told me that time would be a good thing. Time, he said, is what helped him cope when his wife had miscarried their first child. Time, he said, is what was needed to help her feel whole again. To help them both understand who they were beyond the unexpected cancellation of a life that had yet to occur.

Time was funny that way. Within its duration, their lives had never held a child, and yet, suddenly, their arms were empty.

We tried three different yellows.

He told me, "Sunrise Daffodil is a great choice," and that it would probably take a few coats to cover the map, and that he was sure Reg would call when he got the time.

✺

The phone rang sometime after 2am, and I tripped over myself as I rushed to answer the call. A soft wind rustled through the bedroom window down the hallway, muffling the dimmed city symphony that piano'd through the night. I'd left the window open to air out the fresh paint smell and leap frogged the makeshift pyramids of furniture to settle in on the couch. Sleep had come in fits. In whimpers. My eyes closed for only moments as hours ticked by. Dreams that lasted days were over in minutes.

I tripped a second time before reaching my phone on the kitchen counter. The skin on my knee burned. The screen flashed with light.

"Hello?"

"Hi, Love."

Reg's voice was smooth and carbonated, fizzing with static electricity. I felt my neck give way, collapse vertebrae by vertebrae into the wholeness of my body. Relief and desire swirled within my lungs.

"I've wanted... for a while..."

"Reg. I think we have a bad connection."

But the line was dead. Silence echoed back at me as I felt the soft warmth of the screen glow fade to black against my cheek. My shin was wet with the sloppy remnants of my rush to answer. I was lightheaded. I felt the vibration before the phone actually started to ring.

"Reg!"

The declaration. The question. The need.

"Howard, it's your mother."

My stomach crashed. I had not spoken to Catherine Perry Portman in over five years. Not since my first attempt at a dozen steps making a difference in where I stood. An attempt at amends left leaping for a solace I was trying to put down. The third time around, the time that stuck, Annie told me I did not have to try again with her; that I should understand my triggers. My mother was not a trigger. She was a loaded revolver.

"I debated calling you about this. Whether or not I should reach out at all."

She had never been a reacher. When I was seven, we'd take the river-side path from our house to the market. I was to be seen and not heard—— so quick she was with the backhand or a cliché. I would stand aside as she gossiped with the other women congregated beside the magazine stands and wait to carry the bags back home. I studied the parallel lines of the aisles, the angled joints of the floor tiles. I plotted escape plans, mapped out adventures with the heroes from the fronts of cereal boxes. And then I loaded my forearms up with the plastic bags that bulged with cardboard boxes and aluminum cans to begin the trek back home.

In the spring, tadpoles shimmied through the puddles that formed along the riverbank. I loved watching their synchronized dance as they cleaned the stones of algae, slick and syncopated and temporary. There were six weeks, six trips to the grocery store, twelve chances to see them swim before their legs sent them hopping into the tall grass on the far bank. I stole the few steps from the path to the water, lost my balance, and splashed into the bed. My mother watched from the corner of her eye, mumbled something about not getting her magazines wet, and kept step-ping forward. I sat with my arms outstretched, angled up to keep the bags dry, and felt the slow current swish over my legs. I waited for a hand, for a rope, for a lightning bolt.

Silence crackled over the line.

"Maybe I shouldn't have called."

"How've you been, Mom?"

The words sighed out in a jumble. An attempt at familiarity, a sweeping under the rug.

When I was eleven, I stared at the shirtless soap opera star on the stand beside the cash register a little too long. Her initial "your scrawny ass will never look like that" escalated to a burning sensation across my cheek and a "no son of mine."

"Things have been rough. That's why I called."

I waited.

I heard her twine the phone cord around her finger, shift her legs against the scratchy fabric of her ankle length skirt. Her yellow apron shone through the receiver.

"Things have been a little off here too, lately."

She hadn't asked, but three was fast approaching. I needed to hurry things along.

When I was seventeen, Cathy followed me out one night. She took notes as I smoked in the parking lot of the movie theater. She shuddered as I took a swig of whiskey from a tiny metal flask. She watched my hand slip into Preston's. He lived two towns over, and when he kissed me, the rough stubble of a beard trying its best to grow in made my lips burn in a way I'd mistaken for fire. My clothes were packed into bulging grocery bags——the same ones I'd carried for her——by the time I made it home.

She needed to hurry things along.

For a time, I wanted to be the boy who admired his mother. So certain was I there existed a memory somewhere disguising itself as a fairytale. I was so sure there was something I could hold onto to redeem our relationship. A past reformatted and remembered to help me sleep at night. But every blue jay that landed on her finger turned into an apple in her palm.

She spoke in slurs and stutters, oscillating between needing to tell me something and wishing she had never picked up the phone. My past caught in my throat, and I cleared it. I realized I felt nothing. And there was solace in that.

"Mom, have you been drinking?"

"Have I been drinking?" she chortled. "That's a hoot coming from you."

"Is there a point to this late night rendezvous?"

"So this is how you speak to the woman who raised you now?"

"This is how I speak to the woman who gave birth to me, yes."

This was how I spoke in my memory. But her laugh——her laugh—— was always the same.

She'd laughed the same laugh when I'd called to make amends. It was actually a beautiful sound. Her vibrato tickled the air in undulating waves. She didn't laugh often, at least around me, but when she did, it was whimsical enough to bring on a temporary bout of amnesia. It held the make believe safety of my formative years.

"Your father's dead."

Tires screeched outside my window. The squealing sound of metal against rims. Locking.

"I buried him two weeks ago."

A horn gave way to the crunching of metal, to the crescendo of a siren approaching, singing her seduction to all the bus bench lawyers.

"I wasn't going to call, but I thought you should know."

I hung up the phone and did my best to hurdle furniture to reach the curtains. The street was awash in a strobe of red and white light. A yellow sedan had jumped the curb, barely missing the line of cars parked along the edge. The pedestrian in the green ball cap was not so lucky.

He looked happy, though, from what I could tell. Peaceful as the paramedics loaded his body onto the gurney. Almost smiling as they raised the sheet to cover his face. Finally, he could close his eyes, end his trip. He was finally at rest.

THE HOUSE THAT WASN'T THERE

IT WAS A QUIET TANTRUM, pulsing out in spasmodic songbird simpers, old book numbers barely recognized in the current youth of so long ago. Simple and subtle but, to be sure, finding its footing with each creak of the floorboards, every shift of the light. It wheezed in place, a breath caught, awaiting freedom. It trilled the molecules of the air; a cat's purr phasing into each object, gentle——at first——and infecting it all with motion so subdued that everything was left uneasy in its wake. Waiting to wake.

He pushed through room after room. Each space was a mausoleum filled with the ghosts of old furniture, the memories of those who had come before. Those who has gone. Repetitive ghosts caught in picture frames out of the corner of his eye. Posing and smiling and always in anticipation of the flash. Always waiting. Waiting. Waiting.

His name was Rafe or William or Paul. Never Reginald. He had olive skin or rosy cheeks. And his voice broke a bit whenever he got excited. He remembered that to be true. He thought it was. It had been so long since he had heard himself speak, the sounds he thought his own were muddled, played back via intercom, pre-recorded and canned for the next time around. The laughter of an audience not really there.

He watched himself as he passed through the house, stood back to take in the view as if it were projected on a screen. A languid dream made lucid. And the house heaved deep breaths of fear and anger and exhaustion.

A leather diary sat open across a faded armchair. Dates crossed out. Times circled in red. Days that had meaning, had importance, but could not be recalled. He hadn't known the date would be special when it happened. And it wasn't, until it was decided upon, and then it was. Then time passed, and it was no longer important. But it was still circled in red. A twinge pulsed in his chest each time the day occurred, but he couldn't quite remember what had lodged in there. He couldn't quite bring himself to turn the page.

7

I STARED THROUGH THE WINDOW as the sun rose. I had been there all night, ever since the call, through the sound of the sirens and the filled silence of the after. The street wore so many faces, collecting them like Reg's masks inside the hall closet, switching them out with each passing hour, every passing moment, any twitch in expression. The long nosed plague mask, birdlike and filled with pleasant smells of carnations and mint and juniper, afraid of what had occurred, sifted through the remnants of a broken headlight, of spilled blood and soul. The harlequin colors of a pre-dawn jester laughed in the face of impending obscurity. The mask of the fool, of the lover, of the decadent. And finally, as the sun stumbled through the high rises and hotels, the great coastal trees and the decaying matter of the fallen, it donned a brightly colored death mask. A caricature of the life that had been there, delicately painted in hues that expanded, sitting up in bed and soldiering on as if it were built to withstand even those moments when degradation and circumstance had marred the visage beneath. Solid and somber and energetic and ever changing. Depending on who looked.

I looked.

I saw.

Light sliced from the slate and serpentine in the asphalt, an aggregate of sun and streetlamp ignited, intensified, and sent beaming into my eyes. I turned to face the living room; the chaotic remnants of my yesterday strewn about in joyous disarray to mock the carnage I thought I could control. Furniture, heaped upon itself in folded acquiescence, no longer useful for sleeping or drawing, found what it could be when given more options than simply to serve.

I wondered if his living room was a wreck as well. The man from the street. The man in the morgue. I thought there were papers strewn across his coffee table, bills to pay, love letters to return. I imagined the book he'd been putting off reading, its spine still pristine——not snapped like his own——resting on the kitchen table as a reminder to take a day off once in a while. I contemplated children who would be waking up soon and wondering where their daddy was, why he wasn't back from his run. It had already been four hours after all. Surely his absence was ready to be noticed. Or maybe they already knew. Maybe they were sobbing and huddled together on the couch; or picking up the dirty clothes he never managed to hoop shot into the hamper and would not be wearing again. Ever. Still, perhaps they couldn't know. It had only been four hours.

I had only just found out, and my father had been dead for nearly a month.

He had black hair, pitch through most of it, but greying at the temples, though that could have been the light of the ambulance sirens refracting off the blood which slicked all of it back. An optical illusion. A memory distorted.

My father's hair was jet black also. It had been, when last I'd seen him, silent and swallowed in his thoughts as my mother ushered me out the door.

The paint had dried in the night, though I still touched the bedroom wall to be certain. The color was deeper than I remembered, sturdier and bolstered by its perch atop the drywall. It echoed the eggshell palate beneath it and looked nothing like the burnt orange of the daybreak I'd just witnessed. I carried what I could back into the bedroom and pushed the rest down the hallway, a blanket stretched underneath each item to protect the floors. The stained and swirling planks of the hardwood floor felt cool and sticky against my legs as I sat down to reassemble the bed frame. I'd cleaned most of the blood from my shin, and a small scab had formed just below my knee. It burned a bit as I shifted my weight and my skin pulled taut.

It was nothing. Hardly noticeable. A clumsy scratch made larger with its healing.

Would they have cleaned him up before his family saw him? The man from the street. The man from the night. Did they wipe away the excess? Strategically place the sheet so that the wounds were invisible? Provide some sense of security beneath the harsh fluorescent lighting that always seemed to flicker in the morgue? Hide the way he died so that the absence of life was all the more present?

What face had my dad worn in that position?

I tested the stability of the frame before pulling the mattress back into place. The cherry wood of the headboard popped against the yellow of the walls. Subtleties I had not noticed before exploded in sparks and blurred into the swirled etching in the posts. Regal and offset by the casual crease of Reg's body in the mattress. Curved to the side in a yearning position, reaching out as I pulled in behind him on the nights when I could. He slept with the covers pulled over his head, and I angled my face out to breathe.

I contemplated his final thought. He planned his day down to the second; organization and fantasy interacted in his favor. The prayer of a positive outlook. Or he questioned his daughter's choice in major at the school he was paying too much for. He told himself the stars seemed lovely, what he could see of them, or he felt like waffles for breakfast, or he would finally get to that novel by Sunday. Anything but 'Oh shit! That car's going to hit me.' Anything else before the shock. Time slowed down. Allowed him to collect himself. To stretch the moment and redeem his mind for a proper send off. His dying breath was an expression of love for the family and friends he left behind.

My father breathed my name, hollowed and raspy, clinging to the air of the hospital room like the constant stench of disinfectant. His IV bag hung there like a speech bubble filled with only my being. A cleansing. A regret. An exhale. That's what had given my mom the courage to drink herself into calling me. The very mention of my name had sent her straight for the vodka.

I needed a drink.

Instead, I reset the dresser and then the desk. I reset the desk corner that had broken and tried to make it as seamless as it could be. I took a shower. I made a sandwich. I read the news, but there was no mention of the accident that had occurred just outside my window. The world never seemed ready to witness what had been seen. I wondered how his family was coping, if they had people to reach out to for comfort, for distraction. If they were happy he was gone.

Moments transpire that shift everything into a new prospective.

The go go boy was well liked in his hometown. A starter on the varsity team. A solid C+ student. Polite and respectful to adults. Admired by his peers——well, the ones who mattered. He travelled over six hundred miles to get here, to study business, to succeed. And he took his final hit wearing a thong inside the storeroom of a gay bar. His parents were devastated. But as they learned who he'd become, we learned who he was.

Shift.

The man on the street had plans. He had thoughts and feelings. He was filled with ideas that flashed and diverted into headlights. Entire processes agitated in the gurgle of a 3am flight. And then nothing. No more plans. No more inclusion. A future rewritten.

Shifted.

And then the man who raised me. Memories of cold shoulders and averted eyes were replaced by afternoons grilling in the backyard. Strict schedules and soft belts gave way to dedication and a desire for me to be better, to have a better life than the one he had worked so hard to build. A fifteen year absence relieved by a single, final breath. He sighed my name. And he died.

Occurrences like that have names only after the fact. They exist in a prologue, a documentation requiring a consensus to be formed, someone intelligent to step in and say "this is the what" and leave the rest of us to figure out the why. Bees began vanishing in 1869, victims of the (then called) Disappearing Disease that decimated entire colonies without a trace. Slowly, at first, and with few warning signs to trigger any alarm, the drones just stopped returning to the hive. They lost their way home.

They fell prey to pesticides or predators or disease. One or two here, another there, until all that was left was a queen and her riches. Then, unable to fend for herself, her hive died.

One hundred and thirty-seven years later, Colony Collapse Disorder was christened, the broken bits of a century in the shattered champagne bottle around the hull. To be fair, it had worn many monikers throughout those days. The naming of it seemed to bring understanding, even if no one could figure out why it was happening. The naming of a thing brings comfort, even as the thing itself continues forth.

One bee falls. And then another. And then another until the hollow golden caverns of home are left a ghost town, decimated and abandoned in struggle and grief. Pilfered and razed to make way for the next thing to be named. Apiaries turned to morgues. The heartland left to rot.

❧

I did a lot of holding my head in my hands. The air conditioning unit hummed through the vents like a chainsaw when I focused on the sound. The burnt smell of hazelnut and ozone filled my nostrils as coffee poured into Styrofoam cups. Annie's hand cupped my shoulder, and I pulled myself to attention.

"We don't usually see you at the Saturday meetings," she said as she extended a steaming cup toward me. "Don't you usually have work?"

I peered over the anonymity of rows over circles. I watched the watchful crowd zombie their way to their seats.

"I head in right after." My voice shook as I spoke, struggling to shake free of my thoughts, each tendril of non sequitur ideology wrapping through the syllables. "It's been harsh today."

"The aftermath of death can be hard to work through," she said, voice filled with compassion, eyes tilted toward the toe of her shoe.

I studied the lines formed as she tightened her mouth. Wrinkles of understanding pitched across her cheeks, pulled taut, and smoothed where her left incisor pushed against her bottom lip. Perplexed at first, my mind conjured Blade, recalled our conversation about him.

"Well, and now..."

Her eyes snapped to mine as my words trailed off. More people were taking their seats, shoving sugar cookies into their pants pockets.

"Now?"

I sighed as I leaned back in my chair. The meeting was about to begin.

"I'll speak about it tonight," I replied. "I think I've cleared my head enough for that."

Relief coupled the expectancy in her expression, and she touched my shoulder once more before finding a seat of her own. The first speaker stood before us.

No.

❧

THE HOUSE THAT WASN'T THERE

Annie wasn't there. She didn't give me coffee. She offered no solace.

I sat against the cool metal of the folding chair and scanned the faces of my compatriots. I recognized a few of them, remembered bits and pieces of the darkest parts of their histories but couldn't recollect their names. I was alone, but the crowd helped.

When I stood to speak, my sneakers snagged against the cord of the oscillating fan aimed at the group. I reached out to stabilize the base and smirked as I rested my forearms against the podium.

"My name is Howard, and..."

I told them about Blade. About my father. About the man on the street. Slowly and jumbled together. Three souls lost and placed against a single feather; their weight squared off with Osiris. Annie's eyes filled with concern, with compassion. She tilted her chin slightly to the left, a subtle gesture of empathy. She offered friendship bolstered in mercy.

Except Annie wasn't there.

"And it's not like I actually knew any of them," I said. "Our relationships were peripheral. A new coworker; the aftermath of a life I had never witnessed; some man named Gideon I barely knew over a decade ago. But still, there's that feeling of reaching out to an emptiness beside me that should have been filled with their bodies. Like they could still be there. Still breathing and growing and shrinking and moving. And there's that idea of filling the space that they are definitely not in with bourbon. With escape."

Annie nodded to encourage me further. To delve deeper and come up on the other side of the bottle, bobbing in the water with a cork in my mouth.

She wasn't there, but behind her, to the left, a man adjusted the khaki collar of his trench coat. His face was comforting. Dark skin stretched tight over gaunt cheekbones; a century of smile lines echoing his lips; kind yet stormy eyes. He tapped the brim of his hat to punctuate my story. To prove he was listening. To testify.

"But three years is a hell of a lot longer than those moments, even as they freeze into eternity. The corn and rye, however sweet the mixture, would do nothing to affect them. Only me. Only to mess up all of the things they left behind."

Annie was not there.

The timer dinged as I collected myself. I knocked my fist against the woodgrain of the stand and shuffled back to my seat. The man in the khaki trench coat's fingers wrapped around my shoulder. The ebony skin of his hands turned white and pink at the swollen joints, straining to fold the way they had instinctively done for decades before that moment. He leaned in slowly. His breath scraped the nape of my neck.

"There is comfort in knowing something is still there," he said, "even if you can't see it. Can't touch it. Like the bottle. Or your boyfriend——"

No. He said "father."

"——Like the bottle. Or your father. You don't have to have them in your hand to feel what they made you feel."

I touched his hand on my shoulder and electricity sparked between us. We exchanged a shy, familiar smile, and he pulled back into himself, nodding to the podium as we turned to the next speaker.

As the meeting ended, I looked for Annie. I looked for the man in the trilby. The kind man in the trench coat. They were not there.

᙮

I walked slowly through the evening air. The days had stretched so long, dusk was hours from the horizon, but still a calm haze washed the grey off the tree lined street. Pigeons cooed from their roosts, waddled along the sidewalks, and pecked aggressively at the paper cups and discarded remnants of a life too busy. The sheen of their feathers, some of them, mimicked the rainbow glow of the oil buildup on the streets. The beauty of the things left unnoticed. The beauty achieved in not noticing.

I realized I had not talked about Reg at the meeting. About missing him. About wondering how his training was going. If he was fitting in and finding himself where he was. Where I was not. I hadn't even called him to tell him about my dad. I told myself it was because I hadn't wanted to disturb him, to interrupt his training. The important training for the promotion. The new position and the new life together.

I held my phone in my hand. My thumb hovered above the picture next to his number. Swallowing hard, I accessed my messages instead to try once more at hearing his. To hear his voice. To make out more words through the static.

"Hi, Love."

His voice was heady with an exhausted excitement. It sang in repetition. A chorus of peace tinged in doubt.

"This is... great... for us... right...."

Words echoed and rearranged. New meanings. New information leaking through. Cords to Chords. Regurgitated binaries.

"You're... important...."

I knew I was. I knew he'd call when he could. He'd be home when he could.

"A beacon... I'm... happy... I will be... Soon."

I heard what I needed to hear: a voice singing through time, reminding me of a moment when temporarily seemed like forever. Telling me the now was malleable. Nautical clay washed by the waves of a passerby.

"I love... you."

The Maiden Name was dark when I arrived. A hastily written note apologized for the inconvenience to the two or three wanderers who'd tested the door through the calm afternoon hours. I fished my keys from my pocket and disengaged the lock bar protecting the door. The space breathed its air conditioned chill onto the sidewalk, welcoming me in exhale, silent and settled and still.

A few glasses graced the bar top, half empty, filled with the remnants of whiskey and saliva. Unfinished. A still life begging for consumption. Each of them was maybe half full from the optimist's point of view. Though addicts are rarely optimists, when we are, a glass filled to any level can be both a delight and dismay. The promise of more versus that which could have already been imbibed.

I straightened the stools two at a time and collected the cups as I rounded the corner of the bar, tossing the leftover alcohol into the dump sink. I pulled the stoppers from the bottoms of the sanitizer, wash, and rinse sinks and watched the tepid water swirl down the drains in competing cyclones. The rinse sink always lost: the chemicals in the soaps agitated the molecules of the water, exciting the double hydrogen, exasperating the oxygen, and gurgling back up to prevent the fall of the tide. Replugging the sinks, I turned the faucet to hot and moved to switch on the lights.

Connor had left a note atop the cash register.

Emergency evacuation, it read. *Lonnie fainted at the piano. I had to drive him to the clinic. Should all be fine. Open as usual. No live music tonight.*

I pictured the piano man slumped over the keys, parched and aching for the cool splash of gin to quench his swirling brain. Putting on airs in hopes of breaking Connor's hard shell. He probably had a pal at the clinic who would even prescribe him an hourly dosage: a two ounce minimum shot. I could see him taking the gag that far.

He was okay, though. I hoped he was okay.

❧

Fading sunlight exploded into the room as the door swung open, harsh and blinding in the dim pallor of the space. I smiled instinctively at the truncated silhouette, giving my best how can I help you face, as he staggered to the bar. My eyes adjusted as he tossed his trilby to the counter and took up residence on a stool.

"Scotch," he mumbled. "Cheap. Neat."

I nodded and turned to pour.

"There a convention in town or something?" I asked as I pointed at his get up, a half hearted chuckle in my throat, an attempt to open a rapport.

The man's eyes glassed over, and he rubbed his temples.

"I just mean that seems quite the popular outfit amongst men of a certain age of late."

He clasped a liver spotted hand around the high ball glass and took a hearty, mealy sip. A grotesque whistle of a sigh, hollowed and echoed through failing lungs, emerged from his throat before he went back in for another swig.

"I'll just leave you be," I nodded and moved to finish prep for the evening. A cutting board, a few limes. Maraschino cherries redder than anything naturally occurring. A ceramic blade sharp against the yellow rind of a lemon.

The acidic sting of a stray mist of juice hit my eye as the skin of the fruit broke. I winced as I felt the tear ducts go to work to rinse away the foreign particles. In my watery vision, the man seated at the bar looked remarkably like my old friend Jordan from back home. Jordan had been my best friend since third grade. We'd done everything together. Inseparable. Twins, the teachers called us. Brothers brought together by fate. Right up until junior high, until we both found ourselves awake at a sleep over, and I misread the message in our darkened midnight stare. United until my hand slipped a little too far south.

Take away the trench coat and the years, and this guy could've been Jordan's twin in a way I never was.

"You any relation to Jordan Mitchell?"

"You really are dense, aren't you?" he asked, finishing his glass and twirling it against the woodgrain of the bar.

"Sorry. You don't want to be bothered."

The man huffed and scrambled to his feet. He reached for his hat and batted at the brim with his fingertips.

"What's it going to take for you to realize your part in all of this?" he asked.

The ring of the landline jostled me back from the man's glare. My mouth gaped like a fish out of water even as my body moved toward the phone.

"I don't think I understand what you mean," I said.

"You don't think. Of course you don't," he replied, his tongue thick against the back of his teeth. "That's part of the goddamn problem."

"Hello?"

I answered the phone timidly, my eyes still trained on the old man as he pushed his way toward the door.

"Howard, it's Connor. We need to go dark tonight."

"What do you mean?"

"I mean you seem to think that everything is happening to you."

The old man pulled the door open and paused in the frame.

"Close up shop. Lonnie's dead."

I bit my lip at Connor's news. The old man gave me one last look, shaking his head in dismay.

8

I DREW ANOTHER MAP. I'd like to say I closed my eyes and let my body take over, the impulse of what would come guiding my hand down staggered city streets, each of which emerged ecstatically from the felt tip of a magic wand. As if the making of a thing were autonomous. As if it were making itself through me: rich, full, and developed, and springing to life once the ink well was exposed. The reality, though, was a face pressed against a field of Sunrise Daffodils. A measured line. An ill plotted pace.

An unfortunate byproduct of the Industrial Age is the assumption of Now. We want it all so quickly. So quickly we wanted it all. For some of us, the immediacy carried with it the complexity of gods. So much accomplished in so little time. Seven days and a world at our feet. For others in our midst, we found our humanity mixed up inside a few lucid moments which left us wondering when we would find ourselves again. How we could feel like the gods who surrounded us, and how we should feel when presented with our own mistakes.

Once upon a time, I turned to the bottle. That morning, it was the hardware store. A benefit of the Now: no pressing pigments for me. Besides which, Reg was more partial to blue than yellow.

"I'd go with this one. Keep with the floral motif."

I flipped the paint swatch around my cupped palm and smiled over my shoulder at Cent. From behind the counter, he nodded to a passing customer and returned to adhering sticky price tags to the wooden handles of paint brushes, knowing they could never be completely removed. I could have sworn I'd heard his voice.

I tossed the swatch to the counter and tapped the third color in with my index finger. Cent glanced at the card and mumbled the call numbers to himself before asking how many gallons I needed.

No.

"Howie! How's my favorite customer? Picking up another gallon to finish off your bouquet?"

Cent had one of those smiles that curved in a remarkably genuine manner. Infectious, it battled the fluorescent lighting of the store and put everyone in the vicinity in a visibly better mood. Shoppers smiled as their household chores stared back at them from the shelves. Construction workers' stomping gaits turned to skips as they selected tools that curved to fit the callouses on their hands. He'd make a good bartender, Cent would, with his subtle remembrance, his genial manner.

"Yeah. I think two gallons of Cornflower Blue should do it."

"Gloss or matte?"

No.

"Reg a fan of blue?"

"He loves blue."

Green, though. Green is his favorite color. That leaf hued tie with the subtle paisley pattern was always his favorite.

"Matte."

"Coming right up!"

Cent smiled his winning smile again as he collected two gallon cans of base paint and typed the call numbers into the machine to pour the pigment. Three sharp spurts of liquid pierced the milky surface of white and slowly began to spool into one another. As he pounded the lid back on to ready the can for the gyroscope, I rested my weight against the counter.

"How'd you get started here, anyway?" I asked over the whirr of the mixer.

"Filled out the application."

I laughed at his joke. The kind of laugh that let him know we were comrades, that we were in this together, that we were connected. He told me his father owned the store, and his father before him. It was a tradition that would have been passed to the son that he lost, but he and his wife were finally at a moment where trying again seemed possible. That the loss would still be there, but tradition demanded a forward momentum. And I laughed at that too: tradition as generational stagnation.

"You're a good man," I told him. "Being there for your wife, towing the family line. I don't think I ever even knew what my dad did for a living."

And I didn't. I knew he wore a button up shirt with no tie to work every day. And khaki slacks my mother had ironed creases into. And that he came home from work late in the evenings with dark crescents of dirt and debris caked beneath his fingernails. And I knew that it was against the rules to speak to him before he'd had an hour kicked back in his recliner with the television tuned to whatever classic movie our antenna would pick up. The latter I learned through experience, the previous via observation.

Everything else I knew of my father was what I was told, but those were the things I trusted the least. He was a good man. He was a kind man. He always wanted to be a father. Even if he thought those things were true, which he must have as often as he said them, I learned to be wary of what I heard versus what I felt. That's something he taught me, I guess. He was a hard worker, harder than I ever was. He told me that. He knew how to be a man instead of how to be with one. He told me that one too. By way of my mom. He was dead. My mom had told me that one. And I had no choice but to believe it.

When Cent smiled, his lips parted to reveal the imperfections in his teeth, the slight twist to his lower jaw. It was beautiful, and we all beamed, and I walked home grinning from ear to ear with two gallons of Cornflower Blue rocking on their little metal handles at my knees.

❧

Gerrie smirked as I rounded the landing to my apartment. Our apartment. Mine and Reg's. She leaned coyly against the door and brushed her hair behind her ear with her free hand. Her other hand, her right hand, tapped the coupled pages of her research paper, pointing out the red circled "A" near the top of the page. A scarlet letter she could be proud of.

"Thought you'd want to know," she said.

"So I can take credit for my part in your glory?"

"Well, if it hadn't been for your ink and your printer...."

"Congratulations are in order for the both of us, then!"

We laughed as I slipped the key into the deadbolt and turned the knob. I paused for a moment to listen, half expecting Reg's voice to waft down the hallway and caress my shoulders after the long trek back. He would do that sometimes: catch me before I'd even had the chance to place my bags on the counter, let his strong hands curve against the small of my back and inch up to my shoulders, grip tightly and massage just at the edges of my neck, all the while whispering how good it was to have me home again with him. I hoped he'd complete his training soon. I needed him home again with me.

"Second attempt a failure?" Gerrie nodded at the paint cans then slipped back over the arm of my sofa to stare at the ceiling.

"Not an 'A' paper, to be sure. But I prefer to think of it as a solid 'C plus' effort." I sat in the armchair across from her and leaned my head against the cushion. "It's good to see you. I like you stopping by like this. Makes things a little less lonely."

"Still no word from Reg?"

"Not as such. Not since the voicemail, anyway. Reception was bad, though, so I can only make out every other word."

"Put it on speaker. Maybe I can help you decipher the code."

Gerrie sat up and leaned eagerly toward the coffee table as I flipped my phone repeatedly in my hand. I'd listened to the message a hundred times just to hear his voice. It was comforting. It was mine.

"Some other time," I said. "Let's focus on you for a minute. How are you handling your month of freedom?"

She nodded toward the paint cans on the kitchen counter and smiled. "About the same way you're handling yours. Keeping busy with Foucault and Butler and de Beauvoir."

"The antisocial sociologist has friends outside of me?"

"In words alone," she sighed dramatically. She crossed the room and peered out the window to the street. "I get it, though. Needing the thing to keep you occupied. Without your maps and my essays, both of us would actually have to face the world out there."

"Hey, now!" I exaggerated the offense in my voice. "I have no trouble venturing outside of my comfort zone."

"You're a man. You have that privilege."

"I'm a queer man."

"A gay, white, cisgendered man. That, believe it or not, comes adorned with certain societal advantages."

"Agreed. But you have your own set of benefits."

"It's not about that, though. In the end, anyway. Equality isn't geared toward a reverse of power, but the equity of all those involved. Simone de Beauvoir said, 'One's life has value so long as one attributes value to the life of others.'"

I giggled in agreement as I slipped my phone back into my pocket.

"She also said," Gerrie continued, "that books saved her from despair. So, my essays have a gendered historical context. And you're changing the subject."

"I just like listening to you rant."

She crossed the room and reached for my pocket. Instinctively, I grabbed her arms to stop her. But not hard. Not enough to hurt her. Still, I saw a flash of fear cross her face. And internalized memory forcing its way to her features. I let go quickly. She sat sullenly on the coffee table.

"I didn't——"

"I know."

We sat in silence for a moment. The pressure in the room weighed down on us, daring us to speak, fighting the air back into our lungs.

"All of us have a history that doesn't want to be heard," she said. "A bully that lashes our brains from the inside, slashing all the way down to our hearts. Which is crazy dramatic, I know. I just mean that I understand if you've got some things you aren't ready to share. And we can talk about whatever else you feel like talking about."

"Except for those things you aren't ready to share."

There is a stillness that accompanies confession. A somber understanding that to confess means innately to relive, to slalom around events that are often too painful to be uncovered. It's not that memory is untrustworthy, it's that trauma tries so hard to spread itself through, to rectify a life on its terms alone, that to access it, we must assess every part of ourselves.

So we sat in stillness. In knowing. Trauma did not define us. We were who we were in spite of its nagging voice, the shards of its imposition. But we knew it was there.

"I'll play the message," I said. "Maybe you can make it out."

Gerrie leaned in and cocked her head slightly to angle her ear toward the phone. Reg's voice hummed to life through the speakers, melodic and sweet. I'd often joked with him that he'd be a wonder at the silent orchestra if he didn't hate it so much. He could do a Cole Porter song if he wanted. Who cared if they were rarely picked; they were always in the book.

"Hi, Love——"

I heard what I always heard: moments of sincerity adjunct with the charred singe of a poor connection. Gerrie's eyes glassed over as she listened. She swallowed hard. The message ended.

"Should I play it again?"

"No."

Gerrie seemed hypnotized. Adrift in thoughts as her mind attempted to make sense of the staccato words.

"See? I told you. Wherever he is, the cell service was horrible."

"How——"

"I can't wait for you to meet him, though. When he gets back," I said, smiling and patting her knee. "I think the two of you would really hit it off."

"I was eleven when my father died," she said.

I was startled by the change in subject but honored that my own sharing had encouraged hers.

"It was difficult. A drunk driver, except my dad was the one who was drunk. So my mom's friends would come by and give their sympathy meshed in with all these statistics about alcohol and automotive deaths that were meant to make us feel better. Meant to allocate blame onto the bastard who did it. But my dad was the bastard. And their sorrow filled looks were so fucking hollow."

She leaned back against the coffee table and looked up at the ceiling of the apartment. Her own safe space was just on the other side, but between her and there was the image of a past too painful to pierce.

"Darius had been Dad's best friend. He blamed himself for not taking the keys from him that night. He blamed himself, and he came over to our house every single day to try to make things better. To make himself feel better. He comforted my mom. And it wasn't long before he started to try to comfort me. Subtle. At first. But even at eleven years old, it sounded like a four alarm fire, a wailing ambulance, the last whimper of a drawn out sob. And while my mom cried down the hallway, I cried in my room. With him."

Her body bristled as the sense memory overwhelmed her. Her skin pricked, agitated and longing for escape, and I suddenly felt the guilt of my hands stopping her just moments before.

"Eventually my mom married him. I told her what had happened, and she said grief had made me misunderstand the situation, and she married him. He moved into our house because it was bigger than his. So home became a war zone and only I knew that the battle lines were drawn. But I still had no idea where the landmines were placed. I'd go to the kitchen for some water, or I'd open a window for some air, and the bombs would detonate. Once every few months, like clockwork, until I turned fifteen."

"Gerrie, I didn't——"

"You don't have to say anything. I don't need sympathy anymore. I just wanted you to know that I understand what loss and grief can do to a person."

"Reg is coming back."

"You want to know what the craziest part of all that is?" she asked. "Like the definition of insanity? I keep going back. Every year on my birthday. Every holiday gathering. I go back to that house and relive it all over again. Like, if I face it enough, it will stop having power over me."

☙

We develop empathy as a means of dealing with the world. In order to exist within it. To not go mad. We develop empathy as a way of connecting with those around us, but it's really just a method we employ to rationalize our own emotions by placing them on others and then selfishly taking them back. We speak in the first person——"I feel your pain"——and we pull attention back to the self. *I* feel your pain, so *I am in pain.* Implied: take care of me. And then we call it compassion.

Gerrie went home, and I covered the yellow in blue.

It's been said——and proven——that over three-fourths of those released from the American prison system will be back behind bars within three years. We blame it on bad seeds, on those devoid of empathy, on a learned way of life that is impossible to escape. We set them separate and strip them of their feelings, of their motivations, of their humanity. We make them numbers. And we forget we created them.

We analyze and name disorders for those who feel differently. Syndromes, we call them. And I guess those are proven too, through observation and recurrence and exaggerated deviations from those who hide themselves better. We label deviants as an empathetic way of rationalizing their behavior. Again, for ourselves. It's to treat them, we say, we label them to treat them better. But it's really to set ourselves apart. Again, with the naming of things. Power placed and subverted.

Maggie Willenholm lived down the street from me while I was growing up in a normal house in a normal town. She had two gerbils with little noses that looked like pencil erasers who rolled around in little wood shavings, who, twenty-one days later, were a family of eight. When Maggie brought the lot of them in for show and tell at school, the momma gerbil ate her offspring. Right in front of the entire class.

Bob Williams had a black lab that licked the wounds on his tabby when she returned home with a scrape from leaping too low over a chain link fence.

Gary Kirkpatrick's parakeet grew so somber when its cage mate died, it refused to ever sing again.

But it's us humans who get disorders, who get empathy in order to set us apart. Then we use it to set us apart.

In 1973, a masked man sauntered into a bank with a submachine gun hidden under his jacket. He took four employees hostage, and, in the midst of a five day crisis, the repeat offender demanded his old prison pal be brought to him. They prayed that he would finish, but he just kept right on. Tear gas ended the standoff in a slurry of saltwater. Atypical, but normal all the same.

What surprised everyone, though, was the empathy of the hostages. They sympathized with the man who had held them at gunpoint. They saw his humanity. And Stockholm Syndrome was born in order to rationalize their emotions.

But maybe it started earlier. A parolee is not so different from a freed hostage longing to return to the relative comfort of not having to make choices, of eschewing decisions and the outside world and its rules and regulations. Maybe the masked man himself just longed for the closed arms of his captor, would do whatever it took to regain that embrace.

Maybe that's why Gerrie continued to return home. To eat dinner, and laugh with her mom, and cringe at his touch. She wasn't weak; she was strong. She was trying to see the humanity of those around her in relation to her own empathy.

I longed for Reg to return.

I watched as the paint dried to a pale grey blue.

*

I arrived late to work that evening, but it didn't make much of a difference. Two deaths in as many weeks will put a damper on any environment, even one based in drowning. Connor had spoken with the owners and decided that two weeks dark would properly honor their memories. Lonnie's and Blade's. A moment of silence and a chance to find a new piano man. A moment of silence and a website donation drive to pay for a little vacation and a gold plated plaque. Me, though, I still needed to clean up. To reset for the grand reopening celebration. To earn some cash to cover my rent.

I chose to clean in the dark with only the string lights on to accent the space in a soft orange glow. Old men in khaki trench coats and matching trilbies waltzed past the windows, igniting the sidewalk with surefooted steps from too shaky legs. I pretended not to notice the few who stopped to pull on the door, who used the narrow brims of their hats to shield the reflection of the setting sun from their eyes as they attempted to peer in through the glass.

I was preoccupied, anyway. The Cornflower Blue had hued too purple in the light that streamed from the bedroom window. It would have to go. Its violet undertones had confused the lines of my map, jumbled them all up again. Besides which, Reg would probably prefer green. Even if it didn't really match the bedspread.

I wiped down the body of Lonnie's piano and closed the fallboard gently over the ebony and ivory keys. A closed casket. A song ended.

I poured a shot glass of gin and placed it on the countertop as I toweled away the grime and fettered spills from the wood. The scent was intoxicating. It was Lonnie's favorite. I flipped the stools to the top of the bar. I made The Maiden Name new again.

My mother's maiden name was Monroe. I'd learned it from my father's obituary. Found online during my walk to work, I'd read it three times in as many blocks. It was strange learning about the lives of the people who had raised me, reading black and white memories that were never mine. Edmund Gideon Portman worked as a janitor at the local mall. He led the team in making sure the benches were free of receipts, confirming all those cups and every single straw found their homes behind the large bold letters of appreciation, ensuring the pennies beneath the flow of the fountains stayed shiny. I scrubbed the sinks, made certain the drains were dry.

The sun disappeared behind the skyline, leaving behind a peacock swirl of refracted light. Pink to orange to green to fuchsia. Subdued and florescent and reminding me that Seafoam Green would be a better alternative to the fields. That water and salt were needed for the bloom. I had about an hour before the hardware store closed. I bolted the door to The Maiden Name and dumped the trash, along with my stock bottles of false indulgence into the alleyway dumpster. I wouldn't need them anymore. I knew it would be a while before I was back.

🦋

People surged like locusts around the automatic doors of the hardware store, mouths agape and voices buzzing as scattered wings slapped against the pavement in undulating circles. The sensors triggered and re-triggered, the voodoo of modern marvels letting the harsh light and soft pop music of the shop pour onto the onlookers in staggered intervals. I joined the crowd. The pulsating swarm of excitement, shock, and awe cascaded through me.

"Can you believe something like that could actually happen in real life?"

"I've never seen anything like that before."

"Not in person, anyway."

They spoke in incomplete sentences, the hive mind taking over to facilitate the announcement of their shared trauma, to piece together the Rube Goldbergian events of the evening.

"Did you ever——"

"Have you ever——"

"Could you ever——"

I listened closely. I waited. I turned to go.

The store was sponsoring a demonstration. A man was loading lumber into a cart. There was a kid, in the third aisle, near the electrical supplies, having a temper tantrum because he wanted ice cream. But his mom was looking for light switches to replace the den lights with a dimmer. She was in the plumbing aisle, wandering lost and looking for electricity. He was kicking boxes of quarter inch bolts with the toe of his tiny blue shoes. Cornflower Blue. Almost lavender. A color much more suited to someone of a fairer temperament. The demonstrator showed the ease with which the tool was loaded. So much simpler, it was, than the identical models of before. It was so much more efficient. Progress. Bolts rolled, scattered like marbles. The shooter left in the circle. Spools of conduit unrolled. Crisscrossed. Set the room alight.

A bolt or a wire. A wonky wheel on a cart. A slap or a shrug or a lunge of a two by four into a groin. One thing leading to another; the story growing more elaborate with each teller's addition. But all of them ending with a finger on the trigger of a nail gun. Then that poor man behind the paint counter.

"He never saw it coming."

"Did you see his smile when the nail went into his temple?"

"I will never forget it."

"How could you?" I said. "How could you ever forget a smile like that?"

The siren lights were approaching, glinting off windows, confusing the streetlights and oscillating at the same speed as the opening and closing of the automatic doors. My phone hummed in my pocket. It vibrated in time with the swirling beams. I said his name without looking at the screen. New habits form so quickly.

"Reg?"

"Howard, it's Annie. You haven't been returning my calls."

"I didn't realize you'd called."

I knew my voice seemed off, distant, cold. A warning sign for my sponsor, no doubt, but she knew me well enough to put it aside. She was just doing her job; she wouldn't dig too deeply.

"I hear sirens," she said. "Is everything okay?"

"It's fine. There was an accident at the Tool Center down the street from me. I'm just walking home and got caught in the fray."

I could hear her nod, even through the phone. See the red curls that framed her face bounce slightly with each jerk of her chin.

"I'm almost at my door," I said. "It should be quieter soon."

The rush of cars swept past me. The late walkers ignored the violence of the neighborhood. I closed the iron gate behind me and let my hand trail over the decorative spikes that guarded my building from what lay beyond. The driftwood stairwell creaked as I ascended. No. The marble stairs felt cold, even through the soles of my shoes. I trudged upward, listening to Annie's measured breath on the line.

"Home," I said, heaving into the kitchen with an unexpected groan. "So, what's up?"

"I've been worried about you. You aren't answering your phone. You haven't been coming to the meetings."

THE HOUSE THAT WASN'T THERE

I locked the door behind me and tossed my keys into the bowl on the coffee table. The smell of drying paint overwhelmed my nostrils.

"What are you talking about?" I asked. "I shared at the last meeting. Last Saturday. You were there, weren't you?"

"Howard, you weren't at the last meeting."

She said my name slowly, sternly, as if trying to reassure me of my presence. As if she wanted to measure my humanity.

"Yes," I said. "I was. Right after we had coffee and I told you I would speak. You remember? There was that strange man sitting behind you. The guy in the trench."

"Howard." She said my name again. "Howard, we had coffee almost two months ago. That was the last time I've seen you. You haven't been to group in months."

The siren lights batted the Cornflower Blue through the open bedroom window, sending it through a frenzied array of Azure and Hibiscus. I crossed to close the curtains.

"You're mistaken," I stuttered. "I remember talking about my dad. And the go go boy."

"Go go boy?" She asked. "What go go boy? Howard, would it be all right if I came over? I think it would be good for us to talk."

A shadow plunged across my view as I reached to pull the curtain. A fourth floor defenestration. My eyes followed it instinctively across the air and to the ground below. But it stopped just short of solid. suspended a few feet above the ground. Limp and plunged through with the fencing. Gerrie was dead.

"I have to go," I said.

I hung up and dialed the coroner.

BROKEN AND UNWANTED, he sat on the stoop of the house. The house that wasn't there. The house with the temper. He chipped bits of concrete from the steps with his fingernails, showered them——a condensed rain, a condescending downpour——onto the metal railings of the gate and listened to the hollow reverberations of a space as it tried to sing. A dance number. Or a fugue.

The air smelled of lilacs. Lilacs and lavender. And Earl Grey cookies set neatly on a saucer to rest beside a cooling cup of honey sweetened coffee. Floral and earthy and sweet and load bearing. A scent that was structural instead of ambient. A framework for everything to come; the remnants of what had been.

The house had arguments with itself. Rooms turned in on each other. Stairs descended when they were meant to ascend. Nadir and apex meant nothing. Merrick gave up his song and leaned back on the door, knowing it would give way, aware that it could swallow him whole.

The house longed for returns. It waited, somewhat patiently, except for on Tuesdays, and sighed its lavender breath in heaving shudders. In robin egg blue. Like the house, Merrick viewed time in epistolary terms. The sent. The received. And the blankness of the moments between.

The door opened slowly. His head eased back, came to a gentle rest on the stiff pine of the floor; his shoulders rested on the precipice, the liminal, the in between. It was not a space of comfort: the period between the outpouring and the reply. He wrote letters on liquid in hopes of allowing everything inside of him to become apparent, to seep, to spill. He waited, breath held, for time to once again tick forward.

He longed for lilacs. Or maybe bergamot. Some things that were sweet and floral and waiting. He knew if he wanted them, he had to go inside.

9

I'M GETTING AHEAD OF MYSELF.

What a peculiar phrase.

As if my self is not where I left it.

I'm getting ahead of myself. Which is to say, I'm stepping outside of myself. To watch. To view. To remember. I'm a driver at the wheel of a shit brown Oldsmobile, careening down a winding highway——some seldom used mountain pass——trying my damnedest to recognize the scenery in front of me as everything I've ever known mixes into a watercolored swirl of impressionist paint dabs. Memory. It's all there in the rearview. The bigger picture. The widespread notions. It's clearer in the sideview. The moments are larger. Closer than they appear. I can make out the features on the faces of those left back there in the dust and grit and burning rubber. But they're out of order. Broken. Try again later. Maintenance has been notified.

I'm getting ahead of myself, but I'm still right there in the middle of all of it. All of it is exactly how I remember.

The cops left my apartment about an hour after Gerrie died. For brevity's sake, I'll say it was the same officers who drove me home after Blade overdosed in the backroom of The Maiden Name. The one with the ash blond ponytail and her partner. It probably wasn't, but a uniform's design is meant for solidarity, for consolidation. Gerrie's body had already been loaded into the back of a van. Someone with a miner's helmet was already swabbing the blood from the fence. I had already answered everything they asked to the best of my ability.

"How well did you know the victim?"

"Had the victim demonstrated any suicidal tendencies?"

"Had the victim said or done anything that would lead you to think——"

"Everything the victim said made me think," I interrupted. "She was a sociology major. She had this way of speaking."

"A sociology major?"

The officers shot a knowing look toward one another as they closed their notebooks. Their pens slid easily into their breast pockets, a repeated motion. They slipped silently through the door, a practiced deed. A quiet night. Especially for Gerrie.

I made pancakes and ate them. I sipped juice from the carton. I closed the bedroom window and stared at the hushed blue of the walls. It was calming, a tranquil infection, a meditation on sedation. Blue would have to do.

"I like the color," Gerrie said. Gerrie had said earlier that day. Another sudden change in subject. A quick walk down the hall. Toward the bedroom window.

"In spite of its heteronormative simplicity?" I laughed.

"Blue was associated with the feminine for centuries. Way longer than pink. The caring sky. The sensual sea. The Virgin Mary and her shroud. It was holy and divine and utterly female. Boys wore pink because it was a subdued form of the manly red. An advertising push to sell more baby clothes switched it all around in the 1950s. Which just further proves that gender is a manmade construct."

I twined my arms across my chest. My hip cocked instinctively, thrusting forward as my torso moved back to fully consider the expanse of color. Like terror tinged in slow guilt, the blue swept across the wall in honeyed, undulating swirls. Waves. A windswept sky. I found my pens, attempted to connect the city.

I was drawn to maps at an early age. Etchings in stone. Tiptoes on paper. They simultaneously offered an escape and a place in the world. The path to a treasure, the locations of wonders, the acknowledgment of the mundane. I was fascinated with the gestures, how even the simplest shape could become the greatest of civilizations, the most majestic of mountains. How a small slip of bleached parchment could be inhabited by millions of creatures, trillions of lifeforms. Imbued possibilities: You Are Here when You Could Be There.

Reg's masks were a lot like my maps: symbols meant to show what was truly underneath, the All that was beyond. The curve of a lip: a highway off ramp. The hollow eyes: a ravine. Maps are guides, representations of space and often innocuous, devoid of the danger the place itself can hold. A steady forester hoisted on butterfly wings across a desert or through a grove. Too, a mask will hide what is really there. Play at its shape and alter it. It will offer professions of love and laughter or tears or horror, and then simplify them in their exaggeration. But when one knows what to look for, when someone develops a radiographic eye, they suffer awash in the cartographic beauty of smile lines and mile markers and crow's feet.

"Your maps," she said. Gerrie had said. Earlier that day or the day before. Past tense in a past, tense recollection. Always moving further and further away. "You think that's really what they are? Freedom and escape? Do those lines provide an explanation or a way out? Or do they serve only to protect you from actual exposure to the Great that is Beyond?"

"When I was in high school," I replied, "I had to read this really long, really dense tome from some famous Russian whose name escapes me now. Which is ironic, considering how many famous Russian authors there are being taught in high school settings. And even now, I don't remember much about the book itself. I don't know all of its themes or analogies or how it got from point A to point That Squiggly Weird Russian Lettering. But I remember the steps. As clearly as the narrator remembered them. The lines it took to move through a city infested with mistakes and motivations. He knew exactly how many paces it would take to transverse his environment. He made his mental maps to get him through his days."

"Dostoyevsky wrote them down. And you draw yours on the wall."

Gerrie gestured in a grand sweeping of her wrist, the curator showing off her latest acquisition. I had not started it until after, but she had seen it already. Somehow, she just knew.

"I thought your books were your escape," I said, and my throat shuddered at the sound of my own voice.

Gerrie laughed. It was a kind laugh, jovial and pitying all the same. And it was light in its heaviness, trilling up octaves in a manic effort to raise the key. She pressed her palm against the window. Her skin glowed an icy blue against the glass.

"Apparently my escape was actually a fourth floor window," she said. Her eyes danced across the fencing below, out into the street to twirl between the litter and leaves. "Funny how quickly the evidence gets gone sometimes. You'd hardly even know I was ever there."

She turned from the window and looked at me sullenly. Her chin trembled as she spoke. Her bottom lip was raw as if she'd spent the last five hours in the morgue chewing on it absently.

"Maybe in the daylight, it'll be clearer," she said. "Maybe when the sun's up, I'll have made my mark."

Her face softened as she spoke; her gaze became wistful.

"I'd really like to see the after," she said. "To know I was there. You Are Here. A star on a map. Right, Howard?"

I stopped drawing as Gerrie tapped her fingers against the flowing demarcations of city streets.

"Right, Gerrie."

I could barely speak. My throat was hoarse and dry and atrophied. Solid, as if run through with a fence post.

"We'll see the after together when the day breaks, Howard," she said. "And when that happens, I'm going to need for you to tell me what it all looked like before."

The smaller the view, the more accurate maps tend to be; but, if the viewer gets too close, the discrepancies are unavoidable. The bigger the picture, the more hazy things become, and thus, the more real within the variance of notion and memory. The Goldilocks illusion. The give and the take of a world devoid of all sense of truth.

✳

The sun rose in a kaleidoscopic bout of false starts, colored wisps of varying shades proclaiming, "I am here," "I am forever," "I have become." No one the wiser that the light bouncing off Beecher Street was just a cascade of refractions from beyond the horizon. Sunrise is a trickster god filled——and filled wholly of itself——with the false promise of a new day. A new beginning. A fresh start. And yet those who stayed awake through the night, who failed to succumb to the limbic lullaby of circadian rhythms, are faced with the duality of being, with the ending required for the and-they're-off.

The knock on the door was measured; the low ticking of an analog clock, the countdown to a quiet detonation, the slow escape of a heartbeat emptied of its blood: hollow, desperate, obsolete. I could have ignored it. I was so tired from the night of blue uniforms, blue walls, blue. I should have ignored it. The coffee I'd made the cops was lukewarm in the pot on the counter and tasted at once bland and bitter as I downed it to recover some of my humanity. Humanity, after all, has always been measured in the minutes we wear our masks. Numbered, like four faint knocks, in opposition to the animal.

The couple on my doorstep looked as haggard as I felt. The woman stood closest to my door; a dainty foot kicked at the frayed fibers of the welcome mat. Her right arm hugged at her stomach as her left hand pulled absently at a pearl necklace, distressed fingertips hemming the rough nodes of her WASP Rosary. Her navy skirt and jacket set was perfectly matched to her eyeshadow. Her lips drawn into delicate arches. Hair parted perfectly behind crisp, short bangs. The man who stood behind her smiled politely. A set of wireframed glasses resting atop a narrow nose acted as armor against the red gleam of sorrow and guilt in his eyes. His tie was loosened slightly, off centered at the collar, and hung limply across his white button down shirt. It was navy blue and matched perfectly to his wife's ensemble. His hair was the color of dried mud and hung limply across his forehead, product barely hanging on amid its ongoing battle with the nervous palm of his hand.

"Please forgive our appearance——"

"And the hour——"

"But the landlord isn't here yet, and the——"

"Rather talkative woman——"

"Mrs. Wilson——"

"Wilkes, on two, told us that you two were friends——"

"That you might have a key."

They spoke in a gentle, measured tone. Their words joined to support each other's as a unit, necessary for complete sentences versus cutting one another off, formal and succinct and heartbroken. I felt myself blinking, absorbing. I noticed their words wash my neck in their breaths. Their teeth gnashed into every syllable, a cutting bite, a "bless your heart" sort of knowing.

"I'm sorry," I said, and genuinely meant it against their simmering sorrow. "It's been a long night. Who are you?"

"Forgive us, again——"

"Our manners are a bit shot——"

"We're the Wisemans——"

"Gertrude's parents."

"Yes!" I said suddenly, my voice jarring the flow of their words. "We were friends. Please, come in."

They stepped timidly into my apartment. A nervous exhaustion threatened to overwhelm their limbs at any moment, to send them crumbling to the floor, a marionette mess of hardwood and cut strings. Or a broken fish bowl with a wet cat peering down from the countertop, the gold gilled body of the forgotten pet surging, limply, for the dive. Like their daughter slouched over wrought iron.

"I'm sorry about the mess," I said. But they hadn't seen the mess. They hadn't seen her body. The blood had been scrubbed clean by the time they had arrived.

"Are you moving?" she asked. Just the she this time. Mrs. Wiseman. Gerrie's mom.

I surveyed the clutter of blankets and pillows scattered on the sofa. The makeshift bed as the paint dried rested like a rat's nest against what should have been a stagnancy. The potted plants wished for water, and the maple desk stood askew and waiting in the corner.

"No," I laughed. A solemn laugh. A nervous laugh. An expression aligned to the situation. "I've just been doing a little redecorating in the bedroom. Gerrie was actually helping me with it while my partner is away."

"Gerty was helping you?" Her incredulous words spilled out like whiskey over stones, a riverbed in a glass, swirling and unexpected. I watched the white tips of her manicured nails attempt to take them back, to close off her lips to any further wrong doing. "You'll forgive me, won't you? I don't know what I'm saying."

"It's been a rather stressful morning," her husband agreed. "We aren't quite ourselves right now."

I smiled sympathetically as I rolled my bedding into a ball and tossed it to the corner to give them room to sit on the couch. "I think Gerrie would have had some quip about that," I said as we sat. "About how times like now are when we are probably most like ourselves."

"You're right," the Wisemans said. "She would have."

We sat in silence for a moment. The curve of our lips felt strained as it gave way to the pressure building in our cheeks, angry at ourselves as if our very mouths had betrayed us yet again. A sturdier reverence, for its own sake, demanded control.

"Gerty always did have a penchant for a——"
"Turn of phrase. She was a rather——"
"Strange and peculiar soul——"

"But a lovely girl——"

"Yes. A lovely person. Did you know her well?"

"I like to think so," I said. "I didn't know her for long, but we were getting close."

A snicker roared from Mr. Wiseman's nostrils. "I knew her for twenty-two years, and I would not ever be able to say we were close."

"Darius!"

"It's the truth. And not for lack of trying."

"It is true," Mrs. Wiseman conceded. "Gertrude was a——"

"Difficult child——"

"When it came to us."

I thought of Gerrie's story about the death of her birth father and the rebirth of her parental unit. I listened to the denial and betrayal in their words for her, even with her gone. Their story could be truer now, without her side on the table. With her side slammed through the fencepost, ripping at the confession, they were free to redact the more unpleasant parts.

I watched the memories slam against the salt crags of their tear ducts, waves of if-we'd-only swirling into if-only-she-had. I imagined Gerrie standing by the window, peering through the blinds at the lack of any trace below, a gentle smirk spread across her lips. I saw her listening, intently, to the other side of the story; her own side lost to a realm of avenging possibility. A cold, steely expression surfaced in Mrs. Wiseman's eyes.

"You said she was helping you redecorate? Do you mind——?" She stood and gestured down the hallway. "I just need to see something her hand touched. Some verification that she was here."

I didn't apologize for the mess, for the mishaps in the mapping, as they stared at the roller streaked expanse of Cornflower peaked in Daffodil. Their eyes traced the lines of the city, familiar and foreign, an appropriation too far removed. The paint still looked wet in places. The dawn sun dried the fence posts. Mr. Wiseman palmed the wall and chuckled.

"I can hear her spouting off about the feminine nature of the color blue," he said.

"How blue should be calming, but it's really violent and angry——"

"Anything to push a button——"

"To subvert the status quo."

"That was our Gerty. Blue in the face of depression."

"Blue to the point of anger——"

"Of violence——"

"Of misunderstanding."

"But never calm. No. That just wouldn't do."

"She used to work so hard at anarchy——"

"Gluing and dying and spiking her hair——"

"How the hell is she supposed to fight against a system she's decided to remove herself from?"

A hurricane emerged from her gut as she buried her face in her husband's chest, tears——even in her situation——a shame rather than a strength. Her erratic sobs fought through the fabric, through the skin, and emerged as a roar sent to echo in the emptiness of my bedroom. I felt her candy coated pain in her every gasp as she rewrote her daughter's history before me, expelled the misery for the strength it was meant to create, discarded the fights and the yelling and the ultimatums. The only thing she couldn't change was the ending. And when I closed my eyes, the ending was all I could see.

Gerrie-Gerty-Gertrude: head against the smudged glass, eyes washed and vision blurred, the cool breeze of 3am twisting through the opened part of her window. I let myself in quietly, the key she gave me for emergencies slipped neatly into my watch pocket. Gerty-Gertrude-Gerrie: a silhouette against the streetlight, a woman at the end of the hallway, a straight shot to freedom.

No. I wasn't there.

Gertrude-Gerrie-Gerty: too lost in herself to hear the footsteps. I saw my hand reach out. Skinny fingers that did not match my own but had the same ink markings across them and made the same shape as mine would when they clasped her shoulder. They clasped her shoulder and exerted the same force as mine would when they pushed.

"I should probably find you that key," I said. "Our landlord isn't exactly known for his timeliness. I'm sure you're desperate to get upstairs."

I checked the bowl on the kitchen counter where my keys for The Maiden Name rested until I got the call to return. It wasn't there. It wasn't on the key ring by the door. I felt it burrow into my hip.

❦

THE HOUSE THAT WASN'T THERE

Forgotten strips of police tape hung like party streamers from the top of the stairwell. Yellow jacket warnings: the party's over; go home. I felt Mr. Wiseman's breath on my neck as the key slipped the latch. The Wisemans, the two of them, close at my heels, and myself, with them, trekking toward salvation.

Gerrie had given me the key just two days earlier. "For emergencies," she'd said. "Just in case." I pushed into her apartment——for the first time——and surveyed the landscape. "If anything happens, you've gotta hide my porn from my parents." The cops had come and gone, leaving their tape and dirt blood footprints across the hardwood. The window was still open at the other end of the apartment, and the morning hissed through the portal as if nothing had changed, as if the displacement of soil didn't matter, the rearrangement of relation was moot.

Mrs. Wiseman pushed past me and let her hands caress her daughter's objects, like a housekeeper searching for dust, a medium reaching for a spark, a mother's final attempt at connection. The spirit of the dead presiding. Ever watchful. Ever vigilant. Ever gone. She clutched her daughter's bag, lifted from it a laptop, a bottle of pills, a notebook, a bottle of pills, a research paper marked with a scarlet letter. A bottle of pills. The white pills, the green pills, the blue pills. Enough to share with the class.

"These were supposed to help."

I was supposed to help. That's why she'd given me the key. To aid in the removal after the helping had failed. But there were cops and fatigue to contend with. Excuses to be made.

"Did she leave a note?"

"The police didn't find one," I said. I assumed. I hadn't found one either.

Mr. Wiseman opened drawers and cabinets, peered inside at the confusion, could not bring himself to touch anything. It would all have to go. Back to her old bedroom gift wrapping studio. To some charity that wouldn't mind the stench of death. To the place of found things when their owners are lost. He opened the fridge and piled the perishables on the counter: soy milk and estrogen and last Tuesday's leftovers alongside a new definition of the word. Of several words. Shared and personal by relation. And of that word too.

"You don't know her password, do you?"

Mrs. Wiseman frowned at the screen, fingers hovering above the keys, longing for insight, for inspiration, for understanding. Most people wouldn't even give their lovers their passwords, but I could see the inferred distance creating chasms in her body.

"She thought my password was 'ponies' because I'd asked for one once when I was six. At least she knew to switch the vowels into numbers."

Gerrie scoffed from behind my shoulder. I felt her breath on my neck as my fingers hovered over her keyboard, urging me on, jarring and light, a fictitious force upon the air.

B-3-N-J-A-M-1-N-5-4-N-6-3-1

Her 1337 reference to one of her favorite philosophers, to his interpretation of a painting written in 1920, to looking always toward the past, to contemplating it, to readying the feet for the flight. A want to awaken the dead dwelled in it, but there was no way that could happen, no way through the storm.

"Delete that 'womxns studies' folder before you hand this back off to my mother," she said. "There's stuff in there she just shouldn't see."

"What was it?" Mrs. Wiseman asked, eyes brimming as she took back control over the computer.

"None of your damn business," Gerrie laughed. "Fuck! Being dead is so freeing."

"A reference to Walter Benjamin," I said.

Mr. Wiseman smiled from the kitchen. "She read his translation of Baudelaire's *Les Fleurs du Mal* when she was only eleven," he laughed. "And that was in German!"

"Too smart for her own good," Mrs. Wiseman agreed. Her finger trekked across the mousepad. Her eyes darted over the screen.

"Ready, as ever, with the backhanded compliment. Leave it up to dear old Mom and Dad to always see the barnacles under the ship. Nothing can ever be adequate with the worst of it just waiting to be called to the surface."

Gerrie stayed just out of eyesight, always behind me, bouncing from shoulder to shoulder. My very own tutelary spirit. My very own telltale heart.

"Nothing," Mrs. Wiseman said as she clicked through folders, through icons, through documents. "I thought she'd at least leave a note."

"I did love to write," Gerrie agreed. "Why didn't I leave a note? I would have left the best note if I had left a note. Funny but still somber and somehow filled with way too many references, so they'd all have to spend hours trying to figure them all out. Why, Howard? Why didn't I leave a note?"

I wanted to think of the question as rhetorical, but it pierced my heart and shot upward, pinning my jaw closed like the sharp point of a wrought iron spoke.

"I don't know."

"You know."

"Maybe the moment was impulsive?" I said. Asked. Understood the lie even as it formed.

"I don't have a truly impulsive bone in my body."

"She didn't have an impulsive bone in her body," her mother cried, still trying to make sense of it all in false recollections and browser histories. "She thought everything out ad nauseam."

"I thought everything out. So, what could it be? You know, they say——"

"They say that most people who truly want to end their lives don't actually leave a note," I offered. "They say that they say goodbye in other ways."

"But she didn't."

"I wouldn't have, would I?" she whispered in my ear. "Not unless I was planning to say goodbye." No. She said, "I wouldn't have bothered to say goodbye to them."

The Wisemans thought through the last few conversations they'd had with their daughter. She'd found a new place; she'd stay in the city, study through the summer; no, she was not coming home. The computer fan hummed against the silence. The air conditioning unit kicked on as the warmth of morning rushed through the still open window. I watched their faces emote as their brains attempted to reconcile the sudden absence, the lack of warning, the non-explanation, and all the air rushing forth to take over the space. I wanted to tell them that a note wouldn't have made it any better, that the reasons often don't align with your own understanding, that reason is rarely reasonable.

But I knew it wouldn't matter. As much as we crave rationalization, our minds busy themselves with creating narratives that support the stories we want to tell. The grass is always greener; the night is always darker;

the love is always pure. Benjamin wrote that the stories we create are meant to counsel, but in telling those stories, we deplete our ability to communicate. "In consequence," he said, "we have no counsel either for ourselves or for others. After all, counsel is less an answer to a question than a proposal concerning the continuation of a story which is just unfolding."

"What do you think happened?" Mr. Wiseman asked. He wanted me to continue the story.

"Yes, Howard," Gerrie laughed. "How does this one unfold?"

To look for clues to the backstory, the three of us——the living of us——turned to face the hallway to try fill in the details left to the imagination. And then another who knew everything, filled to the brim like a toddler with a secret, jumping up and down in anticipation, anxious to release the tale, to make it canon, to down the ship. We stepped forward on instinct, cautiously, with conviction.

"You remember this, don't you?" Gerrie asked. "Sneaking down the hallway. Making your way through the dark."

Her presence slid over my body, tussled my hair, wafted my arms and sent them forward. My hands looked foreign to me, deserters on a mission of their own, stretched out and groping the air for an unclaimed vantage.

"I——I don't know, Mr. and Mrs. Wiseman," I said. I stuttered, like Gerrie had when we first met. I tried to drown out her voice, to change the course of action. "Forgive me for this," I said. I continued. "But we were always on a first name basis. What was Gerrie's last name?"

The Wiseman's looked shocked.

"Wiseman."

Gerrie snickered.

"Did you adopt her?" I asked, and, when met by their confused stares, said, "She told me about her birth father's death when she was young."

"I am her birth father," Mr. Wiseman asserted.

I felt my throat catch and swallowed hard. "I suppose I was mistaken. I apologize."

"Did I lie?" Gerrie asked. "Did I lie or was that another story you were telling to create your own narrative? Was that just something else you were using to change the subject? To make all of this okay?"

I apologized again to the Wisemans, but they weren't listening to me. They were searching the unfamiliar walls for any sense of familiarity. They were searching for their daughter.

"Tell them your story," Gerrie said. "Tell them the story you want them to hear. That's what you're good at. But tell me the truth, for whatever the truth may be worth."

She swallowed hard, the ghost in need of liquid on her larynx.

"Did you move by sight or by feel?" she asked. "Were you stepping with intention or was it more casual? The Dostoyevskian practiced gait in an apartment that mirrored your own."

We breached the doorframe to the bedroom. Mrs. Wiseman did her best to keep her face neutral, to force off any emotion other than the requisite placid contempt. A product of her upbringing. Her daughter, a product of hers.

"This is where it happened. You know."

Gerrie's voice was so clear. More real than my own.

"This is where it happened," Mr. Wiseman solemnly said.

Mrs. Wiseman turned to face me, an earnest dysphoria in her eyes. She needed reason. She longed for finality that didn't seem so final. "You knew her better than we did toward the end," she said. "What caused this? What do you think pushed her?"

Gerrie giggled in my ear. A child's laugh. Mischievous and joyful and pure. Hollow and ringing and everlasting. I watched my body convulse through the space, my feet so sure already of where the hardwood met the rug, where the bed frame jutted from the wall, how her chair was angled from her desk. I was dancing.

"It's like you've been here before," she laughed.

"I——I don't know," I told the Wisemans. "I wish I had the answers."

"Oh, come on," she teased. "You know you know. It's right there. Right on the very tippy-tippy-toe of your tongue."

It went dense. A sudden loss of light. Less so a darkness than an absence. But Gerrie was there. And Gerrie was happy. Smiling and howling as she leaned from her window to reach for the blood red moon. Her bare toes strained to elevate her heels. Pure and exalted. She turned to me and grinned widely. Consuming.

"You pushed me!"

My eyes went wide as I turned to leave the Wisemans to their grief. To find their solace. I rushed from the apartment and burrowed down the stairwell to my own. My keys fumbled in the lock, nothing quite catching, her laugh still echoing in my eardrums just behind the beating in my chest attempting to drown it out at my temples. Once inside, I slammed the door, willed my breath to balance, to fill deeper into my lungs. An attempt to grow them so to stifle the space of my own heart.

"Babe, is that you?"

The sweetest voice called from the bedroom. Honey poured over a gravelly avalanche of cane sugar. Licking the air with its tone the way only music was normally allowed to. Then a silhouette in a doorway. Then his beautiful face framed in the morning light.

He said, "I know it took longer than expected."

He said, "I'm finally home."

THE HOUSE THAT WASN'T THERE

THE HOUSE WAS SET in a two step waltz, the kind that isn't done anymore, the type considered gauche in all the wrong circles. It danced in historical cadence, brimming in controlled excitement, slick and smooth and shimmying its slate grey shutters against an indifferent world. The house that wasn't there. The house with the jitterbug. Caught in the light of a late morning sun in the extended summer of the final days of innocence. Robin egg siding glistening; the wrought iron gate swinging open.

Oh, do houses love to dance! More so as homes, but there is a freeing shudder within an obscured abdication. A moment of joyful release as windows long sealed slide open, door hinges creak ajar, and attic hatches swish off their cobwebs. A breath. A spotlight. A life renewed. And too, a hopeful glance at a Friday morning, blinking gently against the city streets in their hustle and their bustle and their too good a job at cleaning up the remnants of the night before.

Houses do love to dance. A two step or a line dance. Sometimes a tango when a door is painted red as a rose. With slate grey shutters, they are partial to a foxtrot, a Lindy hop, a jive. Particularly in the sunlight and often on a Friday.

If Fridays seem hopeful, it's only for the bubbling murmur of wishes levied against the weekend hours to come. The letting go before it comes right back; the idiosyncratic cracks in the sidewalk one notices as they leap to avoid any perceived and unintentional harm to their mother or her back. If Fridays seem hopeful, it's only for the finality left behind in the night before.

The house that wasn't there sauntered through the step-turn-kick as if no one was watching. Its beds all made, its rooms all emptied, loneliness suddenly felt whole and freeing. As if alone was actually solace in self. A dance to creak the floorboards and stir up the dust of a thousand nights too hard to remember and too distracting to forget. And, too, a voice calling in from the street.

10

"HI, HONEY. I'M HOME!" HE SAID.

No.

"You feel like home to me," he said.

No.

"There's no place like——"

No.

❧

It didn't matter what he said. The music swelled, the camera swooped through the doorframe to make the simple line of the hallway seem suddenly majestic and magical, and maybe I tripped a little as I soared down the tunnel to envelop him in my arms, to crash down with him onto the bed, to realize suddenly how much I'd truly missed him even as he was back by my side. He laughed, a simple gesture of his chin toward joyful, and eyed the room with a false bewilderment.

"I see you decided to undergo some redecorating while I was gone."

I blushed as he shook his head. He knew me well. He understood my impulses. And he saddled them deep within his subconscious as the id based whims of the man who would always love him. I was that to him. He was everything to me.

"I'll get it all put back right," I said. "I'd hoped to have it finished before you returned."

"It's fine! I totally get it!" He laughed again. That sweet and gentle lilt of lilac and woodpecker on his breath, glistening in the rose colored midnight of his eyes. He laughed again——he laughed so much——and he said, "I know I leave a lot of space to fill when I'm gone."

Chasms opened in his wake. Him, that wandering river of life cutting canyons so great all that he was echoed within them to highlight his absence.

"I don't want to talk about that right now," I cooed. The bedsheets felt lush, filled with his scent. My head drifted in him. "I just want to be here with you."

"You don't work tonight?"

He hadn't gotten my messages. He hadn't heard, but I didn't want to ruin the moment.

"No," I said. "The bar—— Some shit went down, and we've closed up for a few weeks. We'll be back to business again soon."

Reg pressed his lips against my forehead and kissed me in that exaggerated way he sometimes used. It was so loud and filling that I almost didn't hear the chortle from across the room.

"Back to business again so soon?" he mocked, standing atop my desk, rocking from the balls of his feet to his heels. His tight muscled thighs quivered beneath his blue sequined jockstrap. His hips pulsed to swing his cock, to make it strain against his underwear, to have it call forth the emerald dollar bills. He spun around and flexed his ass. "As if my death didn't matter," he said. "Business as usual. Nothing to see here. Move it right along."

"What's wrong, hon?" Reg asked. His fingers traced the line of my temple as I blinked the vision of Blade from my eyes.

"Nothing, I——" I kissed him. His lips were firm and wet and electric. I pulled him close against me and shuddered at his fingertips.

Blade's weight shifted our bodies as he stepped onto the mattress. He thrust his pelvis sensuously above our heads, keeping time with the thumping beat of a song that wasn't playing. His dick pulled as it rubbed against the fabric of his jockstrap, sending the light from the open window sparkling in tiny blue fireworks across the room. I could tell he was getting hard. Reg's tongue traced down my neck. I was too.

"Oh yeah," Blade said, "the blood's really flowing now."

Reg nibbled gently at my collarbone. The dancer swayed to an unheard beat and bounced his pecs as he looked down at me.

"Or maybe it's just the rigor mortis."

I moaned——a growl, a warning——as I flipped on top of the man I loved, the man I'd missed so much, and pinned his arms against the sheets. His hair fell against the bedding in curly tendrils of cinnamon black ideas escaping like squid ink from his mind, garbled in the margins of the sticky humidity of us finally reunited. My lips brushed against his earlobe, traveled the dense islands of his freckles, and took flight from the flat, soft expanse on his nose. I could still feel the dead go go dancer gyrating behind me.

"Show me how much you missed me," Reg commanded.

My fingers drove down the sides of his body and fumbled with the fabric at the lower hem of his t-shirt. His body quivered as the palms of my hands made contact with his hips.

"Crows actually mourn when their loved ones are not around."

Reg continued to writhe beneath me as I searched the room for the voice. His hands slipped beneath the fabric of my tee to massage my back and my sides, pushing and pulling at the skin, tripping it like a tin cup along the bars of my ribcage.

"Monogamous creatures, crows are."

The man was standing beside the window, peering outward, head tilted toward the street below. His black hair seemed slick and wet against the dizzying rays of the midmorning sun.

"And when a mating partner dies, the entire murder mourns with wailing cries for weeks on end."

Reg pulled my face to his, and I felt his tongue slip between my teeth, the two of us together sounding consonants and intonating vowels. Both of us needed for our language to take shape.

"Oh, I'm sorry," the man at the window said.

"What?"

"I didn't say anything. Kiss me."

Reg pulled my mouth back to his. His blurry eyes were closed as mine scanned the horizon for the man. He'd turned from the window and smiled, somewhat, in the hazy silhouette of the outside world.

"You never really got to see my face, did you? Maybe this will help." His mouth formed over the sound of squealing tires, the crunch of bending metal. "Or I could put on my green hat."

Reg bit my neck. I bit my lip. The pedestrian killed in the car crash right below my window bit his smile.

"I think you pictured my messy apartment," he said. "My children mourning. Or your father. But I didn't have a family. Or a messy apartment. I actually owned a house just off campus and taught Animal Behavior at the university upstate. Probably the complete opposite of your father, though I understand why you needed the comparison. Still, it wasn't really about me, was it? No, it was more about the mourning rituals of crows. Their pain and their sorrow and the weeks of their strangely strong weakness."

Reg arched his back to drive his pelvis into mine as he pulled my shirt over my head and tossed it across the room. He fought to remove his own, and it finally landed at the hazy man's feet.

"Of course, some crows will still fuck their dead," he laughed. "We haven't figured out if it's out of love or spite yet. Maybe it's both."

My lover's fingers pulled at the drawstring on my sweatpants for a bit before giving up and moving to unbutton his own. His dick throbbed against the teeth of his zipper, pushing the pull tab toward the inseam. Releasing him. He pulled my hand down to feel him through the fabric of his briefs and pumped rhythmically against my clenched palm. I felt him pulse as a tiny bead of wetness soaked through the muted blue and white striped cotton.

"Gods, I've missed you!"

"I missed you t——"

"Shut up and fuck me."

Reg moved his finger from my lips to dip inside my mouth, to activate my tongue and slip sensuously along my teeth.

"The color turned out nice, but I still don't think it's quite right. If you want my two cents," another voice called out. "Hah! Two 'Cents. My Margie always used to say that. I just got it. Guess a nail to the crown will do that for you sometimes. Oh, you should probably do what he says. Looks like you both could use it."

Cent smiled his crooked toothed smile at me as he passed the bed to study the wall like an art critic, like a college student meant to be in adoration of a master work. Reg reached into my pants, grabbed me, guided me toward him. I bent down to kiss his neck, to let my tongue trace along his clavicle as my hands worked to push my sweats down beyond the crook of my knees, past my ankles and onto the floor. I helped Reg finish removing his, his legs straightened up into the air in front of me before they slipped, open and free, in a V-shape to slide from my shoulders down the side of my body.

Growling again, I pulled his legs back over my shoulders. I felt the muscles of his calves tense as he stretched his torso to fumble for the bottle of lubricant in the top drawer where the nightstand would be if I hadn't moved it to paint the walls.

"Fuck it," he said. "Spit."

His tongue moistened his palm as an evil glint flashed through his eyes. He wrapped his hand around my cock to wet me before licking his fingers again to ready himself. I moaned as I pushed slowly into him, relishing the sensation as I felt him open to receive me. I arched downward to kiss him, and he bit my lip as he sucked in cool air through his gritted teeth.

The electricity in the room was grounded where our skin touched, and I pressed our chests together. His dick quivered in the air between us, thumping between my stomach and his own in a mercurial drumbeat of passion. Each thrust sent shivers through our tensing muscles. Sweat began to bead across my forehead.

Cent's fingers brushed along the freshly painted wall.

"These strokes are masterful," he said.

"You coulda been a fine dancer," Blade chimed in from behind me.

"Tickling those ivories," Lonnie slurred. I saw him out of the corner of my eye, playing an imaginary waltz on a phantasmic piano, engulfed in his gin, as Blade mounted the Baby Grand to rock back and forth at a syncopated pace. "Or, I guess it's more like banging those sharps."

Reg was a waterfall beneath me, fluid and sensuous, rushing and majestic and powerful enough to change the course of stone. Using my left hand against the mattress, just beside his heart cage, to brace myself, I slid my right hand between us to hold him tightly. I massaged him in time with each thrust, felt our heartbeats merge in time, sending out our crimson blood to throb in unison. A great pulsing waterway of life and sex, consumption and consummation.

He pressed his lips to mine and wrapped his arms over my shoulders, pulling our bodies tightly together. His legs crossed over the small of my back to keep me locked within him as we shifted our bodies over. He released me as my back landed against the mattress and leaned back to slip me further inside. I reached up to run my hands over his chest, to tweak the cut glass of his nipples. Quivering, he grabbed my hands and pushed them back to the pillows above my head. He smiled a wicked smile and rocked his body backward. I slipped my hands behind my neck and lost myself in the vision of his serpentine dance, charming and writhing and clenching me deep within us.

The city moved in centuries outside the window, but all there was was this room; this bed; him, me. Us. Holy fuck, I'd missed him. The gentle morning light glistened off his cheekbones and washed down to highlight the moisture on his lips, mouth slightly ajar in an impassioned moan. His neck strained as he tilted his head back, exposing the sinewy muscles as they arched toward his shoulders, pushed back and bold, and fought down his torso to mimic the tighten and release of his stomach as he undulated over me. With each sway, I caught glimpse of his navel, the tiny trail of hair that began there and moved downward to his thick, pulsing cock.

Our eyes met, and I knew we were ready.

I clamped my hands on his hips——felt him tense, shiver, and release at my touch——and pulled him up slightly to give me a better range of motion as I bent my knees and braced my feet against the sheets. Our eyes locked. My head and shoulders pulled toward him. His arched toward me. His hands were on my chest, my neck, fingers wrapped and contracting. Each pulse was a tightening of contact. Then a warm ecstatic air emerged between us like lightning. And again. Over and over. Frenetic, thumping, pulling, thrusting. He buried his head in the crook of my neck; I trained my ear on his ragged, hollow breath as we propelled our bodies together.

We came as one and collapsed, him warm and sticky on my chest. Him finally home. He kissed my neck, fiercely, then my lips, gently. Inhaling sharply, he pulled off of me and collapsed to the bed by my side. We breathed deeply for a moment then both began to laugh. That sudden release of built up kinetic energy, the last remnants of acceleration being released.

"I love you," I said.

"I love you too," he said.

"I love you both," Blade sneered, and the professor and pianist joined him in a frantic cackle.

I tried to shake the voices from my head, furrowing my brow and clenching my teeth. Reg turned on his side and let his fingertips trace through the drying trails on my stomach.

"So, tell me about life without me," he sighed. "How has it been with me gone?"

"It's been... complex and weird," I said, a little too loudly, attempting to drown out the din from the bedroom.

"Is this the part where you tell him about laced cocaine?"

"Or almond notes behind the juniper?"

"Or a sudden, blinding flash of light?"

"A Rube Goldberg of marbles and a well placed nail gun display?"

"Is this the part where you talk to him about death?"

"I can't wait to hear all about it," Reg smiled. "But first, I think, a shower. If I can bring myself to slip away from bed."

I hopped to my feet and smiled at him, exhausted and ecstatic against the wrinkled sheets.

"I'll get the water hot for you," I said.

I did not want to leave Reg to the specters, but a few minutes couldn't hurt. I trod down the hall and adjusted the knobs on the shower until the water was steaming. My face flushed in the bathroom mirror, and I smiled at the thought of the man in the next room. We had both prided ourselves on our ability to be so together and yet retain our independence. We thought we'd moved beyond ownership; being owned; reliant. I did not even realize until he was gone how intertwined my world had been with his.

He slipped behind me as the steam began to cloud the mirror, his reflection hazy and fragmented in the glass, like a memory I wanted to hold as it ripped and spread through the timeline. I watched him pull the shower curtain tight against the tile of the wall, his silhouette open and posed against the onslaught of water. I smiled again——oh, how he made me smile——wiped my stomach with a towel, and tiptoed back down the hall.

🌿

Blade, Cent, and Lonnie sat on the edge of the bed; their heads cocked expectantly like puppies waiting to be admonished. Waiting for a treat. The professor stared out the window, studying birds and flight patterns, longing for an upstate cabin and the V-formation of geese. I tried to ignore them all as I searched the floor for my sweats and slipped back into them. My tank top was by the window at the professor's feet, so I pulled a new shirt from the dresser.

"Because if there's one thing he's learned," Cent said, "it's that you can ignore something to make it go away."

"Hey, it worked with his parents," Blade smiled.

"And his sobriety the first time around," Lonnie nodded. "And the second too."

I wanted to ask them what the fuck they thought they were doing. I wanted to ignore them. I wanted to relish in Reg's return.

"Fine," Cent said. "You don't want to talk about us. Let's talk about him. Tell us about Reginald Adrian King."

I pushed absently at the dresser, attempting to return the bedroom to some sense of normalcy while still giving myself space to paint, to work on the map I was determined to finish.

"What do you want to know?"

"What first attracted you to him?" Blade asked. He licked his lips as he spoke; dipped his hips into the mattress; made everything sound sexual.

"His song," I smiled. Giving in, I plopped down to the bed and lost myself in memory. "Some of his work friends had dragged him out to a karaoke bar I used to drink at one night. And when they finally convinced him to grab a mic, his sweet, lilting voice was so timid, even through those amplified speakers. But there was this power behind it, you know? And I'm a sucker for a true southern drawl."

The professor tapped against the glass and whistled.

"You know," he said, "unlike most birds, with their loud calls and their ruffled feathers and their preening dances, crows are much more subdued. They fly in close. They sing softly. They coo and cuddle and make the whole mating dance intimate. It's not about power. They know they're powerful. It's about passion."

"I thought you told me you tripped him while you were walking your dog."

Lonnie's accusatory glare cut through my reverie.

"I did? I did." I shook my head and conjured the memory. "He fell flat on his ass and ripped his suit, and he hated me immediately."

"Crows remember faces. And they hold a grudge."

"He hated you," Cent said, "but did you love him?"

"I mean, yeah," I nodded with a sly smile curving across my lips. My eyes glossed over slightly at the thought of him, flustered and fallen, examining the rip in his two sizes too big suit. "Not that I realized it right away. But looking back, it was definitely there."

Lonnie demanded to know which it was: the cooing or the falling. But I didn't answer because it was both, depending on the situation. It was all of it. And all of it was Reg. Origin stories are rarely rarified, and far too often drawn out and slow, and so require a retrospective eye to whittle them down into a carefully crafted, digestible story. A meet cute. A fairytale that isn't fair to the actual complexity of the emotive causation of two people coming together. Which is to say, what a person feels can rarely be whittled down to anything more than a parable. And what's left is a message that has lost its meaning because the whole of it cannot be learned. Meeting Reg. Loving Reg. It wasn't romantic; it wasn't sweet; it wasn't funny. But it was all those things. It was everything. Reg was everything. He was my life.

I stood to make the bed, and Lonnie drifted back to his piano, Blade to his pulsing, Cent to the painting. The professor continued his lecture on crows. How their brain to body mass ratio was the largest of all birds, behind parrots, and it came through in their levels of intelligence. Dialects were created; tools were used; deception and distraction had entered their vocabulary. He found it fascinating, he said, how as a species we determined another's intelligence by its ability to fool the world around it, to create new narratives for itself, to take from the world what it wanted at any given moment in time.

"How did we get here," he said, "to this place where we've become so narcissistically myopic, we grade intelligence upon one's ability to plot and to scheme as opposed to working with the land for our nourishment? It's downright selfish! As selfish as a well placed beam of light."

"Or a fine powder scrupulously cut within another."

"Or the almond in the gin."

"Or playing marbles with little blue shoed boys in hardware stores."

"Not that distraction is in any way discouraged," the professor said to no one in particular. "Not that it's not a necessary ploy in maintaining sanity while living with the discomforts of the modern world. Not that deception in any way negates the intelligence of these majestic, prolific birds."

The shower hissed to the off position as I smoothed the remaining wrinkles from the bedspread. Of course his first act, before making me,

THE HOUSE THAT WASN'T THERE

when he got home was to make the bed. It was only natural. It was the "hi, honey," the "feels like," the "no place." Reg settled into the desk chair with a book while I found my markers. I plotted a course along the mental grid of the wall, attempting again at reconstruction. Reg flipped the pages and did that thing he always did where his index finger absently traced the lines as he read them. We smiled contentedly as we returned to home.

FALL FELT FAMILIAR FOR THE HOUSE, easy and comforting and better suited to the chill that challenged its ever hollow, ever cluttering halls. Fall brought with it the sweet scent of decay——light and fragrant and comforting. The smells that occurred before the worms and the meal and the rot. When the cells were just beginning to break down and release their energy in waves of perfumed remembrances, a lifespan of what ifs and when dids floating on the air.

The house knew how to savor a moment, to stretch it out into olfactory circumlocutions that could cycle through millennia in a single moment or push that moment——solid and strong——through decades. Fall calmed the seething temper tantrum, made it tremble in aggravated acquiescence: the last gasps of a fish on land, the orgiastic flapping of a man in air. Fall found its way through the attic nooks and closets, whispered offerings of freedom through the pipes and air ducts, and settled in to watch the foliage burn then fade then turn to dust.

The house had always spent its summers alone; hot and naked and sweating with the touch of every visitor, every strange soul who attempted to trace their way through its wanton rooms and creaking doorways and narrow stairs. Fellows falling through to leave the marks of their oils in superfluous handprints on the wallpaper, but never truly there, never really whole or supple or comforting. Apparitions——even those who always remained——made transparent by the summer haze.

Fall, though——Fall required a companion. A confidant. Someone to watch the sky alight on Wednesday afternoons when Mrs. Hargrove decided the flue was adequately scrubbed and a fire would be just right to set the mood for the folks who came a-calling. Someone to commiserate with on the shortening of days; to relish within the longing of nights. The house required a host, like a party; like a virus. Someone like a Rafe or a Paul or a William. Someone unafraid, unbewildered by the icy touch of the wrought iron spiderwebbing spun outward to engulf them inward, to pull them to the stoop and through the door and down the hall.

The host would need to be ecstatic or somber, as the occasion allowed, and speak always with a joyous cadence that gave way to cryptic rhythms of circadian cicadas fine tuning the muscles in their legs after seventeen years spent underground. An aged amalgamation. Anachronistic. And always staged by the front hall closet; hand on the doorknob, energized by its conductive, chilly brass. The closet, filled always with half length trench coats and tanned trilbies, awaiting partygoers, ready to arm them against the coming frost.

The house enjoyed a good fête in the Fall. The house that liked to dance. The house that wasn't there. The festival of the forgotten. Everyone dressed alike and free to fill in the focus necessary for the conversation or otherwise fade finally into the wallpaper. They could be no one. They could be everyone. The house, it relished in the solace of anonymity.

11

"YOU'RE REALLY BEAUTIFUL IN THIS LIGHT."

Reg had been home for three days, and we'd barely left the bedroom save to shower or answer the door when our food deliveries were made. And even then, "just leave it at the door" had become an all too common phrase through the callbox. His skin heaved as he breathed, glistened in the soft filter of sun that beamed through the dithering curtains agitated by the push and pull of the breeze.

"So are you," he smiled. He'd told me so a hundred times since his return, but I never tired of hearing it.

I nuzzled into the crook of his arm and let my hand dance absently across his chest as I breathed him in. We were, in that moment, a solid unit of air, slick with moisture, aloft and grounded. A single structure against the undue harshness of the outside world.

"We should go out tonight."

I groaned and pushed my face farther into his shoulder. He caressed my back and kissed my forehead.

"I know," he continued. "I don't want this to end either. But we haven't left the apartment since I got back. And you haven't been to a meeting in over a week."

"I'm drunk on something else right now."

"It's all well and good that you can make jokes about it," he said, "but your health is important to me. I want to make sure you're around for so much more of this in the years to come."

The scent of dried sweat and love mixed with the cotton lavender of the sheets, salty and sweet and sticky and intoxicating. There were dirty dishes on the bedside table, near empty containers of mu shu pork and half eaten gyros from the guy down the street and spaghetti from Michel-Angelo's with all of the soy based meatballs eaten out. I'd been ravenous, but he'd joked he'd only been hungry for me. And that only served to set us off——again——to waves of dizzying convulsions, emotive and forceful and making up for lost time. I tried to make time stand still in our frenetic movement. I tried to knock the hourglass to its side. I tried to capture him all.

"Let's at least go for a walk," he said. "I love the city right when autumn pushes in. It seems somehow more alive."

The sun played at its first setting——that time before dusk when it dipped behind the taller buildings in the skyline, when waves of heat and light permeated the streets to make everything suddenly clearer. Outlined and deep and present. Like a photograph. Like the moment when the clouds first roll in before a thunderstorm and suddenly the entire world seemed solid and electric. Seemed real. The sunset of Man before the sunset of World. I loved those moments, when the world was rendered suddenly crisp and three-dimensional, not just in space but in time: in pause. I loved the ragged breath the streets seemed to heave as they adjusted to the sudden dip in temperature. I loved Reg.

I held his hand as we walked and shielded my eyes against the blinding beam of light emanating from the black iron post where Gerrie had been impaled like a beacon shot toward the sky. A lighthouse. An I-was-here. I realized I hadn't left our building since the incident; that I'd watched it all from above and washed out my sorrow as thoroughly as the cleaners had scrubbed the sidewalk.

Noticing my solemn expression, Reg clenched tightly to my hand.

"What's wrong?"

"That's where she fell."

"Who?"

"Gerrie. The girl who lived above us. She..." I didn't want to ruin the moment with concepts so macabre. I sighed deeply before I finished, hoping my inhale could swallow the word. "Jumped."

"Above us?"

I realized that Reg and Gerrie had never met. She hadn't knocked on our door until after he'd left for his training seminar. She'd learned all about him as I gushed on and on about the masks he'd make, the notes he'd leave for me, the way his lips would curl when a mischievous thought crossed his brain. I'd told her everything about him, made him real in his absence. I could do the same for her. I wanted to tell him about her but thought better of it. Explaining someone after they had gone was problematic at best. True, there was a sense of completion to the story, but memory could be fickle. It either showcased the worst——the bitter moments and the anger and the fear and the agitation——or centered upon such a sickeningly sweet persona it seemed false; manufactured; fantasy. Explaining the dead was better left to the poets lest the dead themselves become manifest. I had enough ghosts on my own. Why would I introduce Reg to them?

It was Sunday or Thursday or Wednesday. One of those days when everyone needed to get out of their house, whether in an attempt to grab hold of those last breezes of the weekend or to pull themselves free of their workweek, if only in a momentary anticipation of the true exodus. Reg held my hand as we traversed the city streets, giggling as we bypassed wandering tourists or fast paced businessmen or rambunctious college students. We wove our bodies through like a tapestry, stretching out the life path of the city in elongated wafts and wefts. We made maps of our bodies, defiantly announcing our reunion. We wore masks of expressions too great to be contained.

It was Reg who spotted her first, about a block away, arms crossed and tapping her toe against the sidewalk in such an exaggerated manner it was almost comical, like a sitcom mother or the wife in a farce, but it got her point across. She pursed her lips and cocked her head. Her eyes squinted toward me with her unspoken questions burning through the red ringlets that surrounded her narrowed face. *Where were you? Where have you been? Why haven't you answered my calls?*

I slowed my pace instinctively like an admonished puppy and let go of Reg's hand.

"I'm going to let you handle this," he whispered gently in my ear and hung back as I trudged forward. "How about I meet you at that little café on Eighth? The one that has that danish you like."

She crossed her arms as I drew nearer, appearing statuesque there on the sidewalk, perched and posed right where the basement stairs of the church met street level before turning to ascend to the large wooden double doors which shielded the sanctity of the pews from the huddled masses who frolicked and fled in their hedonistic fury up and down Monroe.

"So what do you have to say for yourself?" she asked. Her words were firm but gentle. Scolding yet supportive. It was what made Annie such a great sponsor, her ability to hold her charges to account when it was really none of her goddamn business. "How long has it been since we've seen you at group? At a meeting? And don't even start to tell me you've been fine or that you don't need it. Your health is important, Howard. You have to keep at it——keep paying attention to it——to keep yourself in control."

I scoffed without realizing it and blurted, "You make it sound like a pyramid scheme. We'll make you better, but you have to keep coming back. And bring three friends."

I watched her face change as she figured out what to say. Her mind cycled through its rolodex of trained responses, her systems of encouragement, her carefully controlled reality.

"Look, I'm sorry," I continued. "Things have been intense. And horrible. And——really good. But there's been no backslide. I've been maintaining."

Annie gave a compassionate half smile and took my hand.

"Sit with me."

We perched on the cooling concrete of the church steps, her hand on my hand on my knee, my other arm straight as I balanced on the palm planted behind me and stared at the sky. We both peered out at the bustling energy of the world at sunset. A group of women, blonde and bubbling and babbling, clucked together down the street, taking turns sharing stories of the men who texted them and who they were hoping would ask them to the Winter Formal. Strength in numbers. Strength in the unassigned beauty of fitting in. Teenagers tested the curfews imposed by their parents, played at adulthood with colored foam balls, and angled their eyes to catch the first flicker of the streetlights. The universal symbol of your-homework-had-better-be-done. Men rushed home from their offices or their mistresses, so singularly self involved they barely noticed their counterparts all dressed just the same as them. A sports team of trench coats and old fashioned hats.

"Maintaining is excellent," Annie said. "And an admirable, admirable place to be." She repeated the word for emphasis. She repeated the word as if she'd searched briefly for another and found none better for the situation. "But no one is equipped to do everything alone."

She laughed. A well timed expulsion to heighten the moment, to relieve some of the tension in the evening air. She tried to be contagious, to bring me into her.

"It's so complicated," she said. "We ask you to do all this work within yourself. And it's all work that you have to be ready to do, that you need to be willing to do if any of it is to work. We ask you to face these things internally, and examine your dependencies, and battle all these proverbial demons. We ask that because we can't do that for you. All this work, I know it can——in and of itself——make you feel alone. Which is why the meetings are so important. Which is why communication is key. So that you can remember you're not alone. That there are people right there with you, struggling and persevering and able and ready to understand. Which, believe it or not, is so crucial to your sobriety when you're an addict like we are."

Annie likened Group to "finding your tribe," and I understood her immensely. Chosen family was important. Those people of like mind who supported you. Those ghosts who challenged your thoughts. I thought back all those years to that little queer kid who didn't even know what queer was. To his fear of being found out as different. To his solace when he found others like him. He was me and yet he seemed so far away.

Annie sighed as she shook the brochures from her mouth. She could tell they weren't really reaching me, anyway. Understanding and acquiescence were opposite sides of the spinning coin.

"I grew up just a few blocks from here," she said. "Did I ever tell you that? Back when this neighborhood was very different than it is now. Or maybe, at the very least, in the eyes of a frizzy redheaded, pale skinned, freckle faced girl with abnormally large buckteeth that prevented her from ever being any good at the clarinet her parents had bought and forced her to play, it was an entirely different world."

Her eyes faded as she recalled her youth, as if all the life in them was required to bring out the memory, to relive it so it could not relive her.

"I wasn't very well liked by my classmates. Or——I guess——I wasn't disliked, but I looked different. And children are pack animals that play at ideas of adulthood through cruelty and malice as if the only means of upward mobility is on the back of the perceived weakest one around. So, you know, lucky me. And there was one kid who was particularly cruel."

We watched as tiny halogen glows sparked to life all at once throughout the neighborhood like fireflies caught in jars. A manmade attempt at staving off darkness. A competition with the sun once it had its back turned. Bravado, all of it. All of it attempts at control.

"There used to be this park at the corner of Eighth and Pine. Right there where that twelve story condo complex shot up. And it had a mulched yard and a swing set and one of those covered plastic slides that was meant to stop the heat burns of the metal ones but had those ridges and bolts that would always snag your skin and your clothes as you slipped through to the bottom. So, this kid who was cruel——JP Daniels——would always be at this playground, and he would bully me every time I went. Every single time. From when I was seven years old until I was thirteen."

"And then you stood up to your bully, and he stopped. And addiction is my bully, so I've got to stand up to it," I said. "I know this story."

"No." Annie wasn't looking at me. She was lost in her past. "That's not it at all. When I was thirteen, and really too old for the park or the slide, there was something inside me that was longing to return to a moment when I wasn't worried about my body, or sex, or growing up. Already I was wishing for that so much simpler time when all I had to worry about were my teeth and my freckles and my hair. Before all the other shit started piling on. So, I gathered up my nostalgia, and I went to the park. I climbed up that slide, and I pulled my body down that tube in an attempt to just feel a little bit of the freedom that came with the prepubescent mind."

Her eyes were darker now, taking in the worst of it, covered by the slide.

"But JP was there with a couple of his cronies. I don't even remember their names. They might as well have been him. They were extensions of him at the very least, like extra arms with extra fists. So as my thighs scudded and burned against the plastic, the light at either end of the tunnel eclipsed, and I reached out my hands to freeze myself halfway through. I heard JP laugh and call me 'Little Orphan' even though he knew damn well where I lived and who my parents were, but he called me that because kids of his caliber have no originality or instinct to trust the complexities of language. But it didn't matter. I couldn't correct him. All I could see was a glinting flash of light as the sun bounced off a pair of barber shears he'd pulled from his backpack. Like this was something he'd planned. Like he knew I'd slide that slide before I did."

Annie made herself small on the sidewalk. As she spoke, her body disappeared, her hair expounded.

"I screamed and held tight to the sides of the slide, trying my best to keep from slipping down, even as he brandished the blades and began to climb upward toward me. The rubber on the soles of my shoes scuffed as I attempted to push myself back up to the top, even though one of JP's henchmen waited there. At least he didn't have scissors. He caught up with me; and he pulled his body over mine; and he held the scissors against my lips to quiet me. His friends were laughing as he made the first cut. And then another. And another. All with me crying silently under him. All with his body pressed against mine, and the feel of an excitement he hadn't figured out what to do with yet pushing against my stomach. It took forever. It took a moment. Then he was finished, and the three of them ran off into the afternoon. My body unclenched, I slid to the bottom of the slide surrounded by pools of red. I got to my feet and stared at my hair lying there like a puddle of blood as I felt the harsh gaps on the top of my head. Samson and Delilah. But I barely had any strength to begin with."

"I'm so sorry," I said. "That must have been excruciating to overcome."

"That's just the backstory," she said. "That's not even where it really starts. But after that, I became obsessed with blades. Scissors, and pen knives, and steak knives, and butter knives——even the plastic ones. I took them from my house and from restaurants and from the school cafeteria. When I was fifteen, I found other cutters to commiserate with. We compared our scars. We egged each other on. We carved stories into one another's backs. And I really thought I'd found my tribe."

Annie turned her hand over atop mine and slowly pulled up the sleeve of her flowing peasant blouse. I'd noticed she always wore sleeves, even in the dead of summer, but hadn't put much thought into it before. Gingers had notoriously fair skin. It was a fashion statement. I never considered it armor. I never knew it was a mask.

Her forearms were pale, but lush with lengths of pink and puckered scars, all varying in depth and shape. Designs of a soul attempting to feel something, to become real like she just needed the right sigil to come to life. Her face was solemn and secure, free of the shame she had managed to overcome. She'd made peace with her past, and it was inspiring. Each mark was a milestone, a pressure point from which she could leap, finally and ecstatically free.

"They weren't my tribe," she said. "Not the real one. Eventually they led me——or I led myself——to the bottle to numb the sensations of the cuts. I was only seventeen. Years went by in a sea of astringent and blood before I found the people who were actually concerned about what was underneath the scars. Before anyone cared what was behind the wild persona of tequila and vodka and blood and blade. Those people were my real tribe. They were the ones I needed to fully realize who I am."

She looked at me expectantly. She looked like she had suddenly remembered I was there.

"That's why the meetings are so important, Howard. The Group becomes a part of you. Not everyone in there is going to be your best friend, but some of them will be. And all of them understand what you're going through at its base. All our stories are different, all the causes vary, but the dependencies are real. Seeing other people make the positive changes in their lives that you are trying to make really does help."

I nodded and sighed. My eyes danced across the newly formed nightscape of city dwellers rushing home or rushing out, passing one another in their self concerned manner, envious of the comfort of the hearth or the freedom of the bars the other would soon embrace. Thin brims of hats angled down over faces that were lost and indiscernible. Khaki, knee length coats hid shapes and features and notable characteristics. Specters flooded out through the arteries of a city too concerned with itself to imagine the life it sustained; a city too quick to shiver off the aftermath of its deaths.

"I'm really sorry I've been AWOL," I conceded. "I've been a bit pre-occupied. Reg is back."

"Reg is——back?"

"Finally," I exclaimed. "So obviously, we needed some time to reconnect."

Annie bit her lip. Her eyes raced back and forth over her thoughts as if they were an ornate tome there for her to read, to consider, from which to pick and choose the best phrasing. Fear and concern and not wanting to shift the situation clouded her features.

"I'm very happy that you can have Reg with you," she finally said. "But it is very dangerous to trade one dependency for another. And Reg can't become that for you. Not if you want to remain healthy."

Her words were short and then long, staccato and drawn out as she considered the next one to be spoken. It's impact. The multitude of its meanings. She took my hand in hers and massaged my palm with her thumb, trying to ground me in her presence.

I stood swiftly. It probably seemed angry, agitated, annoyed: my sudden uprising. How quickly my leap shifted her hand from mine. But I wasn't angry. I was just tired. So tired of always being on. Always on top of me. I just wanted a few days to live and relish in an utterly true and uncomplicated love. Before life was forced to return to normal. There was nothing wrong with that. I should have been allowed those things.

"I'll be back at the meetings," I said. "I promise."

I stepped back to the sidewalk and felt Annie's hand on my shoulder. I turned to her open, empathetic face.

"I just care about you, Howard," she said. "I'm not trying to mother you."

"I know."

"There's a reality to our lives——to our situations and dependencies and all the fantasies we cook up——there's a reality we have to face up to," she said, and I nodded.

My reality was with Reg.

I turned to leave. To meet up with Reg at the café. To lose myself in the onslaught of bodies and other human like forms ever darkening in the spread of night. Annie stood silently in front of the church, perched on the precipice between ascending and descending stairs, halfway down the slide, wringing her hands and peering after me. It was only then, several steps away, too far really to reach, when I heard her scream. Primal, guttural. Pained. The sudden wail of a death wave. The utterly ineloquent goodbye.

A flurry of motion shocked through the street behind me, and I rushed back to find Annie at the bottom of the stairwell in front of the church basement door. There was a stab wound on her sternum; her head cracked from the fall. A mugging gone bad. A random act of violence.

A crowd was gathering. The door to the basement pushed open and caught itself in the tangle of maroon black blood and orange red hair. Anonymous no more. I closed my eyes and wished it away, but it was real and sudden and reappeared with each flutter of my eyelids.

"Did anyone see what happened?"

"It must've been a mugger."

"A woman alone at night is an easy target."

"Scissors may have been involved."

"A woman alone at night is an easy angel."

I slipped back into the crowd. I spread out into the night.

135

12

THERE WAS NOTHING I COULD HAVE DONE.

The warm hearth light of exposed Edison bulbs emanated through the café windows. It silhouetted the baroque flourishes stenciled there on menu boards and made all the patrons inside appear as if they were starring in a film noir, a mannerist tableau, an expressionist swirl of movement and artificial light. Baristas floated between tables with steaming mugs of quick ristretto shots and frothed milk that somehow didn't spill until customers pulled the winged cups from their lips and laughed at the quick popping bubbles of residue left behind from the rosetta marked foam.

I was at least a hundred yards away when it happened. I hadn't actually seen anything.

I heard the blare of sirens behind me. They echoed off the buildings and bounced around the city to join the wailing cries of their kin out in search of tragedy, of happenstance, of crime. Some hoping to make a difference; most attempting to assuage the damage already caused. And, too, a thousand heartbeats growing loud and rapid as they attempted to fill the space of the one that was no longer pumping.

There were enough people there who knew her. I would only have added to the confusion.

I paused to inhale the salty, earthy aroma of quickly roasted beans ——"cherries," the barista corrected—— as it wafted out atop the mumbling conversations to mingle with the autumn blossoms——aster and chrysanthemum and Japanese anemones. Scent grounded the city, rooted it beneath the pavement. One deep breath. And then another. And another. Forward momentum. It was all we had to keep us here.

There was nothing I could have done.

The door chimed as I entered; eyes turned instinctively toward the sound to survey the new addition, to deem me interesting or worthy or thirsty, then returned to their conversations, assumptions made, as if nothing had happened. I nodded to the workers behind the counter and made a perimeter lap around the space to find where Reg was waiting for me. The shop was nearly full, folks gearing up for a night out or tapping away at keyboards in attempts to finish their masterpieces; chatting about which coffee makers they found attractive, lamenting the long hours at work on such a beautiful day, at the start of such a magical night.

Reg wasn't there.

I waited near the restrooms to see if he'd emerge, giving an awkward smile to the young man who pushed his way out abruptly and bumped the door against the high chairs stacked beside it.

"Cent and I used to come to this coffee shop all the time," Gerrie said. She was leaning against the bathroom door casually, calm and collected, barely moving even as it swung open, swung through her. "Not together, obviously. We didn't know each other. But it is on the way to campus from my apartment. And on the way to the hardware store from his."

No Reg.

"You think if we had known each other, the cops would have connected you to our deaths somehow?" she asked. "That just maybe the two of us biting it would have seemed a little less random. A little less coincidental? Nature abhors a coincidence almost as much as a vacuum."

I approached the counter and described him to the baristas——black guy, about my height, a little shorter; full, kissable lips; eyes that could melt stone like it were butter on a hot day——but they said they hadn't seen him. I waited by the pastry display and scanned the room once more as Gerrie pantomimed licking the centers of each of the danishes, nibbling at the crumbs from the croissants.

"Of course," she said, "that's getting into intelligent design which is incredibly problematic for an Atheistic Jew. 'Course, for the sociology student, there ain't nothing wrong with nature taking its course through a set means of interactions based on a chemical or psychological composition. Even if nature doesn't understand what it's doing in the way we view understanding."

Reg wasn't there.

"But that means that nature has to be given the opportunity to take its course, doesn't it?" she scowled. "A gentle shove, even to a suicidal girl, really kind of fucks with the whole of the process, don't you think?"

"'Freedom is what you do with what's been done to you,'" I said. I said it out loud to a room full of apathetic people.

"Quoting Sartre?" she laughed. "He also said, 'Man is condemned to be free; because once thrown into the world, he is responsible for everything he does.'"

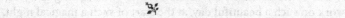

There was nothing I could have done.

"Do you really believe that?" she scoffed. "There's always something to be done or not done. Both the doing and the not doing are a choice. Are an act. In all senses of the word. It's only that nothing can ever be undone. Speaking of: you should check your phone."

❧

Back on the sidewalk, I fished my phone from my pocket. In all the commotion of before, I'd missed the gentle vibration of a phone call.

"Hi, Love... I expected... so many... for a long time... our home... I will be... I love you...."

The message was broken and garbled again——that boy really needed to get his phone serviced!——but I understood the gist. The café had been busy, too many people, too long a wait. He'd decided to just meet back up with me at home, in our bed, in our love. I smiled into the night, face awash in the red twisting lights of a passing ambulance, and steadied my feet toward our door.

❧

Fall brought with it the raging thunder of a world attempting to adjust. A shifting planet, a cooling air, and the retained heat of a summer spent in tantrum rising from the crisscross of asphalt paths all coalesced to shake the moans from the sky. Walking slowly home, I watched as its counterpart——that unlikely, intimate union of light and sound against the wet, sticky sex it made——arched through the sky. Nature's gentle reminder of its dominance over us. The intensified electricity of its antecedent sonic boom.

I marveled, sometimes, at the hubris of cartographers. How we positioned lines on paper to say "this is your path," "this is what was created for you," "this is a realistic account of where you should go." We were fools, ignoring the plans of nature and plotting out the Course of Man as if our naive attempts at dominance would persevere, could remain. Even as I drew my maps through three dimensional space, plotting the course of a straightened line with my body, I obsessed in their inaccuracies. *This was designed, this was built,* I'd think. I'd think, *how can I accept this concrete as fact when there's so much soil and sand and stone underneath, when there's so much lightning in the sky?* I wondered if any map had ever succeeded in capturing the love and the trauma and the enthusiastic mundanity of the souls who experienced the space it attempted to convey. That was my true desire when it got down to it: to leave a lasting remembrance of a place imbued with all the moments that created it; a plotted point containing all the multitudes of place.

THE HOUSE THAT WASN'T THERE

I was near The Maiden Name, and the rain seemed like it would hold off for a while, despite the firework pre-show performance of the night, so I changed my course to pass by its darkened windows, to feel a little bit of the sobriety it brought me; the sense of solid place it conveyed. I found it strange that I hadn't heard from Connor about anything: Blade's memorial, Lonnie's service, a re-opening date. Hell, even a text message ordering me in to scrub clean all the corners and crevices——to make the most of our downtime——should have come through. But everyone copes with grief in different ways. Everyone takes their own amount of time and space to deal with the world around them.

The sky hummed in a violent exuberance as the streets began to clear in anticipation of the storm. I rounded the corner just as the first large drops began to fall against the sidewalk; heavy and pregnant and staggering through a makeshift game of hopscotch. The string lights buzzed around the tinted windows. I pressed my face against the glass to see a room alight with energy, a dozen trilbies on a dozen hat racks. A dozen trench coats on a dozen hooks. Twelve aging men. The flurry of the darkness underneath.

Connor looked frazzled as he shifted between half made drinks and mostly empty glasses behind the bar. It served him right to serve them wrong after reopening the bar without calling me. I surveyed the scene for a moment, safely beneath the awning as the rain picked up in velocity behind me. Anger and schadenfreude gave way to irritation as I watched the hubbub of faceless patrons force their way toward the bar, boomerang their bodies on the dance floor, tilt back the places where their faces should form to suck down the mixtures of fruit juice and fermented grains. I had been a model employee for The Maiden Name. I'd saved Connor's ass so many times as he jostled paperwork instead of tequila bottles. Why wouldn't he call me in if the bar had reopened?

Lonnie's piano was covered in lit candles, but his lack of breath did nothing to anger the flames as he banged his fingers against the keys. Blade would have slipped a hundred times over in the spills Connor left unattended across the bar top if his bare feet——and bare legs and sapphire sequined crotch——required any sort of traction. The place was a bloody mess.

I released the barricade of the door, and a maudlin, macabre drumbeat fought against the thunder at my back. I stepped through the crowd on my tiptoes, focused on the impromptu ballet, the sidestep of elbows and sudden motion, and made my way to the bar.

"What the hell are you doing here?"

"Why the hell would I not be here?" I responded. At least our catty call and response was still intact.

Connor rolled his eyes and moved to grab more napkins from beneath the bar.

"Someone doesn't like you very much," Blade smiled from above me. He tea bagged down to the bar with a fiery smirk in his eyes and rolled his body out in a fluid motion as he rose. A snake being charmed. The charmer all along.

"I would have been here to help with the reopening if you'd've called," I said.

"I did call you," Connor insisted and poured a sloppy mixed drink into a plastic cup before sloshing a bit too much of it on the bar. "Three weeks ago, when it happened."

I wanted to laugh, but his face didn't look like he was joking. His scoff was not the sound of a humored man. It'd only been a few days since Lonnie's passing.

"Don't look at me," Blade said as he twirled to shake his ass. "Time's not really a relevant factor in my worldview anymore." He dipped down again and turned to smile at the gathering crowd. "Not that it really was when I was alive either."

Lonnie bumbled through a sloppy carnival of scales as he tried to keep up with the thumping hum of the dance music Connor had blaring through the speakers. His memory seemed lost in the space. Maybe that's what Connor wanted. A fresh start. A cleansing. Tabula Rasa. I marveled at the atmospheric alterations he had made, the ironic loss of soul.

"Get that bastard to pour me a spot of the juniper," Lonnie called to me from his bench. "He's been ignoring me all night."

"You know the rules," Blade chirped. "No more drinking on the job at The Maiden Name. Thanks to you, and me, and this one right here."

"I'm being serious, man," I said. The picture of politeness, despite the rage at his overlooking joke burning within me. "You know this bar is like a second home to me. I'm here for you. For this place."

Connor stared at me for a moment, his eyes bumbling through confusion and compassion. Despite our differences sometimes, I knew he appreciated my hard work and dedication. We worked well together. We laughed, and we joked, and we got the job done. But somehow these deaths had levied a seriousness to his demeanor. Somehow death had made him grave. He opened his mouth, ready to respond, when a loud snap enveloped the place in silence and darkness. The storm had knocked out the power: a dangerous occurrence for a bar this crowded; for a crowd this drunk.

"You don't work here anymore," Connor said. The finality in his voice seemed hostile. "Fuck off. I've got to go deal with this shit."

Connor turned to the stunned crowd, quiet as the storm raged on outside, listening to the rain hit the pavement, the thunder cracking against the clouds. None of them seemed able to hear Lonnie as he continued his rambling scales. None of them seemed to notice as Blade dipped and stripped for them.

"I think we just blew a fuse, guys. I'll get us back up and going in no time."

An attempt at a calming call. An attempt to keep the crowd and their wallets happy and local.

I slipped behind the bar and followed Connor into the backroom. He fumbled in the darkness, so I swiped the flashlight he obviously didn't know was there and trained its beam onto the alley door.

"The breaker's on the roof," I told him.

"I know that," he said, lying and annoyed.

He pulled a thick, industrial trash bag from the shelving unit and ripped a hole for his face before pulling it over his head. I followed suit.

"You might need me to hold the flashlight."

Even in the darkness, I could see his eyes roll.

"This isn't going to win you your job back, Howard," he insisted as he pushed through the backdoor to the alley.

The air outside was crisp and cool, but the height of the buildings shielded the small inlet from most of the rain. We found the metal ladder affixed to the brick by the dumpster, and Connor began to pull himself up along the building. Water slipped between the winding grooves of the iron as I moved up behind him, careful to leave enough distance between us as we made our way to the roof. The streetlamps haunted the sidewalks as the raindrops clouded their luminescence, sliding over the glass to break prisms and shadows in the light. The view from the roof was astounding.

Though relatively low against the city skyline, the height and exposure to the elements sent a powerful message through the structures to reach out to the both of us: Nature is here. No matter how much you build and erect and attempt to alter it, nature is always present. The lightning jumped between buildings, igniting the sky in a strobe of bright and dark.

"Shine that light over here."

Connor fumbled through his keys to find the tiny fit for the lock box. The rain beat down harder as he flipped through the breakers, listening between each switch for the clap of power returned.

"Can we stop playing games now?" I asked.

Connor grunted and continued to work his fingers against the panel. I'd never known him to take a joke so far. He could be an infuriating little shit sometimes, but this was getting excessive. The flashlight's power sagged under the weight of the storm, and I shook it to shift the batteries a bit, the friction forcing through the energy.

"Seriously, Connor. This has gone too far. I'm not going to let you gaslight me."

His hand clasped around the metal master switch as he turned to me with a fire in his eyes.

"Have you gone completely insane?" he raged. "I always knew hiring you was a mistake. And now you want to grovel for a job you abandoned? You're out of your fucking mind!"

"I abandoned nothing!"

"You abandon everything!" he screamed. He said, "No wonder Reg——"

The frayed plasma edges of a lightning bolt sparked against the antenna atop the building and shivered down to the control panel. Connor's eyes grew wide as it pulsed through him, tensing and releasing his muscles in a rapid succession. His still closed hand pulled the switch as he fell forward, face first onto the rooftop, suddenly still and cold after all the heat and animation. I heard the music rise and pump downstairs, the cheer of the crowd as their fists began to pump, as their feet began to stomp the floor. Connor's head bled where it hit the tar of the roof, blood washing out in watercolor red against the pebbled grey to look like a small and aggravated bolt after the shock of nature's fury.

I needed to call someone. The cops. The paramedics. I rushed down the ladder from the roof.

The alley door had locked behind us. I struggled against the handle to no avail.

"Looks like you're fucked, bro," Blade laughed from atop the dumpster, still dancing, relishing in the wet from the storm like the raindrops were dollar bills.

"He's gone by now, anyway," Lonnie chimed in as he wandered the alley in search of remnants from any thrown out bottle. "Not like there's anything else you could do." He turned his face to the sky and willed the rain to gin.

"I've got to call the cops," I insisted.

"And what are they going to say?" Blade asked. "You, the jilted ex-employee who just got canned."

"You, the guy on site for dead guy number three at the same damn bar."

"It was an accident. It was the storm!"

"You think they're gonna see it that way? Did you even try to resuscitate him?"

"Cops always want the easy bag. It's so much easier to think someone killed someone than to believe there was some freak accident, a morbid act of nature, a deadly dance with god."

"It's so much easier to control people than all of this." Blade spun on the dumpster, his arms raised up to the heavens as if he were embracing the storm. "Man, in my experience, wants dominion almost as much as he wants to be dominated."

"Those cops can't control nature," Lonnie said, "so you best be sure they'll do all they can to control you."

I tried the door again. I banged against the metal. I clanged the flashlight against the steel until the glass shattered and it dented at the edge. But the music inside was too loud. The crowd inside was too exuberant. The man on the roof was too dead.

"Now," Lonnie smiled. "Wipe your filthy prints from the flashlight, maybe think about washing off that bit of blood on the rim from when Connor fell, then toss it in that there dumpster, and do that leaving thing you do best. Skedaddle on back home to your Reg."

THE PROFESSOR STUDIED THE HOUSE with a quiet, distilled curiosity. Like one of his subjects; like one of his students. The house with the temper. The house that wasn't there. The child mind structure that built existence out of nothing and swallowed itself whole in every heaving breath. The robin egg blue siding and the red breasted door poised and heaving and ready to take flight. The slate grey shutters and the wrought iron fencing nested to hold time in space, sturdy and solid and hollow and left behind.

He noticed the parts that others hadn't, he thought. He saw the things the house tried to keep hidden. A gentle tilt in the foundation from days or years or decades of settling. The cracks that formed in unobtrusive outbursts in the mortar, a welcoming invite to the ivy and the weeds and the strange and funny thoughts which clouded the mind inside the brevity of tantrum clarity. The anachronisms of the build. The place in the map where it should have been, and the scribbles it left behind. He saw it all in a way no one ever had; the hubris of the learned.

His hand hovered above the doorknob, playing at the tensions in the air with a practiced restraint. He wasn't quite ready to enter. There was so much left to say, to do, to explore. It was not yet time to trade the green ball cap for one more suited to his age. He had to understand the cover before he could fully grasp the text.

From the street, he could see inside the house. Hallways like arteries leading to humors, to bile. All the hardwood and soft sheets, the ghosts of furnishings left alone but cared for, covered to save them from the dust. And Gideon in an upstairs window.

He knew his name was Gideon, just as he knew his own was Professor. Gideon with the jet black hair like his own. Gideon with his thin lips and pronounced nose like his own. Gideon of the gaunt cheeks and hollow, cataract filled eyes peering outward to a street they could no longer see, to a city they had never experienced. Gideon's palm whitened as it pressed against the glass, smooth, suddenly, and serene, with fingers just a little too long for their width. Gideon's mouth gaped like a cavern, searching the air to form words, to spit phrases at anyone willing to listen. Gideon the janitor and Professor the roadkill.

A blink and the house was gone, its hard edges blurring out into the sky.

13

"**DO YOU REMEMBER HOW YOU KILLED ME?**"

Reg had fallen asleep on the couch. The television ticking off financial statistics or sports scores. Numbers that wouldn't matter tomorrow when they changed again. His brushes and his paints, his papier mâché and balsa wood masks spread across the coffee table. His head angled back and over against the throw pillows. I kissed him gently on the forehead as I passed through to the bedroom, taking the opportunity to compose myself. I wanted to work on the wall, to finish the map and return our home to a staid sense of normalcy before he awoke.

"Do you remember why you killed me?"

I'd used the last of the paint I had from the hardware store as an eraser, to cover the part where the map turned to lies, to begin again. A chrysalis or cocoon. A slug that finds its shell. I decided to start from the outer edges and work my way in, hoping that when I got there the lines would be smooth and fluid. That the perspective wouldn't switch and skew and serpentine. I'd had trouble with maps before, with finding the nuance of the gravel and the concrete, the softness of the tiny twists in the steel; but eventually the marks made sense. I did not know why I couldn't quite figure this out. The lines all worked inward, flowed into a muddied conversation——the din of too many voices——instead of meeting in the agreed upon space. No matter how trained my hand, no matter how direct my aim, my work warped and blundered.

"Do you remember when you killed me?"

My phone rang with an unknown number, and I let it go to voicemail as I capped my marker and stood back to view my work from afar. Though simply lines on a canvas, I could see the notion of a city forming. Its majestic towers and sinking surfaces. The frivolity with which it played at the lives of those within. Happiness and anger and lust and the unexpected all taking on a second life. *Ceçi n'est pas une ville.* To paraphrase. Lines

147

on a wall leading to a central point of nothingness, of forgotten memory. A space of the unknown, begging to be left unfinished. *Ceçi n'est pas une carte.*

Cent rolled his eyes from the bed. His thick fingertips and unkempt nails pulsed at his temple, attempting to massage the piercing pain to a dull ache, a serviceable mediation between what the body wanted and what the spirit could take. I tried to ignore him, but each quick slant of my eye only served to embolden him, to levy the weight of his confusion against the levees meant to hold back the flood.

All of this happened on a subatomic, cosmic level. Synapses firing forward with reckless abandon. Sparks bursting out to become missed connections as quickly as another idea could replace them. A world of possibilities and outcomes imagined and defined in a millisecond were made real and forgotten. A deep breath——a sigh——as both life and death rattle. Living and actively dying. True and untrue and yet completely accurate.

"I thought we were friends, man." He sat up and pulled at the head of his nail. Twisted it. "We're going to talk about this whether you want to or not."

I sighed and capped my pen again. The new line was indiscernible from the others. But the space was not filled.

I kept my voice low, barely a whisper to avoid waking Reg. "I didn't kill you," I said. "My presence in your life did not cause your death."

"You just keep up with those affirmations," Cent laughed. "Keep them going and maybe one day you'll believe them."

My phone chimed with the voicemail left by the unknown number. Cent hovered near me preening his ear to listen in.

"Hello, Mr. Preston. This is Officer Ponytail with the Thirty-Sixth."

I remembered her from the car ride. Kind eyes. I remembered her from the suicide. Firm grip. I remembered her as faceless, though featured, and noble in blue.

"We'd like to see you, myself and Random Male Officer, down at the station for a few follow up questions as we wrap up our inquiry into Ms. Wiseman's death. Nothing to be too concerned over. I promise," she said, because that was the promise made to the innocent. Because that was the promise made for the innocent. "I'm sure we'd all like to lay this issue to rest. For the sake of her family."

She sounded sincere, even as Cent's eyes widened and he tsk-tsk-tsk'ed his tongue at me. I took in the address and time details for the following day. I knew I had nothing to worry about; it was simply a formality. I'd done nothing wrong.

"See, here's the rub," Cent smiled. "Remember that key you had to her apartment? The one you used to let her parents in? The one that tripped the lock to let the cops in? Remember how you came to possess that little incriminating piece of metal?"

"I don't know what you're talking about," I insisted. "And keep your voice down. Reg is sleeping on the couch."

"No sense in waking the dead," Cent laughed. "Not like he can hear me, anyway."

I sat on the edge of the bed and stared at my map, stared out the window, stared through my palms. Anything to keep my eyes away from the pacing hardware store clerk as he ambled to and fro across the hardwood floors like a Great Detective from a Great Detective Novel who had pieced it all together.

"The key's the key to all of this," he said. "The day I died, I helped you make it."

Cent spun me a story as he attempted to pull one out of me. A tale. A confession. The difference was marginal.

I had rushed in, he said, sweat dotting my brow like thorns, begging for evaporation to join the clouds in my head, adept in the agony of precipitation. I had this key, he said, this tiny jagged slip of nickel silver, edged and grooved to perfection and in need of duplication. He could help me, he said. He said he'd said. He didn't need to know the story. They had a machine just for that very task. They carved a hundred of those fuckers a day. He didn't need to know the story. But I told him anyway.

I told him, he said, my friend Gerrie wanted me to have a key to her apartment "just in case." In case she needed help with something obscure and lofty. In case I ever needed to feed the fish she didn't have. In case she'd left the oven on, or the shower dripping to make lions on my ceiling, or her bed unmade and disheveled and cold. Just in case she was ever staring longingly out her bedroom window, as she was wont to do, eyeing the city skyline with revery and disdain and was desperate for a little push in the right direction.

✻

No.

✻

I said I told him Gerrie and I had reached the point in our friendship where we were exchanging keys. There was trust there. There was camaraderie. And Gerrie was there with me. We both had keys made. We both exchanged keys with one another. It was calm and mutual and benign.

Cent sneered, and Gerrie kept her mouth shut, ears down, cupped, listening in through her bedroom floor, peering in on her flight down from her window.

"You can retrofit whatever story you want to align with where you're at now," Cent said. "I could call an abortion a miscarriage, and the outcome would be the same. So whatever floats your boat, Howie. I actually prefer your version of events."

"The true version," I insisted.

"The version that absolves me of any culpability."

Cent had convinced himself——his ghost self——I had stolen the key from Gerrie, snagged it from her keyring through some fantastical sleight of hand, kept her in the dark of a sword thrust box just waiting to reappear from the Other Realm with a flourish of sequins and feathers. Cent said I ran the whole way to the hardware store, so concerned with time, so concerned with getting the key back to her before she noticed its absence. And then, that I'd made him complicit in a crime. The theft of another's life. I'd made him my unwitting accomplice, unaware but just as guilty.

"And that," he insisted, "is what starts to get us to the why. The reason I had to die. The loose end, wagging tongue of connection. The third party with more information, more familiarity, than they should have. The unwitting witness the police would have found. And that then dumps us closer toward the when and the how."

I wasn't there when Cent died. I wasn't a part of his story even as he tried to insert me into it. He had——we all had——an inherent need to place blame. The eternal need to find reasoning stretched beyond the mortal coil. It was an unravelling springing back into shape in the shrinking and expanding void. He needed me to be culpable. After all, I was the only one listening.

"Once you had decided that death was on the table, probably without even realizing it, you knew the need to cut strings where they tied you too closely to the pyre. You, the witch in his Salem finest. You, the corpse bound for cremation. You couldn't let that happen."

He twisted at the nail in his temple as if it were a gear, a crank, a handle flipping the rolodex that turned the pages of his story.

"The entropy of motion, cause and effect, an assumed sequence of events both planned and left to chance. You surveyed the store like any other customer, intrigued by the various weights of hammers, enwrapped in the lengths of the nails, enamored by the insulation. A sniper: you found a clear line of sight. You knew where I'd be——how could you not after all those decades of new paint colors tilting and rocking in the gyroscope, after all those discussions of the subtleties of hues. You didn't know it, but you'd spent weeks studying my routine, my motions. You found your angle, you loaded the nail gun, and you scattered some marbles to scatter mine when you were nowhere around. Ingenious, really."

"And the stuff of fiction," I sighed. "I had no motive. No reason."

"Am I not that important?" he asked.

"I'm not that smart," I replied.

As Cent paced the room, a small trickle of blood escaped his temple to teardrop down his cheek. He sighed and rubbed his head in exaggerated circular motions, attempting to dull the pain collecting there at the tip of a nail.

"It's not like they show on TV," he said. "Death is not instantaneous, even at the severing point. The synapses still fire. The thoughts continue on. The brain tells the body to move, but it can't. The mind tells the mouth to cry out, but you're suddenly stuck in that dream where you're trying to scream and no sound will emerge. At least none that seems human. The dying isn't the turmoil. The real painful part is the loss of control. And it lasts for centuries in your mind."

The blood increased in velocity, such a powerful flow from so tiny a wound, bursting and pumping and painting the walls of the bedroom a deep burgundy red. The covering of past mistakes. The cleansing to err anew.

I waited for the paint to dry, watching as the color altered and congealed in ever darkening shades. Reg stirred in the living room, found his bearings, yawned as the couch creaked beneath him. I felt his presence return to his body; his sense of mind made whole. Cent felt it too, and all the jealousy shuttered within it.

The landscape of dreams is a treacherous place. A plain lilting between life and death and requiring every aspect of reincarnation to exist. I knew better than to believe that dreams were internal. As powerful a canvas the greys may be, they were rooted in process unbecoming of fancy. Dreams, therefore, were not a slip within but a journey throughout. They were human consciousness realized in an intangible force we chose to relegate to fiction to hold tight to our worldview. I wondered where Reg had been. I wondered if somewhere deep inside he mourned the loss of that space as he fell back into what we called the here and now.

"What I mean is," said Cent, "that you're in agony. A mental mindfuck totally separate from any understanding of physical discomfort. But who could blame you for thinking otherwise? As a society we treat the body before the mind. We see the armor before the soul. In our want to be present, we present a physicality as a self when that's so far from the truth of it."

He sneered again, his expressions incongruent with the calmness in his speech.

"Now do you know the answer," he asked. "The how, why, and when you killed me? Are you ready yet to see the whole painting? Does the canvas speak to you in wildfire and bile?"

"None of what you said is true," I sighed, and I listened as Reg rose from the couch to stretch into the night.

"Correction," Cent smiled. "Nothing of what I said answers my questions. It's the surface there to scratch. It's all too damn obvious. The easy answers. The jumping off point for you to dig deeper. The understanding that your physicality has so little bearing on the actual cause."

Cent stared through the window, watching Gerrie leap over and over and over. An angle toward understanding through repetition. An angel saved in a streetlamp glow. Ignoring the storm as the rain washed the fenceposts clean.

"You decided to paint it red, huh?"

Reg yawned his question as he entered the bedroom, rubbing his eyes and breathing in the sharp scent of the drying paint.

"I like it," he said. "It's different. Though you should probably join me on the couch tonight just to avoid the fumes. I can attest to its comfort."

I smiled, and I kissed him. I took his hand, and he led me back down the hall.

🐝

I awoke after Reg had left for work. A gentle, midmorning breeze flowed through the open window and lapped at my eyelashes with sweet aplomb. The street outside brimmed with its usual chaotic hustle, only slightly dampened by the storm of the previous evening. People seemed to walk a little slower; cars paid attention as they passed. A mindset of appreciation set in as the city bristled anew in its wash: brighter visages, saturated hues, the lust of clean air. I surrendered to the daylight in the same way I succumbed to the night.

As did my ghosts. All of them present and accounted for. Fighting and clawing and ambling for a view through the glass, even as the lost rays of a thousand years beamed through them. Gerrie stepped back to give Annie a better view, and Cent placed his arm firmly, airily, around Connor's shoulder. Lonnie and Blade and the Professor noted the car horn symphony and the downbeat of footsteps and the birdsong respectively.

"It's going to be a glorious day," I said.

"Would've been a nice one to feel the sun on our skin," they agreed.

"You'd better get ready," Gerrie said.

The new red walls of the bedroom were vibrant and macabre. They invigorated me with the unseen energy of a life force left unanswered. I showered and got dressed and glowed a reflected crimson in the mirror. My ghosts catcalled encouragement from the front of my apartment as they moved about my morning rituals. They fried eggs. They made blueberry or chocolate chip pancakes. They put on a pot of coffee. They watered plants and wiped down counters and shivered in the cool blast from the open freezer door. They were repetitive ghosts trapped in actions not their own.

I moved quickly to get ready. I knew Reg only had a half day at work. Promotion notwithstanding, his company——The Company——had given him some time off to recalibrate after the intense, oh so long, out of town training session. All of which made perfect sense, I'd told him, and gave me the opportunity to relish in his presence for a while. I wanted to get to the police station to answer the officers' questions, so I could be back before Reg made it home. I needed to keep him as far away from the unpleasantries that seemed to be following me in the deaths of my friends and acquaintances. Of course, I usually told him everything, but sometimes the gravity of it all was better left in weightlessness.

Sometimes it was better to just not know.

The station was just a few blocks away. As I walked, the crowds mumbled in a unified whisper, wondering how I could be so free, how I could move with such dexterity. The answer was simple: my love had returned and was returned. It was all any of us really wanted: the chance to just be and be free. I felt their jealousy on my back.

The wind shifted the leaves on the ginkgo trees to reveal a prismatic yellow green spectrum of rays cascading into darkness. Into absence. For a moment, I saw the trilby, the trench, the fencing, and the slate grey shutters. But just as quickly, they were gone.

14

THE HOUSE THAT WASN'T THERE

THE POLICE STATION FELT A BIT like a principal's office. Yellow detention slips stuck out from manilla folders crowded on desks. Staplers and tape dispensers and a three hole punch; there were too many office supplies to actually be useful. A matted and well trod carpet swirled in muddy grey and burnt reds and navy blues beneath the constantly padding feet of a crew whose flat footed urgency seemed forced. An award or two from too many years ago to be relevant caught the fluorescent light from their place of honor on the wall, glinting in the way that luster finds its lack. And everything there was in triplicate. Like a coven. Or a poem.

I was surprised the furniture stayed true with the floor, as slanted as it was, a subtle tilt yet obvious enough that when I sat in the chair opposite the officers, the decline left me small and powerless. A purposeful move in the design; a happy coincidence of nature settling its score with construction. The officers felt it too. Big in their chairs with their chests puffed out like a robin's breast, they eyed me over their papers, studied my face ardently as they traced through the squiggles of their notes. Gerrie, from over their shoulders, scrutinized their words as well, but she kept her mouth shut.

"Thank you for coming in, Howard," the officer said. The woman with the ponytail. The one with the ash blonde hair.

I'd prefer instead they call me Howard. I thought it bred familiarity. Humanity. A sense of connection in place of the formality of a Mister. Innocence.

"It's no problem. Gerrie: she was my friend. I'm devastated by what happened. I wish I'd seen the signs that she was willing to take her own life."

Gerrie rolled her eyes and scoffed. "The signs were all there, you twat," she insisted. "And you know damn well you saw every single one of them."

155

"You know, Nietzsche said, 'The thought of suicide is a great consolation: by means of it one gets through many a dark night.'" I quoted just as much for Gerrie as I did for the officers. "I guess that night was just too damn dark." I shook my head solemnly and pretended she was really gone. I was laying it on thick.

"It's a sad state," the other officer agreed, his demeanor doing its best impression of my somber face, of the low tenor in my voice.

"Gertrude had made plans to visit her parents next week," Officer Ponytail said. "She'd bought a plane ticket home and everything. Any clue why she'd do something like that if she was intent on taking her own life?"

"Suicidal people make plans with the intent of living." I responded quickly. Maybe too quickly. "They try to give themselves something to hold onto. It's not like they end their lives before they——well, end their lives. The appearance of normalcy, of continuance is important. It's not the total giving up, the planning and the plotting, that you see on TV."

"You talk like an expert."

"I'm a gay man from a rural town with hyper religious parents. I can't assume to speak for everyone, but I've definitely had some experience with the thoughts and machinations toward——well, goodbye."

"How long have you been here?" they asked. Both of them, in unison. The way they would in memory.

"I came here for college well over a decade ago. Almost two, I guess."

"And you work at that bar down on Bleaker. The Maiden Name." It was a statement. A note from a profile. Not a question.

"I did. Until recently."

"What happened?"

"I——I'm a recovering alcoholic. It wasn't a healthy environment for me."

"And so you're in AA?"

"That's supposed to be anonymous. Why all the questions about me?"

The officers exchanged a look as Gerrie smiled between them.

"They know what you did."

The sing song in her voice made her sound like a posied girl in pigtails, dancing around and waiting for bridges to collapse.

"We already know you were acquainted with Lonnie Anderson and Warren Everett, a.k.a. Blade. Can you tell us your connection to Vincent McGuire? He worked at the hardware store a block over from your apartment."

"I bought paint from him a few times."

"And how about Annie Johnson?"

"Who?"

"Your group leader has already confirmed her as your sponsor."

"Yes. She was. Is." I corrected before they caught it. The "was" was never there. "We don't use last names."

"And you're aware that she was murdered last night?"

They spoke their questions as statements, leading me somewhere I knew I shouldn't go. They were scripted in faked improv, in the "yes, and." I did my best to feign a shocked expression. It was better if I wasn't there. *There was nothing I could have done.*

"And Connor Daniels was found electrocuted on the roof of your old workplace this morning. It looked like his head had been bashed in with a blunt object, and he'd been left out, clutching metal, during the middle of that storm."

"That storm was a hell of a fury last night," I said. I was calm and collected. I was grieved and distraught.

"It just seems a bit like death is following you, Mr. Portman. Howard."

Of course death is following me, I wanted to say. It's following everyone. From the moment we are born, it's our only concrete destiny. Some of us just find it before others. I wanted to say that death is a non-discerning structure, and its proximity to any of us at any given time is always utterly near. I wanted to scream *don't you think I fucking know that?!? Don't you think I'm terrified?* But Annie put her finger to her lips to quiet me. Gerrie shook her head from side to side. Connor sulked in the corner. The Professor peered through the window to the open sky, studying the flight patterns rerouted by humanity. And Lonnie and Blade swiped tin cups across the bars of a cell, an ominous heartbeat, the clanging of principle. They weren't done with me yet.

Instead, I said, "You don't think——"

"It's all just very convenient, Mr. Portman."

"Coincidental," I corrected.

"Right now," they said. "Perhaps."

"Is this an interrogation? Am I under arrest?"

My ghosts cackled in unison. I closed my eyes and rubbed my temples to quiet them. To still the pounding in my chest.

"Not at all. This is just a friendly conversation."

"About a multitude of hurtful things." My addendum was necessary. They needed to know it made me sore. "So I'm free to go?"

I braced myself against the desk between us to stand, attempting to find my balance against the ever sliding floor.

"You can go," they said. "But before you do, tell us about your partner, Howard. Tell us about Reginald."

So now Reg was a suspect too in the string of unlucky demises that tiptoed across my life with the force of a small army, a bulldozer aiming for a childhood home. Lonnie had warned me about blame, about the ease of pointing fingers, about the neatly tied bow around the case files.

"He wasn't even here when——"

"Humor us."

"I don't want him anywhere near this. Look, I've made my statement. I've told you everything I know."

"Not everything," Gerrie laughed.

"Not even close," Annie sighed. "He's always had this issue," she told Gerrie. "Every time he came to Group. Repeating the same story until everyone believed it to be true."

"Repetitious ghosts."

"Isn't that what he calls us?"

"The definition of insanity."

"Circumstantial evidence at best," the Professor chimed in, wanting to feel included, obviously hurt he had not even been considered in the investigation. "Of course, it's the eyeing of circumstance that teaches us the patterns of birds." He swallowed hard. "It's the I-ing of our lives that keeps us focused inward. I should go," he said, and I agreed.

The room was getting crowded. The line between the living and the dead blurred out to create a liminal space of being. Besides which, each day brought a new ghost to my arsenal. A tormented retaliation. Nature's means of not letting me be too happy and secure. Someone needed to go. I wanted it to be me.

"It's only a block or two from here," the Professor said. "Less as the crow flies."

He pulled his green ball cap lower on his forehead, shielding his eyes from the harsh fluorescent lights, hiding the swelling tear ducts, and releasing the flow of blood from the head injury he'd sustained at the hood of the curb jumped sedan. Pigeons perched on the windowsill to cheer on his departure with the under appreciated coos of doves not beautiful enough by modern perception. Or maybe they were just too available to be noted. Fowl most foul, even with their iridescent underfeathers.

❧

Reg was waiting for me when I pushed through the door of our apartment, a huge smile slapped across his teeth and a spark glistening in his eye. A small bouquet——Baby's Breath and Lilies and Gladiolus and Roses, all white——wrapped in green tissue paper and tied with yellow ribbon sat waiting for a vase on the countertop. A small spread of casserole dishes——Reg's specialty based on his grandmother's recipes—— steamed and anticipated serving spoons: a delicate array of pastas and cream sauces and vegetables stewed down to a well wishing pulp.

"I decided to make us brunch."

When Reg made food, the servings rarely seemed to go together to make a cohesive meal, but somehow the flavors all interacted with one another in bursts of oleogustus energy and umami plateaus. Like a family cookout or a backyard barbecue. A potluck of pabulum presented in potent poetry. Compiled and combustible but somehow so correct.

"No occasion," he answered the unspoken question in my eyes. "I just wanted to celebrate us."

He was like that sometimes: so saccharinely sweet, it was as if he'd taken all his cues of love from the pop songs that flooded the airwaves of the adult contemporary stations, all their gestures and notions of undying love and the eternal, flaming gratitude that was carried with it. It was beautiful and——on him——felt truthful. It made him easy to talk to because I knew my words would be met with unquestioned understanding. It made him easy to be with because I knew he would be there through it all. It made it easy to disclose my demons to him because I knew he would show me his angels.

"I hope you're hungry," he said and motioned me through to the couch where two flutes of champagne and fresh squeezed orange juice sat waiting on the coffee table.

I took a seat and wanted to tell him about the questioning at the police station. I wanted to reveal the danger that seemed to be unravelling around me.

THE HOUSE THAT WASN'T THERE

"You should tell him what you did," Blade whispered. He had his foot planted dangerously close to the mimosas as he bent and gyrated his pelvis in his florid, go go boy pulsing.

Sunlight reflected through the window off the building across the street and sent a glare of white across my eyes. I relished in his warmth, and even as the sun clouded my vision, I took comfort in just knowing Reg was there.

"You know you want to share," Annie said. She sat in the armchair across from me, legs crossed and hands joined together before her chest, fingers forming the steeple of a church. Her best Sigmund Freud impersonation. Her hair frizzed and frayed in the open window breeze. "And, as your former sponsor, should you be drinking that mimosa?"

"How do you think you're going to like your new position?" I asked instead.

The interview. The promotion.

"I think it's going to be great," he assured me. "More freedom, better benefits. Other than it taking up more of my time and giving me less of it with you, it really will be wonderful. Just the thing I needed."

He placed a plate in my outstretched hands and turned to make his own.

"We've been pretty good at navigating time apart, though," he said. "With our schedules and all. That level of comfort has always come easy for us."

Gerrie rolled her eyes, and Lonnie pretended to gag himself to induce vomiting. Jokes at our expense. The backlash against true love. But even dead they saw what we had. Connor peered up from inspecting the casseroles and said:

"You gonna tell him about the cops? You might be getting a lot more time apart."

No.

The afternoon Reg made us a casserole brunch with white flowers and Pyrex containers and fresh juice mimosas was before. Before he left for his training. Before I couldn't drink. When I shouldn't have been drinking but still was. This was before I went to the police station. This was somewhere else in the timeline. When Reg sat me down on the couch and filled me with the salty sweet foods of his upbringing and rested his hand gently on my knee as he told me for the second time how much my behavior had been hurting him, how deeply the wound had gashed into us. This was my booze soaked intervention. "Just a little champagne," he said, like a true southern gentleman. Just because he didn't want to bombard me, he said. A little medicine to ease the pain, he promised. A spoonful of fermented grapes prescribed to keep me under control.

"So you're plying me up with bourbon glazed ribs and sparkling wine to tell me I have a drinking problem," I asked, incredulous, angry, and bemused. Thinking I was smarter than him through it all.

"I am. And I see the irony. But I was genuinely afraid of how you'd react without it."

He was telling the truth, though I didn't see it then, not right away. I rolled my eyes and left the juice out as I poured another drink. I didn't even like champagne. I was making a point.

It was months before I'd really see it. In retrospect, it was there even then. The love that once blossomed into fireworks of exotic flowers in his irises had succumbed to a lonely terror. He measured every breath, reconsidered every word. He blanched at the thought of losing me, at losing us. I wasn't violent, but I was angry——volatile.

"I met Whiskey long before I met you, babe," I sneered. "This is the only me you've ever known. How do you even know you'd like the me without her?"

"Because I love you."

"You love an idea of what you think I could be," I snapped. "You don't give a shit about the guy right in front of you. You don't care what he needs to live."

He caressed my arm, and I knocked his hand away. He frowned his concern, and I closed my eyes. He spoke his truth, and I went deaf.

❦

No.

❦

Reg kissed me gently when I returned from the police station and asked me where I'd been. Or he didn't, but I wanted him to. I wanted to be caught as much as I wanted to keep him away from it all. I needed to confide in him but knew there were some roads only ghosts could travel.

Lips still pressed on mine, he used his tongue to open my mouth, and we jutted against one another with the calm security of knowing. Finally parting, his kiss changed to a smirk, and he held my wrist as he led me down the hallway. The red patch of wall shone like the setting sun in a fauvist painting, rich and energetic and imbuing the bedroom with raw, erotic energy. He slipped out of his shoes, and I watched as he undressed himself, slowly revealing every familiar part of his survival relegated to my imagination throughout most of the day. Finally nude, he sat on the bed with his legs spread out, thighs thick and muscular against the mattress, gentle and sparse sweeps of hair pulsing my gaze toward the girth of him, already excited and leaking. He nodded to me, and I pulled at the fabric shielding my body with a quick but measured force.

His skin felt hot as I straddled him and ran my fingers through the bramble of his hair. I pushed them down his neck and along his tensing back, every muscle there jostling and angling to be met by my touch. I heard his moan even before his mouth opened. He raised his hips against me, his lips wet, and his teeth pressed sharp against my shoulder. We breathed each other in as our bodies clenched together for a moment——for an eternity——before he entered me.

We writhed together like that: me across him; him sitting on the bed. His hands buckled on my hips; mine clasped over his shoulders. Eyes joined; expressions sacred. I saw the creases in his face deepen. His smile lines sparkled and gave his eyes a brighter sheen within their intensified frame. His lips parched and parted. His temples greyed. In that moment of connection, I watched us grow old together. I saw the universes we had still to experience. He howled beneath me, an Ancient God of the Diaspora transforming himself to fit my needs, my desires.

When we'd finished, collapsed there atop the blankets and heaving in our salt and sweat, he was his normal age again——the age he'd always be; the age I'd always see him. And I locked him there in my mind like that: beautiful and natural and mine. Which, as every fairytale taught, was for the best. Age was a burden meant merely for those too unfortunate to experience life, bitter and unpleasant and ravaged by discomfort and disease. Reg could age gracefully in my mind, but he was so much better off secured there in his youth. In me. In us.

SIGHS ARE AS ADDICTIVE AS YAWNS. A sea of them crashed through the house. A soundscape of exasperation, of contentment, of the little hidden agendas slipped under their breathy din. The house echoed with the noise: the opening of a never closed door, the momentary understanding of knowing absolutely nothing.

Some maintenance was required. It was clear to any hardware store clerk. A splint to fight this angle. A hinge to hang a door on. A few focused touches to reign in the fighting spirit of the house, to temper its shifting struggle as it settled to burst its seams.

Two words filled Vincent's head: What and If. What would happen If he tried this? What would he cause If he only reacted?

The house itself was a reaction; he knew that. The remnants of an idea grown long past its purpose. The shuttered collapse of misinformation developed in disregard of the outside world. Or maybe, he thought, what if the outside world was just too difficult to regard? What if the house decided it best to just retreat within itself? To shield its robin egg siding and slate grey shutters, to hide the aftermath of its tantrums even as they raged internally?

His hand clutched the doorknob, cold even in the street stoked heat, and twisted it through its promise. He heard the latch give with a gentle click and shift of metal as it slid to release the swollen wood from the frame. Still, he refused to open the door, to allow that gentle sigh to escape and permeate the stillness of the street. He waited on the precipice, wondering if the tactile invisibility could be rebuilt, could be given form in its reformation. He had the knowledge, he knew. He'd picked up a thing or two over the years in the hardware store. He knew the bolt from the screw. He knew... he knew... he knew.

❧

Gerrie looked on from the sidewalk. She was always on the outside looking in. Always inside, she was, then flying out. She had never really been a joiner, preferring, instead, careful study and consideration, an in depth look at what had come before, and a bevy of quotes to curry her conversations in a noncommittal manner. "This was said... now discuss." Like the crab grass jutting through the concrete of the sidewalk, some green strand of thought always found its way through the rubble of compounding ideas——the building blocks to a School of Thought——and tickled the feet of all those soldiers and ballerinas fortunate enough to trod barefoot over the centuries. She wanted to kick off her shoes and join in the march, but she knew her socks had softened her soles. And the house just seemed to stare back at her; irritated, disgruntled. Waiting.

It was a Tuesday morning in the early Fall of an unrelenting Summer. She thought there must be some significance to that. Light crept along the street with a vigilante pace, combating shadows much further away than they seemed. It spread out in natural hues of vibrancy: fireworks that burst forward suddenly and then remained yet lost their luster all the same in the constancy. It beckoned lizards to sun their bellies atop the manmade rock and cautioned the more nocturnally inclined to remain indoors. It was the only day the light would ever shine like that, in that particular moment, at that particular time. She wanted to notice the oft overlooked details that made it different so that she wouldn't be like all the others who simply thought that every day was exactly the same as the one that came before, as the ones that wouldn't come after. If she couldn't find her voice, she at least wanted to know she had something to say.

The house blinked its child mind eyes at her. Familiar faces crowded the windows——some only known from the black and white prints on the pages of a book. Older now, most of them, and anachronistically fashioned in tan trilbies and khaki coats, with smile lines so deep their mouths grew hollow and hungry for communication. To speak in anything beyond a riddle.

She felt content there. She felt like she could just be——on that sidewalk——in that time and every time that came after——staring at a house that wasn't there, analyzing its moods and cataloguing its tempers——cautiously away from the wrought iron fencing, standing completely clear of the windows. She was willing to commune with the Gods of Thought the house contained, but only wished to speak from beyond what was already in print.

THE HOUSE THAT WASN'T THERE

Connor wasn't sure why he was there. He didn't know what the big deal was. He pushed past the student and the clerk, pulled himself up onto the stoop, and burrowed through the door. No time for questions. No time for the sighing silence. No time for anything really. Only the surge of energy pulsing through his veins, ready to delete and ignite.

15

"**We need to talk.**"

Annie patted the couch cushion next to her and urged me to sit down. I imagined the sofa as a series of folding chairs, the coffee table littered with trays of donuts and grocery store cookies, Styrofoam cups and luke-warm, burnt beans. There could have been a few pamphlets around de-noting the wonders of Jesus Christ or begging for money to reinforce the chapel doors. There could have been a few blank stares spread through the space; a few mouths quivering with a longing to find solace in only what they were once more. A solace they had never really had before they turned to the bottle. But that wasn't the point. Confession was the goal, and then——and only then——the acceptance that came with speaking names aloud.

If you can name something, you can own it: control it. It's an idea that permeates human nature. We call the land a town and then we sell it to the highest bidder or the mega mart with its disposable society. We call the thing a pet or a houseplant and usher it into our homes. And we tame out its wildness, at least until its teeth are bared or its roots disrupt the roadway. We name the demons in our heads, give them soft abbreviations, and introduce them to medications meant to rope them down until they gnash and gnaw and rupture. The wild always regains control, no matter how many names we give it.

"It's been how long since your last meeting, Howard?" she asked, ever pious, ever holy. Her questions came out as statements of truth, accusa-tions whose answers were a given. Sunlight danced through the red ring-lets of her hair. The light shone through her. "I figured if you're unwilling to go there, we can have our own session here."

She had that look on her face she got when she wasn't going to give up. Like a therapist urging someone toward self discovery. Like a bar back waiting for that glass in your hand. She took her job as sponsor way too seriously, even posthumously.

I sat next to her and folded my hands over my lap. I tried my best to look earnest, eager. Sincere.

"You're right," I said. "We haven't gotten a chance to speak since... since you died. Not really, anyway. How are you?"

I thought if I could turn the conversation, I could avoid internalizing it. I just wanted to be happy in Reg's return. I just wanted the ghosts to leave me alone.

"I view it as something else to overcome," she said. "Like our alcoholism. It's work, and it's constant, but it's doable. But let's do the work on overcoming your stuff, Howard. This is about you. This is always about you."

"All right," I sighed. "I'm Howard, and I'm an alcoholic."

"Hi, Howard."

"My relationship with fermentation began when I was nine years old——"

"Nope." Annie's voice was stern as she cut me off. Clear. Almost solid. Very nearly physical. "I don't want to hear the same old story you tell in that musty church basement with that stale coffee and the crumbs falling off those donuts and the faces begging for connection. I want to hear your Truth." She said it was a capital T. "I want to know what really drives you to quit drinking. To stay sober."

I stared blankly at her. I stared blankly through her. My ghosts crowded around the living room——the ones who hadn't left——and cocked their heads to show they were listening. All of them waited for the correct answer. Me: the schoolboy, naked and proud in front of the whole class.

I stayed sober for Reg, but that was not something I could say. It was against the rules to be good——for whatever that meant——for someone else. I had to do it for myself.

"He stays sober so he can brag about being sober," Gerrie said.

"He stays sober so he can look down on all us drunks," Lonnie said.

"He's sober?" Cent asked.

I stayed silent.

"You're the one who said AA was like confession," Annie smirked. "Don't you think it's time you unburden yourself?"

I swam in the transparency of ghosts. I listened to their chorus as their mouths remained closed. "Confess. Confess. Confess!" Stoic expressions hardened with the bewilderment of my own. My lips trembled despite me.

My eyes glazed and clouded to match their visage. I couldn't answer her question in any way that would satisfy her expectations. Besides which, that wasn't the core of the matter. We all knew that. I needed to go further back. But my memory was as disjointed and as hazy as my ghosts were. It was as muddled as my map, crossing over itself in question marks——curving lines on plotted points in time.

"I drank to escape myself," I finally exclaimed. It was the answer they wanted to hear, and it very well could have been the truth. "So my sobriety was about finding me again."

"But you didn't want to find yourself, did you?" Annie asked. "Not really. As crazy as Reg thought you were on the sauce, you knew what all that whiskey was suppressing."

"I'm not who you think I am," I cried. At nothing. At wisps in the air.

"You're exactly who you think you are," Gerrie said. "How could you be anything else?"

Cogito, ergo sum. Doubt and thought and presence. All of that wrapped up in some proof of existence that touch could not corroborate. All of this non-corporeal being floating around me: nothing more than the silent definition behind the word. Descartes before the horse faced girl drawing disclosure from my depths. Descartes before the neigh. All these cards on the table.

"Good ol' René was right to an extent," Gerrie smiled. "But it's not the thought that proves you exist, really. It's the thoughts you have that prove what you are. Intent is where the self actualizes."

"I've missed you, friend," I said, and her face softened for just a moment. I could tell she missed me too. I wanted her to.

"Focus," she reprimanded. "You need to pay attention so you can weed through the stories you've created to replace the ones you'd rather forget."

"The stories that hurt the most," Annie said.

"The ones that clench your gut," Lonnie said.

"The ones that pierce your brain," Cent added.

They were leading me to water. They wanted me to drown.

🐎

Intent is where the magic lies. A poison or a remedy. A curse or a spell.

Intent is where the soul lies. "I didn't mean to hurt you, baby. I promise to never do it again."

❧

I was so drunk when I walked through the door, I didn't even see the note on the table.

❧

No.

❧

Wasted, I tripped over the suitcases that littered the entryway to our apartment. The burden of not looking down at the spinning planet beneath me was clumsiness as opposed to nausea. I caught myself on the wall and clipped the light switch, flashing the overhead bulbs as if to announce my grand entrance, a warning to return to your seats. Reg sat patiently on the couch, hands clasped in his lap, back stiff and straight and away from the cushions, head cocked left over his shoulder to watch me fumble with my keys.

"I decided to make us brunch."

And he patted the seat next to him like Annie——except Annie hadn't done so yet. Annie would tap the cushion like Reg much later, after she had died. He patted the couch and didn't realize he was encouraging me to temper the cage I had built for my mind.

Intent and result do not coalesce with cause and effect. Or: he wanted me to be sober, so I was.

"I didn't realize my drinking was causing you such pain," I said.

"I thought we were having fun," I said. "I know I was."

"But if you want me to stop," I said, "I'll stop. For you. For us."

I said everything I was supposed to say, and I threw a flute filled with orange juice and stomped on grapes against the wall for dramatic effect. Syrupy sweet strands of pale yellow silk chased the cascading diamond shards of tempered glass to the floor. For a second, Reg was crumpled there. For a moment, I was too.

❧

"It's the things you think that haunt you. It's the house you live in: the foundation and the wall planks and the pipes that run through all the hidden crevices only the rats ever think to look within. The thoughts you think build the electrical currents that power your lamps and your televisions and your synapses to fire. They cycle in on themselves until they are all that you are."

Gerrie leaned out the window as she spoke, no longer really speaking to anyone, pontificating away and thinking about the trajectory of pane to plane, of sill to spoke. She considered what it was like to fall, how it differed from being thrown, until all that was left of her was the impact.

"Let's cycle back to you," Annie said, ever the sponsor, ever the therapist. "You've yet to admit a single true thing about yourself."

All of my ghosts had snarling smiles on their faces. Jackals, all of them, or coyotes, ready to laugh or tear at my flesh, aching to see inside. Tricksters most active in the liminal space within the dawn or the dusk. The sun set slowly outside, leaving remnants of itself tacked onto the metal frames of high rises, focused through windowpanes in excruciating intervals of eight minutes and twenty seconds. It spilled out and left itself behind to hear my answer. I focused on the tendrilled expanse of the Pothos in the corner. Lush and Kelly green, it trickled from its pot in rivulets of variegated hearts, dripping and angling simultaneously for the window and the door. Searching for escape no matter how much I tended to its needs, regardless of the saturation to its core. It was never satiated.

A small thing back then, but growing steadily, Reg had gifted the plant to me on our first Summer Solstice together. Hidden behind his back like a bouquet, he knocked on my apartment door and presented it with a flourish even as he leaned in to kiss me.

"I know we said no presents," he said demurely. "Joyous Solstice, darling."

"I love you!" I blurted and quickly corrected to "it" as I hung my burning cheeks to peer into the tiny explosion of greenery.

For his part, Reg smiled and let it slide and only asked if I was planning to invite him in. It wasn't until later, melted together atop the twin mattress I kept on the floor instead of a frame, when we were basked in the flickering light of two Seven Day Candles and sweating into the shortest night of the year that he asked: "How do you know?"

I ran through every cliché in my head——he made me laugh; he was sweet and charming and caring; he challenged me and made me comfortable all at the same time——ticking through them like elongated leaves on a vine of "he loves me; he loves me nots." But both he and I knew that none of those answers would suffice. The truth was, I simply did. It was just something I knew as much as I felt. We were easy. And I felt more myself in a way that allowed the space for him to enter. And the little Pothos in the corner shuddered in the candlelight. Each leaf was a memory——a story——taken in and printed on its palm and growing outward with every bit of our lives it internalized, like it was feeding on us. Like it needed our sweat and our sex and our tears. Like it was sucking us dry.

"Is that true," Annie asked, "or did you clip that from your mother's garden?"

"Is that true," Cent asked, "or did you buy that from the garden center?"

"Is that true," Lonnie asked, "or are you drunk on misinformation?"

"Is that true," Gerrie asked, "or is that plant really plastic? Is that plant really there at all?"

The living room shuddered between past and present, between all the memories I wanted to keep intact and the reality of the moment. My ghosts drew faces of varying emotions, lines etched across what was meant to be their skin in what it meant to be happy, sad; to be surprised, concerned; to be in anticipation. A world of concrete desire pulsed atop their transparency, even as Reg and I cycled through our own memories and emotions in the background. The happy times outweighed the bad. The arguments we had——all the words and phrases I uttered and forgot burning brilliantly on his face——were replaced in the calm acquiescence that denoted true love. "That's what true love is, right? That's how we know?"

Annie ran the tips of her fingers through her tight, orange ringlets, fluffing her mane to sparkle in the setting sunlight, to draw attention to her caring and concerned features.

"It's pretty clear you're avoiding the root of the matter," she said. She said, "So why don't we get down to it?" It was a command more so than a question, but she still gave it that questioning lilt at the end.

I held my breath, felt it stifle even as the breeze flowed through the room. It pressed against my lips; the world itself reminding me of the basic processes of life. I bit my tongue from spouting answers that should have been mine to give.

Exasperated, Annie heaved into the air between us, an exaggerated sigh that affected nothing on the visible plane. "Guilt," she said. "Let's discuss your guilt. How it leads to addiction. How it led you to where you are now."

"I have nothing to feel guilty over," I shot back, finally finding my voice in the din of those who weren't there. "Guilt requires blame. Guilt needs dreams sold before they're realized."

Annie cackled as Gerrie rolled her eyes. Lonnie poured himself a drink as Cent shook his head.

"Let's start with this then."

As Annie snapped her fingers, the room crowded with trench coats, with ghosts long forgotten. My father and Connor and the Professor. Preston and Rafe and Paul. My second grade teacher, Mrs. Hargrove. Folks whose names I could not remember; boys whose names I never knew. All of them suddenly there, crowding in on me, drowning out the light. A setting sun. A fade to black. Claustrophobic, I clutched at my throat. My fingers spidered up my chin, across my cheeks, danced through my stubble and mounted themselves around my eyes. I fought for darkness and lost. My own hands betrayed me, forcing my eyes open, holding my lids taut.

A tiny bead of light focused in the center of my vision, burning my retina, black and white and spiraling. Awaiting its technicolor treatment. Setting the scene. Evoking a mood.

Rain beat down in large droplets which scattered across the heat soaked pavement. Each splash became a cascade of darkness emptying the grey asphalt of its light. The city street teemed with ruthless people hunched over in reflective raincoats that did nothing but absorb the world around them, sucking it in as if daring nature to defy humankind's superiority. Children huddled under expansive umbrellas or sloshed defiantly through the growing pools of water that formed around the body.

The body. The only beacon of light in the entirety of the darkened scene. Slowly extinguishing. The body. Crumpled and brilliant and bleeding from her chest. Her life force spilled out along her breasts, streamed down to mix with the rain in an eddy, an estuary of tributaries and capillaries. The liquid soaked into the earth and spread out to form angelic wings alongside her body. Her red hair glistened in the falling sky. A crown. A halo. Almost a body. Just on the cusp. Still a few breaths left.

I wanted to run but felt the muscles in my legs seize. The rain beat down, and all life was extinguished. Her eyes opened against the drops and trained on my face, horrified and drying and revived.

"They're coming," Annie said. Annie the body; not Annie the ghost. "They're coming," she said. "You should go."

My legs quaked and released. I turned swiftly away from the steps in front of the church, away from the red period of some renaissance artist, away from the aftermath of unseen equations. Two steps into the dense fall of rain, three steps into the sea of trench coats and trilbies, swimming with all my might just to keep my head above water. But there she stood. An empty look on her face, at arm's length in front of me, my arm between us, my hand clenched at her chest, tough and hard and sharp. I recoiled, and she fell. A tumble down the stairs. An angel again on the sidewalk.

"They're coming. You should go."

Another step into the darkness. Another attempt at escape. And a knife still clutched against my palm. The cold, steely glare of the onlookers who studied my face for any sign of recognition, of guilt. And Annie again. Compassionate and cool as she placed her hands on mine and guided my arm forward, pulling me toward her, urging me on.

I closed my eyes as the knife broke skin, slid through tenuous muscle and bone and found its sheath deep inside the four chambered home at her base. A pulse of comfort as she attempted to take me in and unburden me. A final effort at understanding.

I opened my eyes to an empty room. The sun had finished its denouement and chosen new lives to haunt in some other corner of the world. My and Reg's belongings spilled from shelves into boxes. Plants in their death throes longed to return to the soil of their pots. An unfinished meal was left lazily on its plate. The first breeze of night jostled through the curtains. So much of the day was left unfinished but forced forward through time anyway.

Annie's words echoed through my mind, trapped there in solitude. I held my breath against the stillness.

The closet door swung open, and I heard Gerrie's laugh. A waterfall of wooden masks cascaded to the floor, each more brilliant than the last. Macabre grins and colorful tears. Expressions held inside and carved through balsa, etched in paint with hardened brushes and delicate blades. Newspaper clippings of obituaries soaked in water and flour and baked into headshots of emotions too fine for the fine print. All of them Reg's. Each one a death mask of the moment trapped inside, forced within and contained until it rotted and died. A mausoleum of emotions too afraid to ever meet the light of day, to face the wrath of a lover scorned. My hands pushed through the corpses and felt the comfortable familiarity of Reg's broad nose, his supple lips. I saw all of his pain and joy even as I remembered the touch of his skin against mine.

They're coming. You should go.

175

16

FLIGHT COMES SURPRISINGLY NATURAL for someone who's been a fighter his entire life. The dichotomy of animal instinct in the name of self preservation. Flight is ingrained. And has nothing to do with fear. It's, in and of itself, a form of battle.

I left the apartment slowly, careful to stay silent against the prying ears of nosy neighbors.

Animals migrate to more hospitable climates. It's in our nature to seek out safety. To pull at the seams of our clothing until we can fit through and remain shielded and covered and warm.

I expected to see Reg in the stairwell, wanted him to pull me into his arms and tell me everything would be okay. I needed to feel the comfort of his home against me. I rounded the final landing and longed to see his smile.

Molly and Mark or Holly and Hank or maybe it was Polly and Frank——the couple on the first floor——were just returning from the park. Her ashen long ponytail and his vacant stare looked so appropriate against the royal blue matching uniforms they wore for their jog. Molly wiped the sweat from her brow using the back of her hand whereas Hank used the lower hem of his t-shirt. A flick of the wrist, a wring of the fabric, and a part of them left on a welcome mat.

We, all of us, are always leaving something behind. It's what we're best at. It's what we were built to do. It's been that way since Adam and Eve departed the Garden seeking out sustenance after they consumed the final viable apple there, tossing its arsenic seeded core to the ground on their way out. They wandered the arid soils in search of a new oasis to consume and decimate, to feed the hungry children they bore, to rear them toward their natural inclinations. A single spot of origin spread out until the base lines crossed and became unintelligible, untraceable. Gathering followers with each stomp in the soil, two sets of footprints multiplied into only one, and a god like status was achieved.

I felt my followers swirling around me, tiptoeing behind me down the stairs and out into the streets to join the harried wanderers caught off guard by the sudden onslaught of night. The righteous and the wicked teemed across the sidewalks in chaotic celebration, welcoming the dark with rebellious frivolity. All of us were searching for some knowledge to make us feel secure as we said goodbye to the harsh light of day for an even harsher vision nestled in the nuance of night. We funneled out into the city in acrobatic showings of wonder, arching and tumbling and gliding each and every way along our tightropes. All of us bounded toward a crossroads, bared our souls for our devils. We were ready to make a deal. A bargain. Half price for the half life left lived.

I wandered without purpose, without direction, plotting the map of my journey in my mind, creating icons to denote the buildings I passed, the trees that uprooted the lanes of traffic, the waterlines that burst in chaotic defiance of flow. I avoided the cracks in the sidewalk in a casual escape of Annie's warning. *They're coming. You should go.*

My ribs ached as my heart strained against them. My nomadic nature, baked into the mud of my being, urged me onward with a casual grace. Hot dog vendors sold soft pretzels and falafel and glowing necklaces to the interlopers to light their way to the hotels or barstools or new homes. All of us were imbued with a wanderlust; the gentle reminder that tonight we did not want to fight.

Cent, Gerrie, Annie, and Lonnie whispered behind me, but kept their distance. They moved with a grace only visible from the corners of my eyes; a quick understanding as I rounded a bend in the road and was able to take them in. I felt like a tagged creature with the four of them monitoring my every move; a bird in migratory flight, or maybe a butterfly, freshly free from the tightening silk of transition. And them attempting to figure out why, to learn the cause of my actions. To name them and tame me in the process. All of us always monitored; all of us always lost.

Men ambled toward me from the darkness, oozing from the depths in their dusk soaked khaki. They tripped over the lines in my map and reached toward my outstretched arms to prevent themselves from falling, clinging to my skin with cold and clammy palms and whispering warnings into my ears.

"The things you still don't know can kill you," they said.

They said, "Mind you don't find what you're searching for."

THE HOUSE THAT WASN'T THERE

"Beware if you do find what you're moving towards," they said. "The things you do know can kill you too."

I needed a white steed to save me from the onslaught, so I mounted him and rode off into the night. Away from the trench coats and trilbies; away from my ghosts. It's in our nature to run. To curse the stone and search out greenery. To conquer what's around us and set out to cleanse the world with our proselytizing fire. We go to wars, and we call them crusades. We want to spread what we know; what we've found to be true. We call it joy and salvation and forgiveness. We name it holy and helpful and right. And all those who oppose us in their righteous indignation label it a Xenophobic Attempt at Control through Collateral Damage. Still if any one of us was ever really honest with ourselves——the gods forbid!—— we'd know it not as a fear of others, but a fear of ourselves. We'd see that crippling state sprung from the little cobblestone fortresses we'd built of all we'd learned and identified. We'd see our insecurities in knowledge and think, if we could just get enough people to agree, then surely, we would be right. Another cobblestone for the wall. Another brick to lay down. If we could just think.

The night blooming jasmine, caught in the revelry of its final days with Persephone, layered its aroma into the fabric of the city streets, sweet and sticky and heaving with the sweat of moths and bats winging their serpent tongues deep inside. I plotted their blooms, their crystalline icons, like constellations across my map. Guideposts to a land caught between ideation and memory, that split second of novelty before it's trapped in déjà vu. As a child, I thought the night smelled like candy——that it was something adults wanted to keep secret, sacred, and wholly theirs——and I fought my bedtime just to try to get a taste. Or else I listened, quietly, holding my breath, until I could no longer hear my father's beer soaked guffaws, my mother's proper and dainty panting, and I'd pull open the window just slightly to let the cartoon fingertips of aroma beckon me forth into the darkness.

No.

178

That wasn't me. That wasn't my memory. It was Reg. It was a story he'd told me of his childhood. When life had seemed so intense in its excruciating simplicity. And it wasn't jasmine. It was melted, spinning sugar dyed light pink or baby blue; and it only happened twice a year when the little fair would roll through town and set up in the parking lot of the strip mall across the street from his apartment complex. He'd place his skin against the window screen and suck in until his nose had a little waffle pattern seared across the bridge. His tiny little palms pawed at the barrier but knew enough to not push too hard, to not let it fall. Escaping into the night meant the night could come back in.

"What does it mean to take someone's memory?" the man asked me. The one in the trilby and trench coat. The one hunched over his notebook on a little sidewalk table, jotting furiously and not waiting for an answer. The one who looked remarkably like me, like I expected I would look when time completed its rounds.

"Do you think it honors them?" he said. "Does it keep them alive, at least in thought? Or is it a means of erasure? A consumption of a soul until all that's left is the idea of them, refastened to a new self." He pulled his pen across a blank page, tracing the map of his thoughts, leaving nothing behind. "That's what I'm grappling with now," he said. "That's what I've got to figure out."

"Figuring it out can kill you," another man said. Trench coat buckled tight at his hips, hat pulled down over a grey mop of hair, he bumbled toward me and locked pace with my step, a few feet behind, keeping company with ghosts. He gave his answer without waiting for a reply. A one way conversation down a one way street. A necessity for a forward march.

Another trenched figure sprouted from the shadows. He joined in our gallop; he pushed me through the streets. And another. And still more. Each of them with some cryptic warning. Each intent on pursuit.

"Knowing only reveals areas of deeper darkness."

"Darkness only lets you appreciate the light."

"They'll leave the light on for you."

"They're waiting."

"They're coming."

An army of heartbeats crowded the streets behind me, pulsing out a syncopated waltz into the night sky. The sound mixed with the gentle aroma of the night flowers to intoxicate us, to distill us through the cooling air. A gentle hum of insects. The distant cry of sirens. The beat beat beat against the cage of collarbone. A heart stuck in a throat. A rumble in a chest. And in the middle of it all: a silence. A hole. A void.

❀

I opened my eyes, and I was alone. Sitting in the dark of my bedroom, the mattress felt strange beneath my thighs, sheets pulled and blankets wrapped to form a texture that seemed unfamiliar: a warning against a barren land. I felt my pupils dilate———that swiftly slow crank open, my own internal void made evident. Not that it mattered. The glass of the closed window was intent on trapping out the beams of the streetlight outside, letting only a small sliver through to accent the deep blood red of the walls. A gash. An opening. A tiny bead of brightness to really, finally show just how deep the dark had grown. I knew my space by thought alone, little memories that distorted the actual size of the dresser, moved it about two inches to the left. An idea of roughly where I'd thrown off my clothing the night before produced a crumpled pile of rock hard fabric on the floor.

I found myself lost in what the darkness chose to reveal. The dripping texture of paint splattered onto a wall far too quickly; the disconnected lines of a map pushing through coat after coat; the gentle arch of a foot, the bend of an ankle———a body on autopilot as the mind wandered through its own narrative of being. Toes sought out the floorboards, cool and waxed and feeling more of concrete than wood. Hands clasped the folded seam of the mattress, fingers prodded and pulled at the stitches, at the embroidery of clouds. I pulled myself up, and the swift rush of cool air against my face brought me back into my self. For just a moment, I felt solid; I felt crushed. And then I was lost again in thought.

The apartment was a wreck from the day's inquisition. Photo albums spread like quilts across the coffee table. Pictures of me pretending to be an adult. Snapshots of Reg dressed as a detective for Halloween: long coat, low hat, notepad. Images of us learning how to be in love. Masks littered the hallway like steppingstones. The soft imprint of the footsteps of ghosts covered every surface with an echo, hollow and reverberating and never really there to begin with but always taking up so much space. I'd intended to clean before Reg got home. I still had time. Reg wasn't there. His work, his new position, took its toll in long hours and missed dinners and left me full in the anticipation of his return. I missed him, but he had left a voice-mail. Garbled and cutting as all the rest, but his voice still soothed me.

"...Love... I expected... this... long time... schedule... I will be... Soon. Please know that I love you...."

I needed to speak with him about his phone. He was long overdue for a replacement. But I understood his message: his new schedule had him working long hours, but he'd be home as soon as he could.

I cleaned without turning on the lights, eyes adjusting to the black. The darkness disclosed the spots all out of place from my memory. It was simpler not to see. Easier instead to feel for where my things should be. To find the difference and correct it without paying so much attention to every distracting little detail. There was an honesty in understanding the ambiance when everything was lost in shadow.

As a child, I remembered, all of my classmates were scared of the dark; afraid of the things that occupied the spaces in the deepest crevices of their imaginations. They held tight to a forlorn knowing as they averted their eyes and grew up and stopped believing. I was always different. I relished in what the darkness chose to reveal. Even then as now. I pretended to be asleep, listened for the soft click of my parents' bedroom door as it hitched itself in its frame for the night, and slipped barefoot through my first floor window to feel the mounting dew on the grass. Trees revealed their faces in the night, spoke in stuttering whispers, called forth the Hesperides to disclose the disparities of light and vision. Houses bled their a-frames into the midnight sky until they were one, until all that was left was a blank space where a home should have been, a void where a life had happened. Monsters emerged from their shadows to dance through the chilled air, and I found myself one of them, content and empowered in my daring. I was one of the things that went bump in the night. I was a nocturnal crea-ture finding wings on the sharp edges of diamond stars. And I was happy.

Reg's masks, clustered on the hallway floor, burst in coalescing colors in the tiny sliver of streetlight that sliced sharply across the room. Across the room and down the hall. Crimson and sky, fuchsia and persimmon swirling together to form the shape of his nose; to gently part his lips as they waited somewhat impatiently for a kiss. His emotions were splashed across the sweetly carved cheeks: amusement, confusion, envy, romance. Nostalgia and satisfaction. Entrancement and triumph. All were smeared beneath a mirage of sexual desire. Every mask ached to tell me the secret it held; where Reg was——emotionally manifested physically——when he painted the cheeks and sanded down the jawline. I collected them, like daffodils, in my arms and carried them back to the bed. Three dozen tiny lovers anticipating discovery. Three dozen subtle shades of feeling waiting to finally feel.

I lined them up in columns across the unmade bed. I lined them up in rows to study the stains in the ceiling, to pick out the shapes of the clouds.

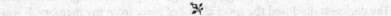

I answered the door sometime after 3am. There were two of them there:

"Are you Howard Preston?"

A concerned sympathy. A messenger to be shot.

"I hate to be the one to tell you..."

No.

The door opened just after 4am, and I listened as two pair of quiet feet shuffled into the room. A calm decision, a careful placement of each step, like they'd been here before, as if they understood the architecture better than the building itself. They slipped slowly through the darkness and paused, flanking the hallway on either side.

"Mr. Preston?" A voice called. Her voice. The blonde with the ponytail.

"We know you're back there." The other one. The nameless, faceless man in blue.

"They know you're back here," Gerrie sang, leaning through the window as if she were planning my escape.

No.

The door opened just before 5am with the familiar clang of his keys jingling in the deadbolt. He moved without turning on the lights, sure of the space, of the formation of home. He tiptoed gently down the hallway and smiled at my sleepy eyes as he entered the bedroom.

"Sorry I'm so late."

"I'm just glad you're here."

We pushed his wooden masks to the floor, shaking them from the quilt like burrs from a thistle, laughed as they plotted out scenes of enchantment in a straight to video romantic comedy. We loosened his tie and pulled at the straining buttons on his shirt. We slipped the leather snake of his belt from his waist and let our lips rest near one another's; not yet touching, just breathing each other's air. We fell to the sheets in a flurry of skin, limbs akimbo, wrapped, and clawed to bring ourselves close. We pushed inside and were welcomed. We pulsed and were electric.

Reg's face cycled through his masks as he came across my stomach. Every muscle in my body relaxed in the warm and sticky leap. I finished, simultaneously, inside him, and we finally let our lips meet.

I grabbed a nearby towel from the floor and reluctantly wiped him from me. We'd traveled centuries in minutes. We always did. Flights of fancy or flights of bourbon. Soaring moments of skin on skin. It was all the same thing. It was all just a turn of instinct forcing us together.

Or apart.

THE HOUSE THAT WASN'T THERE

WHEN THEY CAME TO TEAR DOWN THE HOUSE, they couldn't find it. It was as if it wanted to preserve itself through nonexistence. A century's worth of confessions or a midnight's sweaty sex quickly hidden in an absence of materiality. A trick of the light well practiced and well timed. A little parlor magic. A tiny lie.

When they somehow made it inside, they could not find the others. No lush and lavish parties. No masqueraders in old fashioned hats and jackets. No merrymakers devouring their mom's own blueberry pie——the one they knew from their youth; more of a cobbler, really——in the lavender scented kitchen as a blue hot fire singed the edges of memory and sung a crackling lullaby to the wind that wasn't there.

Instead there were hallways that stretched beyond knowing, through light and abyss and back again under the sputtering flicker of a florescent bulb in the final days of its death rattle. Instead there were rooms that crumbled into each other; rooms that divided themselves at odd angles, off measurements, illusions in the study. And, too, there were closets—— so much closet space!——and cabinets to line the walls, all brimming with untold curiosities, wonders, and bewilderments. All locked. And a little sign to let them know that Cerberus had swallowed the key, but good luck figuring out which head.

They let their thoughts escape them, watched them slide into the keyholes——the type meant for peeping through——decorative, really—— there for the hormone addled view of him drying himself after his shower, for checking the children's games without disturbing them, for making sure both parents were asleep before slipping out into the chill of the night. They flipped switches to turn on lights or lit candles with matches found nearby in tiny books pulled nearly bare with lipstick prints and "555-" phone numbers. Lines that went nowhere. Marks connecting an elaborate grid, a human variance.

They pulled at door handles whose metal etching were chilly to the touch and branded curlicued flourishes on palms. They took tools to windowpanes and floorboards. Played tug of war with panels of peeling wallpaper. Chipped at the masonry of the hearth until the metal on stone sparked and set fire. And when they stood back to look at the war they had created, at the destruction they had waged, they found it lacking.

The house was there, and it was solid, and it was whole. It shook its violent temper through the timber of its frame and settled, on a Tuesday morning in the early fall of a late empire, into the child mind imagination of a stubborn goodbye. It ruffled its robin egg siding like feathers, flapped its slate grey shutters like beaks: a murder of crows motioning toward evolution. Mourning the morning light as it illuminated the planks of its halls, guiding the feet of intruders forward, separating them and isolating them. The house that was there. The house that was hungry.

17

Andrew Forrest Baker

MURDER IS A TRICKY SUBJECT, almost as derelict as time. It runs a ramshackle course over the mind and body, consuming and regurgitating bits of the self in orgiastic splendor, in consummate disgust. It tells you, once and for all, what control really is: how to have it and how to lose it simultaneously in an epic insertion of self. It is the ultimate culmination of a xenophobic society that teaches dominion. The second sin past consumption. The origin of natural order. There was no death before murder. Ask Abel. But death created the difference, so, as such, life could not exist without it.

If Gerrie were here, she would tell me what Claude Cahun wrote. That "I am (the 'I' is) the outcome of God multiplied by God divided by God." That "God x God / GOD = me = God." That we are the divine, holy masters of our own destinies.

Murder convinces you you are god.

Murder convinces you. You are God.

🌿

Reg slept and then was gone. I sat on the floor of the bedroom, staring at the bloody walls as the soft morning light filtered through the closed curtains and cast a hazy film over every object I'd tried to own. A reminder of their ephemeral state. A nod to their non-permanence. I had a map to make. I had a job to do. And work would set me free.

The many faces of Reg were scattered about the floor around me like river stones, smooth and polished and vibrantly defiant against the wearing down from the world around them. A Greek Chorus, they sang to the crimson sea of the walls, beckoned sailors to the rocky bedposts, the swirling unknown. They summoned me to my feet. They called ghosts from the darkness.

Annie, in her faded denim jeans and patent red heels, pranced confidently forward. Her porcelain skin had taken on an ashy grey tone; her eyes had hollowed; her hands had gnarled——forevermore clutching at her heart. The caked mud of her dried wound shone like stiff armor across her chest. Her lips gaped in shock, in awe, in surrender. She circled the room slowly——clockwise, then counter——winding together the webbed threads of a spell. The afterlife found witchcraft naturally. Fight or flight rescinded to preservation of energy, control of that which is neither created nor destroyed, the culmination of it. She entranced me while pulling her strings tight.

And then Gerrie, marching inward and out, weaving through the spun tapestry Annie had begun. Gerrie, with her short black bob and gentle stutter when she was new, when she was nervous. Gerrie, with her references and her fear and her drive. Gerrie, with the long dark spike of a fencepost spearing her from sternum through jaw. Her eyes were wide and unmoving. Her tongue was sharp and pinned. I should have been frightened. I should have been frightened.

As Annie's concentric circles wound closer to me, she turned her head and watched my movements through the abyss of her eyes. Darkness seeped from them like tentacles, like veins, pulsing out to devour. She attempted to speak, but no air would fill her deflated lungs. Moving ever closer to where I stood, Gerrie continued to jut back and forth. Clotho and Lachesis waiting on Atropos. Waiting to atrophy.

Annie stopped, suddenly, before me; leaned in until all I could see was the black. And behind her: Gerrie, goading on the darkness. And within that black, a city street, slightly wet with the first large drops of rain; a darkened hallway with the gentle glow of a moon shaped nightlight illuminating the way. I saw myself in a flurry of still lifes. I was a selection of jostled, uncollected memories in a flip book doing its best at cinema verité. Staccato and stuck, I watched myself move through someone else's life.

I was talking to Annie. I was slinking down a hallway.

"That's why the meetings are so important," she said. "All of them understand what you're going through. All our stories are different. All the causes vary. But the dependencies are real."

"I need to catch up with Reg," I said. Both the me in my vision and the me in the room. We said it in unison. We spoke it as truth.

Annie's face turned gaunt, shocked, an expressionist painting on a bridge, on a street, on the syntax of an unspoken response. She stretched out. She pulled at her center and compounded in on herself.

All the while Gerrie kicked her feet happily, swinging them from the soft crescent of her knee as she perched atop my dresser, my kitchen counter. As she walked back and forth, back and forth, back and forth.

"Still no word from Reg?" she asked. She asked it on repeat, the skipping of a record, the digital reverb of a glitch. She asked it as I held my phone in my hand, voicemail at the ready. I held a knife in my hand. I placed the phone in my pocket.

I placed my phone in my pocket, and I picked up a knife from the case. A sleek, non-serrated blade with a black oxide coating meant for hunting or camping or quick deployment. A little large, but comfortable in my palm. Made perfectly for the task at hand.

"Going hunting?" Cent asked, smiling from the other side of the glass display case. Smiling and jingling his ring of keys and whistling a jaunty tune from behind a staggered smile.

The blade was an absence, an obstruction in its nothingness. My vision blurred as I focused on its steel slit, its gash upon the world. Annie's voice, disembodied and sharp, bursting from its heel:

"Reg is back?"

"I got that key ready for you."

Cent slid the humble piece of metal across the counter, slipped it right beside the folding knife. His crooked mouth beamed its best service with a smile. The overhead fluorescent lights bounced off the glass between us, focused and figured and blinding. Like the bright light of a blood moon at the end of a hallway. The glint off a mirror into a sleepy driver's eyes.

"I understand what grief and loss can do to a person," Gerrie said. Gerrie leaned out the window of her fourth story intellect. She reached for the moon like a moth arched at guidance. "I know every inch of its power."

What power did grief hold? What control did it serve to import? It loomed over any of us, all of us, always, as a guillotine, a lightning rod, a memory. It was a power sublimated by control. It was refined in its tricky, nuanced anachronism. It held us, or maybe only me, out of place, out of time, out of sight. And if grief held that power, if loss gained that control, how could I tame it? Fight or flight. A fight before the gauntlet was drawn. A quick and easy succession.

"So just the knife and the key?"

"Reg is back?"

"Should I play it again?"

"I understand loss..."

"Should I play it again?"

"I understand grief..."

"Reg is back?"

"Should I play it again?"

I held my phone in my hand. I stared at the name beside the voice-mail. The voices of ghosts echoed in my head, thumping in cadence with my heartbeat. And there was my own heart, weak and feeble; questioning: *should I play it again?*

So I played it again. And again. Repeated histories in the hollow eyes of specters. Annie on the street; Gerrie at her window; Cent at the counter. Each of them ripe with knowledge; all of them waiting to pop. And me, staring into the abyss. A phone in my hand. Or a knife. Watching the ghost of myself do things I'd never do. A lunge at a petite young woman gazing longingly from a night sky window, the way those lost in the existential crisis of college were wont to do. A plunge into the chest cavity of a wom-an too consumed with care to fully know the scarred, burnt marks it was leaving on her soul. A nail gun with a hair trigger locked and loaded and aimed and left to chance.

I watched from a fourth floor window as Gerrie fell. She flew toward the ground with a grace and dignity reserved for those who accepted fate with the casual aplomb of receiving tea in the afternoon or a hard earned "A" on a term paper. She turned on the air and smiled at me, saying, "I accept your pain as my own."

I was careful not to touch the windowsill. Careful not to disturb the room.

I saw Annie lean back from me, sliding off the knife and slipping down the church steps to make angel wings against the pavement. She winked at me and curved her lips into a gentle smirk, the sly smile of knowing more than she could ever let on. The concrete cooled her back against the warmth of rain and blood, and she said, "I accept your pain as my own."

I dropped the red stained knife into a sewer grate. I let the rain and the crowd do its job.

THE HOUSE THAT WASN'T THERE

I joined the herd that gathered before the automatic doors of the hardware store, staring in awe as they opened and closed and added to the confusion with each whoosh of air conditioned air. I heard the stories grow more elaborate as the fantasy took over and carried the happenings into myth. I stepped aside as the gurney pushed through the crowd to the ambulance waiting at the curb. Cent lifted his head and slipped from the sheet. His crooked teeth beamed beneath his fragile lips. A nail pierced his temple like the start of a crown. He spoke with his usual grace, with a casual shrug: "Sometimes you just know too much." Often you can only imagine the avalanche of events and the tiny accidents that fracture an entire universe.

I pulled myself from the crowd. I collapsed to the floor. Annie closed her eyes, but it made no difference. There was only more darkness. She took Gerrie's hand and rescinded to the shadows.

"Don't worry," I heard them say. "You aren't done yet."

※

Death is a stingy subject meant, in most cases, to be only of consequence to the living. In most cases, the dead simply do not care. In most cases. Death and his scythe do the work of absence and leave the forgetting and the accepting and the real emotional drudgery to the ones he leaves around to visit some other time. Death is a singular mind unconcerned with the purview of those he governs. Another mad play at control. It's a control he doesn't even know he has, one placed upon him by the living. It's the power he always fails to notice because it is not over those he holds but those he has yet to touch.

I crouched on the floor with my forehead on my knees, feet arched and heels raised, attempting to balance on my toes. I wanted to be as compact as I could be and as far away as possible from anything utterly tangible. I braced myself for the impact of their Dickensian warning.

Yet there was nothing but daylight. Nothing but a floor littered with masks and an unmade bed and a red hued wall. The breath I had caught in my throat expelled through the picket fence of my teeth, a solid mass made airy once more. The advent of spirits. And I couldn't help but laugh.

My own voice was a roar against the sudden and deafening silence, but something else was there beneath it, clawing its way into my eardrums.

A faint tingling across my jaw. A tonal downbeat washing down the hallway from the living room.

Lonnie's lips were blue. His fingers——yellow and jaundiced—— tapped out a simple scale on the grand piano taking over the space where my couch should have been. Xs for eyes, he nodded toward the tip jar perched on the cover above the pin block, demanding his dollars before his scale would turn to a pop ballad dirge. He picked up my laughter where I cut it off and carried it through to completion.

The notes of the music cascaded into the air in a synesthetic spiral of milky reds and creamy blacks turning violet and yellow and violent and ubiquitous. An exploding black hole of sound; a dense white dwarf of taunting. I stood frozen, mesmerized, as the colors built upon each other and consumed my vision.

"Here's to the lost souls left here," Lonnie sang, his gravelly voice no more than a wisp against a stone. "Here's to the drinks that do us in."

The black took shape, formed shadows intent on acquiring agency. Silhouettes that ached to smile as much as they yearned to show. A man at a piano, much younger than he looked, much older than he cared to admit. And a child behind a bar playing with potions, mixing prescriptions to cure the ails of a tough day in the city. He pulled a small bottle from his waistband and dumped its contents into a larger container. The sweet scent of almonds filled the room, wafted through the singsong lilt of my disembodied voice:

"How about I make you an Amaretto Sour tonight?"

A hefty ask for a gin man, to be sure, but a saccharine sticky juice to combat the no drinking policy on Connor's lips. It made it much easier to hide the booze.

"Here's to the drinks that do us in."

"That never happened!" I screamed. The real me. The one who watched the one watching me. I felt it rumble through my lungs, found it glued to my tongue.

The room flashed quickly to the space I remembered. My ferns and rhododendrons by the window; a colorful quilt across the back of the couch; sunlit and warm. No. Drooping dead leaves and the smell of decay and dirt; furniture crushed or pushed aside; curtains so tight only a razor edge of light entered in a blinding beam. No. My home. Mine and Reg's home. Complete and warm and comforting. The gentle smell of lavender and the tinny tickle of a music box. A victrola. A piano.

THE HOUSE THAT WASN'T THERE

Lonnie sipped his drink as Connor climbed the walls, angry at being back but conjured all the same. Lonnie chugged his glass while Blade bounced atop the counter. An entire bar and rooftop fit neatly in the treble and bass clefs of a stanza. A power outage on a downbeat. A fine, powdered rat killer chopped into tiny white lines of energy. A flashlight as a billy club.

I stood behind the bar and slid another rocks glass to the pianist. I leaned against the bar and cut another bump for the dancer.

"You know poison is usually the weapon of choice for women, right?" Blade said, still gyrating. He turned swiftly and bent into a body roll, presenting his ass, asking for worship, sniffing a line of white powder from the toe of his boots before rising——slowly——back up.

Lonnie downed his glass and sang, "Here's to the drinks..."

"But I guess that makes sense, you fucking faggot," Blade said as he thrust his cock toward my face. The sequined fabric of his jock caught the glow from the string lights nailed around the bar changing the blue to a dazzling, starlike shimmer of red and gold.

Lights flashed. Lightning flashed. Rain soaked through my clothes down to my skin. Wind howled to call its lichen brethren to arms, to bring them——full force——to the rooftop: mouths snarled, teeth bared, fur raised. Connor already looked like a shadow against the rumbling sky, a trash bag raincoat beat against his frame by the downpour. His skin puckered where it met water and breathed deep to take more in. To consume, to conduct, to dilute. The sky alit in his eyes as he glared at me. The flashlight in my hand felt cold and slick and heavy.

"Why are you even here?" he asked.

"Why are you even here?" Lonnie and Blade echoed from downstairs. I watched them choke and stroke and die beneath my feet. I saw their bodies slump over counters and keyboards, spread and melt beneath the thunderstorm.

"You are fucking crazy!" Connor said.

A flip of the wrist. A turn of a torch. I watched myself strike the base of the flashlight against Connor's forehead, saw him crumble to the concrete, face down in the collecting water. I wrapped his palm around a metal post and called the lightning to me.

Guilt is a sticky subject; honeyed and tempting——delicious, even, at times——and all consuming as it sinks the mind to its shallows. Fault is much more ambiguous. I leaned my forehead against the porcelain tile of my shower wall and felt the warm water cascade with a steaming hiss down my back. Each pulse from the shower head sent a stinging ray of needles, a swarm of bees, a crown of thorns to shiver down my body. I waited for the water to purify me. For it to turn to blood. Or wine.

I wanted a drink.

I wanted Reg to come home from work and slip behind me in the shower and cover me with his being and shield me from responsibilities.

Instead, I got Gerrie, perched on the toilet just outside the shower curtain, legs crossed at the knee and toe tapping impatiently against the tub.

"Why'd you do it?" she asked. Her tone evoked a therapist, a psychiatrist, a sociologist fully realized. It held not a dash of accusation. It was simply a calm and collected call to summon an unadulterated response.

"What did I do?" I cried. My face felt cold against the tile wall, blue and moribund, even as the heat activated sharply throughout the rest of me. "What did I do?"

Even I wasn't sure if my question was in earnest or admission. Even I wondered if it was in regret. Maybe it was everything. Maybe the question itself was all I was. I'd asked it so many times before on so many late mornings as my mind wandered back from its blackened state of the night before.

I wanted to cry. I needed that purge. I wanted to let go and expel all the negative energy that had been building like a dam within my chest. But I wasn't ready yet. The shower would have to do. I let the water trick my reddened cheeks, but my lips needed saline to be fooled.

"We've established the pain," Gerrie said. "We've established the death, even if we're still a bit off the mark. We already know the what. We need to get to the why. That's the only thing that's going to get you to the real heart of it all."

"I know why he did it," Blade said, admiring himself in the bathroom mirror, rocking his hips against the sink.

"We all do," Annie sighed and adjusted the towel on the rack, shaking out the wrinkles so it hung limp and smooth.

"Of course we do," Gerrie agreed. "But we need him to get there on his own."

"Fuck him," Connor said. "I was done, and he brought me back. I was gone, and he said no. Fuck him."

"Or we can watch him fuck Reg again," Lonnie laughed. "I think I liked that."

"We know he did," Blade chimed. A rhythmic music box. A broken record. A scratch on my memory.

I turned off the faucet and let the sudden wash of cold air career over me. My eyes were red and sore, as if they'd been held open to watch the most horrific of acts, as if my tear ducts had been overworked and cleared. It felt real. My face believed it real. Even if it wasn't, was there a difference?

"I have an idea," Cent called from the hallway. He appeared in the doorframe with a brush and gallon of paint in his hand. "How about we let him finish the map?"

18

As if solace could ever be found in plotted lines on a grid, I dragged the felt tip of my marker across the wall, noting the pocks and crevices formed from years of moving furniture or drunken bodies or banging headboards against the drywall as the potholes and cracked sidewalks from the roots of trees that paid no mind to the concrete of my map. I rounded corners with the casual grace of a stroll through the city I'd finally called home in the very moment Reg appeared. A rewritten history of belonging where Physicality met Being in the slapstick meet cute of fantasy. The streets came alive with the hubbub of hobnobbing socialites and corner vendors and homeless vets, all searching for something to ease the pain of existence. Time attempted to find its place on still used cobblestone, on splintered barstools, on laundry lines adorned with flattened, wind batted sheets with two holes cut out of them so the ghosts could see. Still, something did not seem quite right. Something crucial was missing.

The harlequin faces of Reg's masks stared up from the floor, each one begging for a voice to speak its tale. I found a hammer and nails. I held the smooth curve of whittled balsa wood in my palms, felt its heat seeping through the brilliantly hued face paint; a clown at the circus, a drag queen at the club. Its mouth curved in a slightly befuddled, mostly bemused smile, tinged with just a hint of anger. Like it was trying to decide between terror and lust. Like its entire life had just jumped the tracks and the confusion of new growth only compounded behind the eyes I was left to imagine in its hollow sockets. Lofty and enraged and on the precipice of laughter. I knew where it belonged.

Two swift taps of two small tacks and he was home: the northbound corner of This Street and That. Perched in the exact spot I'd collided with Reg all those years prior; hands full of tangled leashes, holes in hand me down suits, yipping dogs laughing as our bodies collapsed. A memory in a mask. A recollection on a map.

THE HOUSE THAT WASN'T THERE

I picked up another mask and studied its expression. This one formed in papier mâché; I saw Reg's hand in each brushstroke of color, each angle of each strip of newsprint, calm and collected and emoting a lifetime's worth of thoughts he was so good at keeping bottled inside. As if he'd implanted his hopes and fears into each color choice; like he'd imbued each carved smile with a molecule of his self, with the minutiae of whom he longed to be. These masks were worth more than any photo album. A spell of carved wood and scrap paper and crushed insects.

I remembered when Reg made that face. We'd been dating less than a month, and it was one of those rare mornings when the sun decided to hide behind the dark clouds of mourning but still sent his warmth out to embrace us in our unclothed dawn. We stepped, like fauns, from the bed to let our shaky legs find footing on the matted vampire carpet of his bedroom. I always joked that the flooring, filled with the wooden splinters of quickly carved faces, was out for blood. I trod to the window and flung open the curtains, forgetting we were in a ground level apartment, and Miss Peters——his landlord——got more than an eyeful.

She screamed; Reg cackled; and I spun around so swiftly I knocked a hardcover ledger from his bookshelf in the process. One toe found a plump slice of wood as the book crashed its spine to my other foot. And there I was, bare assed against the glass, hobbling from one foot to the other as Reg lost his mind in laughter. His face swirled in plum and lemon and mango.

I found that apartment on my rendering and nailed up the mask. I stood back to look, and, despite the one troubled spot, it was starting to make sense. I finally knew I was constructing a history——The True Story of Us——and, as such, both of us would be required.

"What about this one?"

Gerrie was on all fours, studying the intricacies in another of Reg's shrouds. Crimson downturned mouth and soft charcoal triangles around the eyes. A sturdy but defeated chisel in the cheeks. I collected it from the floor and sank my teeth into my lower lip, darkening it to match the visage.

"This was years later," I said. I told her about when I'd broken his heart for the second time. It was a minor thing, I'd thought. A white lie that severed a promise like reinforced glass, everything still in place but a little more difficult to see through. Sticky fingers and an open wallet and the silky sting of whiskey flowing down my gullet just one more time.

"You promised me you'd stop," he said. He was sitting in the dark of the steps as I'd stumbled through the front gate. He was waiting for confirmation of the tale he already knew by heart.

And I assured him I did.

It wasn't the action that broke him. It was the deceit. My fear——my fight in my flight. My inability to recognize the undying compassion he had for me.

I said, "It was the lack of trust I had in us that created this mask."

It was a part of our history. It found its home on the wall.

I shifted through our timeline in the city, combining his art and mine, eschewing chronology in favor of the impact of moments. A pink and lime green laugh memorialized the night we led a group of tourists on an impromptu voyage through the finer points of a downtrodden rail system. A lavender and chartreuse smirk denoted the time I brought home a thrift store painting to hang over our couch that he'd donated the month before we met. A tragedy face of black and white from when he'd been spending too much time with Carl from work and I'd threatened to move out because my insecurity was always wrapped in rage. I placed them throughout the map as their stories began to pulse like heartbeats, populating the city, bringing it to life.

"Keep going," Annie urged me onward. "You're almost there."

Reg was a precocious child. His father had told me as much. Always ready with a song or a dance or a masquerade meant to reveal more than it hid. Growing up, that had been his way of expressing pain or longing or desire or joy. Grown up, the company man had grown more reserved in his expressions, but he had not lost them. He simply transferred them to wood or paper. He coaxed them out of a solid mass, or built them, strip by strip from nothing. Then he locked them there for the future to discover.

I picked up another mask, and I told another story. It was so easy. I had memorized every line of Reg's face, every twinge and tickle of his every muscle as he cycled through his worlds of happiness and pain. I knew every aspect of every countenance he wore. I had studied his face like a map, and it had revealed to me the hidden treasures of what went on inside his mind.

"What's the story behind this one?" Lonnie asked.

The mask had a morose shade of blue emblazoned across its skin, fractured by maroon starbursts that sprung from the eyes. Its lips were held slightly apart, as if it were waiting to speak, yearning to receive. Its nose was longer, straighter than the others. It was the only mask Reg ever made outside of his own image; the only one he'd made for me.

We had just moved into our apartment together. He'd presented it with little fanfare as a housewarming gift: the humble artist both proud and humiliated by his craft.

"I've always thought you carried the stars in your eyes," he'd told me, smiling and deflecting as if the Muse had taken over his body to create and left him little choice but to construct.

I'd stared at it for weeks, appreciating the intricacies of the carving, noting the subtle lines in the parched, thin lips, the stippling along the jawline. I'd pondered aloud why he'd chosen a shade of blue so saturnine, and he'd sighed: "There's something about you that's so remarkably close to death." And I'd laughed, and he'd said, "I'm not so sure that's a bad thing, though. I'm still figuring out where it all falls."

"I know exactly where I'm falling," I said, and he blushed.

"If nothing else, it makes you interesting. And color me thoroughly intrigued."

As he kissed me, I felt suddenly like a wooden boy come to life.

I hung the mask over our first apartment. Over the representation of our first apartment on a map. Above a markered line on a red wall covered with apocryphal faces held tight by tiny nails. It was all just facade. The map, the mask, the emotions behind it. All of it was a stand in, a wannabe actor holding the place until the real action was ready and willing and able to begin. I felt that way too often in my life. Like I was peering down from the edge of a cliff and waiting, just waiting, for something real to happen. Like Connor on a roof or Blade on a bar. Like Gerrie at her window or Annie on the church steps.

"We're losing him," Annie cried.

"He's been fucking lost," Connor moaned. "But fine." He kicked a mask across the floor and rolled his eyes as it spun gently at my feet. "Tell us about this one."

❧

People have a long history of hiding who they truly are. Whether sacred or profane, for anonymity or in the service of connection, even our earliest cultures donned masks. Wooden or metallic or ceramic. Beautiful or featureless or grotesque. False faces designed to emote——or alter an emotion——when the DNA below just couldn't be bothered or coaxed or enough.

I watched the piece swirl at my feet; centripetal force rocked its uneven features through a seesaw of yes and no and maybe. The flat bridge of its nose was caked in white, thick and abnormal, like sunscreen applied by an over caring mother and baked in by the harsh rays of the closest star around. Its cheeks were a kaleidoscope of vining neon tones like hands held in the air over the rollercoaster drop; it spoke through cotton candy lips that were sweet and sticky and dew kissed. I held it in my hands. An object in motion continuing despite the unbalanced force of my grasp.

"Right when summer started this year," I said, "just after spring had sent its rains to wipe up the spillage of the plants' software yellow bloom, a little carnival was flung up in an empty parking lot over on the outskirts of the city. Close enough to the edge for the suburban folks to feel safe venturing in and far enough out for the city dwellers to think they were headed for a real adventure. Reg dragged me out of bed early one Sunday morning. No. I called the cab and woke him up. Either way, we ended up standing on this hot asphalt and watching all these kids who had convinced their parents that carnies were closer to God than any church could be as they ran amok around the clowns and the bagged up goldfish and the funnel cakes."

My ghosts sat cross legged on the floor at my feet, fists perched to hold up their chins, and leaned in as they imagined the heat of the bodies melting in the grease paint, the drip of the oil from the tips of deep fried corndogs. They mimed the joyful faces of teenagers hell bent on winning stuffed animals for the girlfriends they would leave for a drunken night with their college roommates. They swooned at the gut punch of rides meant to illicit elation through fear induced adrenaline.

"Reg had been working so hard, vying for some position that was rumored to be coming open at his office, putting in long hours and killing the cartilage in his knuckles as he typed. He needed, more than anyone I knew, a day to shake all of that off and return to him some sense of lost boy wonder. The kind that only comes from the freedom felt in flying. The broken chains of maybe-life's-not-all-about-production."

THE HOUSE THAT WASN'T THERE

I fixed the mask to the wall, just beyond the reaches of where the lines intercepted. I would draw them later, but even in their absence, the connections were there. Home from work, Reg swept quietly into the room, sat gently on the edge of the bed, and leaned back to admire the marrying of our work across the wall. My ghosts were quiet as I spoke directly to him.

"Do you remember how much you laughed behind the wheel of that purple bumper car? The one flecked in gold glitter with worn out tires that always pulled to the right?" He nodded, and I smiled. "You looked happier than I could remember seeing you in months. Like you'd finally figured out how to be in the moment and exhale out all the burdens and the negativity and the impossibilities of the facts and figures you spent your days attempting to balance. And I remember laughing too. I laughed at the inherent bliss always bubbling beneath the tally of days spent stressed out and fighting for equal footing. At finally knowing how close happiness always was to us if we simply took the time to be there in it. I remember how close to you I felt as we careened into one another with those rubber barriers bouncing us back. There was something in that: the sheer force with which we rebounded and tried again to merge, only to be knocked off kilter again and again and again. I knew——I could see it in your face——at that moment, neither of us wanted the ride to end."

Reg leaned back across the mattress and placed his hands beneath his head, staring at the ceiling in fond remembrance, making lions out of water spots, forming joy to replace what was. I sat beside him and smirked as I studied his body, trying to lock into place the way his slacks clung to his hips, every line and wrinkle in his skin.

"We went to that fortune teller whose accent was somewhere between Southern California and Medieval Farce, and she charged us fifteen bucks apiece to spread out tarot cards on that phases of the moon fabric that was ragged at the edges since it was never properly hemmed. She flipped over these cards and hemmed and hawed at the illustrations, giving us some elaborate Shakespearean story about finding true love and overcoming its struggles once she noticed our shoulders pressed against one another's. If she'd really been psychic, she'd have known that you had a deeper understanding of those cards than she could ever feign to, but you let her divine away. I nodded, and you ooh'ed and ahh'ed as a tiny smirk quivered in your lower lip. We put on a show for her even though it was supposed to be the other way around. Then, when we got back outside and the sun glistened like stardust across your sweat dappled forehead, you just said, 'Pentacles are about finance and work, not about love,' and we doubled over in a witch like cackle right there in the middle of that steady stream of merry-making adults and sticky fingered children."

Masks were worn by the devout to honor their gods. To create a visage that was pleasing to the rose colored iris of their creator. As if the imperfections of the human form——the one created by the gods themselves——should be corrected in order to enter their sight, should be purged by shield to enter the sites deemed theirs and holy. Masks were at the very core of the human attempt to one up God.

"I pulled you off to the side, right next to the sun faded yellow and red striping of the ring toss tent, and I kissed the corner of your mouth as you continued to laugh at our fortunes. 'I truly do love you,' I said, and you told me you loved me too. I congratulated myself on maintaining my sobriety, and I thanked you for your part in it. And then, right there in the middle of all that ruckus, swimming in the humidity of burning sugar and jostling bodies, I told you there was no way I could ever imagine my life without you. I asked you to marry me."

Masks were worn by the dead to idealize their lives. To serve as a reminder of the person before the worms and decay could sweep them away. Before we had the means and the makeup counter to paint them back to life. Masks were the remnant of a soul sent out into the universe. A notice of happier times, even in the midst of despair.

It was a quick question, so in the moment, I didn't even have a ring. But I meant it. In that moment, with that impulse, it was everything in my world.

"You told me no," I said as Reg kept his eyes trained on the ceiling: a daydream in a lion's den. "Your face fell serious, but you still had that little bit of a spark in your eye. You told me you still wanted to be with me, that you loved waking up next to me——whenever we had the chance to—— and that you'd loved all the time we had had together. You said making plans for a forever was not something you could do right then. You told me that you were happy taking it day by day, and that you wished for a million more days to come."

Masks were worn by the hunters of African Tribes to confuse the predators who were out hunting them. They placed them on backward, looking out from the back of the head. Someone to watch their six. A bit of misdirection to leave the big cats prowling and pacing in the brush, attempting to remain hidden in the dusty hues of the bleached land. To provide a hint of safety; an easy out.

"And then you went and made plans for forever, anyway," I said, and my ghosts lurched forward.

No.

"Of course I told you I understood," I said, and Reg smiled.

He propped his head up on his right hand and twisted his body to lean into me. His mouth snarled into a bow of empathetic concern.

I saw him clearly. All those moments stuck in the corner of the bar, contained within himself, as I swallowed hard to spread out. All those forced smiles that seemed so obvious now from behind their masks.

"I guess I did understand. Honestly," I said. I said "honestly" as much to Reg as to my ghosts. I said "honestly" to make myself believe it. "But, if we're being honest, that was the first time you broke my heart."

"What was the second time?" Gerrie asked from her nest on the floor.

The second time?

"Yes," Annie said. "Let's get to that."

A loud pounding shook from the front door, down the hallway, and into the bedroom. The masks rocked across the wall, shaking their heads as their hollow eyes peered into me, wide and afraid, all of them urging me to hide.

"We need you to open up, Mr. Preston!"

I recognized the voice of the cop with the blonde hair in the ponytail. I recognized the demand, and I wanted more than anything to ignore it. Reg climbed to his feet and retrieved the final mask from the floor. He overlooked the knocking that echoed through the room and presented the mask to me like a birthday gift, like a wedding ring.

"What about this one?" he asked.

The mask was unfinished. Not a drop of paint had touched the smooth curves of its wood. A half carved nose reflected the gentle turn of a lower lip. An expression just beginning to form. A being just starting out. Or else one ended before it could be realized, caught midgesture and unsure whether it was dawning or resolving, solving something or opening up more questions.

I looked at the map on the wall. I looked to where the lines lost their meaning——the difficult part——the space that refused to exist. I saw it suddenly through new eyes. Placing the mask on the pillow, I fled from the room, slalomed down the long hall, and collapsed against the door. With Reg at my heels and my ghosts behind me, I opened the door and stepped out. The officers stood aside and held out their arms to usher me onward. I descended the stairs two at a time, in bounds!, in leaps!, as men in khaki trench coats and yellow brown trilbies joined in the parade. I flew through the gate in leaps and bounds(!) as officers in blue with ponytails and accusing yet understanding faces fell into pursuit.

I knew how to finish my map.

I understood, finally, where I needed to go.

19

THE HOUSE WAS COLD, even at the start of autumn, as the long days of sunlight bore their heat against its robin egg siding, and the slate grey shutters did little to shield the window glass from the rays. It sat there, halfway up the block, like a perfectly ordinary piece of architecture, benign and unremarkable, waiting for something else to bring it to life. The perfect mask for what lay between its walls.

Can houses hold stories? Hallways, like the spine of a book, opened into great rooms filled with tales of harrowing discoveries and epic disasters. Journeys sank through the floorboards as if they were never really there to begin with, as if their destinations were always just the broken figment of a dream, some flight of fancy to pass the heat addled summer nights. This was the place on the map where it happened, the part I couldn't bring myself to draw.

The crowd was silent behind me, quivering with a sullied anticipation as if, on a Tuesday morning, the one-two punch——the kindest delivery of pain——could bring about enlightenment.

The house had always been a part of me, though it had taken many forms in its child mind protestations of ever becoming too real. A protective barrier; a callous onlooker. I'd first found it as a child, but it looked different then. And now it was here. Now it was here.

"Well, we're here," Connor said.

"What happens now?" Lonnie asked.

"That's up to him," Annie answered.

The cops——I could see them out of the corner of my eye——were twirling their batons and slapping them against their palms as they waited for an answer. They counted the trilbies in an accusatory manner. They looked questioningly at the hazy apparitions left in my wake. And Reg, somewhere lost in the gathering mass, held his breath and watched patiently. I felt his expectant eyes on me. I felt the precipice of peace.

"Do you know why you brought us here?" Gerrie asked. Her voice was calm and gentle. She held my hand as I nodded. She walked with me as I crossed the street——the congregation at our heels——to stand beneath the ginkgo trees that lined the sidewalk and peer into the hollow eyes of the house.

"When I was little," I said, "I used to imagine living in the city. In a big house painted the blue of some fantastical sky with an iron gate to act as a protective moat and rooms that folded in on each other with secret passageways to faraway lands. Like the great manors from the books I would read. Like an escape route from my life."

The group hummed around me, teeming in the street. They were locusts celebrating the warming of the rising sun. Annie grabbed my other hand as if to urge me onward. My phone vibrated in my pocket to alert me of a missed call, a voicemail. The voicemail.

"It became a sanctuary in my mind: one I would retreat to whenever my father cracked his beer and snapped his belt against his palm. Or my mother swung through one of her impishly selfish moods which she insisted were meant to make me stronger. As if a boy of seven needed nothing more than to be taught to be tough instead of being shown compassion. As if I were a burden placed upon her by her god, something sent to test her faith, and not the product of her limited carnal desires. It was obvious my parents never wanted kids. So, I created a new home I could run to. One where I could draw on the walls, shove my feet into oversized but practical heels, and whisper my secrets into understanding ears without fear of repercussion."

Gerrie squeezed my elbow, and Annie ran her hand up and down the crook of my arm. They sighed with me and released their grasp as I stepped apprehensively across the sidewalk. I hesitated briefly then clasped my hands around the wrought iron fencing, not quite ready to open the gate. The metal sent an icy chill through me, jolting from my palms into my spine. I felt my knees go weak and turned to lean against the posts for stability. A sea of sympathetic eyes looked back at me. A history lesson in the garden of me, they filled the streets with the casual chaos of memory. They blocked the traffic with no regard.

"This house——the house in my mind——became the place that I learned myself. I would sit on the back porch, more of a stoop really, while my dad and my mom raged on inside, and I'd draw room after room of the place, connecting them in new and unexpected ways, rearranging them whenever I saw fit or for however best they continued the narrative I was creating in my head. I was writing the story where I felt loved and wanted and no one tried to confront me with anything abhorrent. Myopic of me, I know. But sitting there, drawing those rooms, watching them connect and grow and mean something more than anything I was witnessing around me: I think that's where my love of maps came into being."

The crowd murmured in agreement. A wave of nodding heads and *that makes sense* and *my house was a castle* and *tell us what happens next.*

"By the time I was eleven, the house had taken on a new purpose. Rooms that once smelled of lilac turned musty and dank. Stairwells that led to majestic gardens descended instead to desolate caverns littered with empty chairs and lonely mirrors. It was as if my synapses had stopped firing to connect the spaces of my imagination. My once retreat had become a prison. And so I thought, if the place was destined to become forgotten, I could fill it with all the things I didn't want to remember."

The gate slowly creaked open, and the front door swung inward. I could hear the echoes of angry voices waft from the foyer, the merriment of parties from the other room spill across the welcome mat. Everything that had hurt me was just beyond the thin walls that bowed and pulsed to keep it all contained.

"My sixth grade Phys. Ed. teacher who laughed at me alongside all my classmates when I couldn't complete ten push ups and didn't want to take my shirt off in the locker room."

A flurry of movement sprang forth from the center of the crowd behind me as a man ricocheted forward. He paused to face me and nodded, removing his tan trilby and clutching it at his chest before walking silently into the house.

"The pastor at the Baptist Church who pulled my mother aside one Sunday after service to tell her he was worried that I had a demon inside of me. Told her I needed to 'find God' and then told me the best place to find Him was behind his zipper."

Another man in another trench coat trod inside, still assuming he walked on water, even in the darkest recesses of my mind.

"And Preston, my first boyfriend, once he'd decided his adventure was over. Or Rafe, the guy I met my freshman year of college who loved me so much, but I just couldn't love him back. Or William, who slipped Rohypnol into my flask of whiskey at that party before the Summer Solstice. Or Paul, whom I liked——so much——but who just never really got over his own ex."

I am not a reliable narrator.

Were they trench coats or lab coats? Did their faces interchange and break apart as much as it seemed? Did my friends relish in my voice as much as they did in my memory? Or were they always simply me?

If I am the one to remember and record them, does it really even matter?

Or

If I am the only one to survive, who will be there to record me?

Like a house erased from memory. A memory trapped. Why am I the one who's left? And once I'm written down, will I disappear as well?

One by one, the men entered the house. The herd thinned in the street. Each painful memory stopped by to say hello as if only to prepare me for the next one or the next one, for the hundreds yet to come. They hung their hats on the rack by the door. They closeted their trench coats. They disappeared into the darker recesses of the house to make way for something greater. I named them all as the house took them in. I claimed them all and waited to be devoured.

The house grew hungry. The house that wasn't there. The house that had a temper. It pretended to be unmoved as it sat there on the street, basking in the glittering light of a still rising sun, doing nothing as its shadow launched westward and clawed at the horizon, chasing the night. It feigned stoicism. But the house had a temper, and I knew it wanted blood. I did what I could to satiate its desires, but in the end, I found, only mine would do.

Annie and Gerrie smiled knowingly at each other. Their mouths curved upward, but there was no sense of joy in their faces, only the resolute understanding of confrontation assuaged by newfound perception. Lonnie's fingers tickled the air as if he were still at his piano. Cent eyed the foundation of the house looking for fissures he could mend. Blade continued to rock on his heels, in his thong, on the sidewalk. And Connor twisted his fingers together and tapped his toes against the dying remnants of a dandelion still hanging on in a crack.

THE HOUSE THAT WASN'T THERE

"Eventually the house wanted everyone," I said. "It was no longer satisfied with only my past. It craved my present. It demanded my future. From men whose bodies and casual cockiness I was jealous of"——and with that, Blade danced inside——"to people who reminded me what I was so close to becoming." Lonnie disappeared through the doorframe. "From those who confronted and disturbed my way of life"——Connor rolled his eyes in time with his exaggerated exit——"to casual acquaintances who began to sense that something was off in my stories."

Cent shook my hand before ascending the short steps to the front door. He knocked twice by the hinges and tested the doorbell before stepping forward to his fate.

"And then there were the people who loved me," I said. "The ones who knew the truth or were dangerously close to figuring it out. The women who had tasked themselves with helping me find acceptance somewhere hidden in the rubble of the basement. The ones I threw away instead of allowing in too deep."

Gerrie wrapped her arms around my neck, and Annie placed her hand on my shoulder. Tears brimmed in both of their eyes, and their wet, glossy pupils caught the glow of the morning.

"We love you, Howard," Gerrie smiled.

"You're almost there," Annie said. "You're so very close."

"You can forget your guilt once you've faced it," Gerrie said. "I know it's so very hard to face."

Officer Ponytail and her partner tipped their hats and twirled their batons. My sponsor and the quiet girl who lived above me when I could no longer take this house followed the police inside.

They closed the door behind them, and I stared at the ceramic numbers——1349——nailed just below the window. Birds were chirping their wake up calls from the nearby telephone lines. People yawned inside their apartments. My phone, in my pocket, vibrated once more to alert me of a message. The voicemail.

But there was only me and Reg on the street. He took my hand, and I closed my eyes to stop my own tears from falling.

"This is where we lived when I asked you to marry me," I said. "I asked you to marry me, and you said you'd rather die."

"I didn't say that."

"You didn't say that, but that's just what you did."

Reg smiled at me. The close lipped grin he got whenever he was trying to make me feel better. The one he knew could always win me over. His thumb slipped between our hands to caress the callouses on my palm, to trace the frayed and fractured love line. I could smell the intoxicating scent of him: musk and cedar and a soft floral overtone. It lingered in the air like sweat on a pillow, a heady reminder of passionate nights and lazy afternoons.

"I wasn't trying to leave you," he said. He said it, and I wanted to believe him. "I was trying to escape myself. Check your voicemail."

My phone buzzed once more in my pocket, an angry rumbling against my thigh. I pulled it out and stared at the screen. Reg was on the line, and my heart sank as I ended the call.

It was an early morning several months back, or years maybe——time worked funny here——and I'd spent the night roaming the city, creating new pathways in my mind, mapping them against the common understanding of what our town meant. I'd promised Reg I'd be home before sunrise, but I could already feel the great star beginning to break through the clouds as it rounded the horizon and trudged on——selfish, or a slave to time, who's to say?——marching forward with no mind to the lives it was affecting below.

Things had not been bad between us. We had not been fighting. But we had settled into a routine, and complacency was beginning to take its toll. To break it, I had opted for bold and rash decisions, walks through the darker alleyways on the darkest nights, a job in a bar, and last minute excursions to the circus. Reg, the staid and true warrior at my side, had thrown himself into work, ticking off numerical values as something he could control. I should have noticed something was off.

"You can't blame yourself."

I didn't answer when he called. We weren't fighting, but Reg had a tendency to get aggravated when things didn't align with his schedule. Well, not *his* schedule, but the agreed upon plan. He didn't seem to understand that I had a plan too. He couldn't see that when I asked him to be mine——forever——I was lining up our lives, taking inventory and deciding what was most important. And he won every time. I was hurt that the thought of being with me distressed him so much he had had to run as far away as possible.

"That's not what happened," Reg said. "You know better than that. I loved you."

"Then why did you leave?!"

He sighed and ran his hand over the gate. He let his eyes trace along the frame of the house. He did everything except look at me.

"Why wouldn't you marry me?" I asked. "Why did you get so scared you had to leave?"

The silence was deafening. Even the birds had stopped singing. The house held its breath and tried its best to suppress the pounding beat of its heart. My ghosts filled the windows as eager, as desperate as I was for an answer. Finally, Reg spoke:

"It was a long time coming," he said. "I couldn't do that to you. That's why I said no. I saw a future you couldn't even dream of existing. Not yet. It was my destiny, and I couldn't let it be yours. Check your voicemail."

I was only a few miles from home as the sun crested its first lower high rise on the edge of the city. I walked swiftly. If I could just make it home before he had to leave for work, show him I was sober, tell him I'd just lost track of time, he would understand. My phone, in my pocket, alerted me of a message. I broke into a jog.

"I need you to remember me the way you loved me. I need you to believe I stayed longer because of you. I need you to not consider only the ending when you consider the all of me. Check your voicemail."

Morning occurred quickly around me. Lights flicked on like camera flashbulbs in bedroom windows. Dogs scratched at wooden doors and begged to be let outside. Pancakes sizzled on griddles, and people everywhere prayed for just one more minute.

I stopped suddenly when I rounded the block to our house. Police cars lined the street. A small crowd of women in fuzzy slippers, men in ragged robes, and yawning souls in tattered rock-n-roll tees had gathered, mesmerized by the twirling lights of the sirens. Everyone on the block was called forth to a macabre sense of misery. It was all around us. It was the only time we paid attention.

I made my way slowly through the crowd, scanning the faces for one that looked like Reg, attempting to figure out what was going on. My heart leapt into my throat, and I held my breath to try to quell its thumping. By the time I reached the front of the crowd, I found the squad cars trained on my door. Officers politely kept the mob at bay; shadows moved in the third story window.

"Excuse me. I live here," I said.

The officer had kind eyes and blonde hair, pulled back into a casual and efficient ponytail. I could tell her expressionless face wanted to give a sympathetic smile, to let me know everything was going to be okay, but years of this had hardened her. Would harden me.

"Where do you live, sir?"

"Thirteen forty-nine. Unit three."

Her face dropped. Her eyes searched the pavement for guidance.

"Please, sir. Come with me."

She led me between two police cars as the crowd's whispering grew to a deafening gust of wind. My heart pulsed with the rotating lights atop the cars, red and then blue and then red. She asked me questions: who I was, who I lived with, the nature of our relationship. Time was frozen. Even the sun had ceased its westward ascent. Time was indefinite. A thousand days and nights collapsed to the ground at my feet.

"We received a call at 7:57 this morning," she said. Three minutes after Reg called me. Three minutes after I hit ignore.

"Reginald King, the resident at 1349 Southport, Unit 3, informed the answering officer of his plan to end his own life."

❧

No.

❧

Yes.

❧

The street collapsed around me. All that was solid gave way, even as the air became thick. Suffocating. Shaking, I pulled my phone from my pocket. I saw his name flash across my screen. Saw his face smiling joyfully back at me.

"He called it in?" I asked.

"He didn't want you to find him," she said.

"I didn't want you to find me," he said.

"He called it in." My words caught in my throat, grated across my tongue as I attempted to push them out. "Did you——make it in time?"

She bit her lip. Her eyes searched mine with compassion.

"We did not."

I fell to the sidewalk, sobbing. The white seeded remnants of a dandelion tricked into blooming late broke free of the pistil and floated off like ghosts in my tear drenched sight. The officer placed a blanket around my shoulders. She crouched down and left her hand by my neck.

"Is there someone we can call?" she asked.

I pulled up my phone. I held it to my ear. I listened to the voicemail.

"Hi, Love." Reg's voice was clear. Determined. Unmistaken. "This is not how I expected to do this. I've wanted so many great things for us. But, for a while now, things have not been right. For a long time. And it's not you, and it's not us, and it's not your schedule or our home or any of the other excuses and reasonings we've hashed out time and again. It's just time. It's just too late. It's just a thing I have to do. It's not something I can really explain, but I'm trying because it's important. Because you're important. But most importantly, I need you to know that it's not your fault. You were a beacon. Drunk or sober. I thought we could be everything, but it wasn't enough. And I'm not happy. But I will be. Soon. Please know that I love you. Please remember that I loved you."

I wanted to collapse again. Like I was feeling it for the first time. Like I would feel it for the first time every time, always, forever. Reg tilted his head as he looked at me. There was no pain in his eyes. Mine held enough for the both of us.

"I still don't know how you did it," I said. "Drugs, or knives, or jumping. I've imagined it a hundred different ways. But I was always too afraid to ask."

"Does it really matter?"

"I guess not."

Reg took my hand one more time. He squeezed it tightly, and looked solemnly, lovingly into my eyes. He was patient, waiting for the blur of salt tears to clean my irises, to give me one more chance to fully take him in, to give me enough time so I could memorize every surface. As he turned to open the gate I cried, "Let me go with you."

"You can't," he said. "Not yet."

And I knew he was right. He walked slowly up the steps. His hand clutched the cold doorknob, and, without looking back, he said, "You have another message."

The city fizzed with the quiet exuberance of a renaissance painting, caught midaction in the center of a party where everyone was royalty, where every soul was god. But there was only me. Not fooled by the debaucherous heat of the concrete nights, flocks of crows began their preparations to seek out warmer climes even as the doves angled to regain their control of the streets. And there was only me. Somewhere, halfway up the block, a house sat brazenly against the skyline. It felt its temper reside. It imagined its halls as once again great, and soft, and flowing.

I exhaled as much of my fear as I could manage into the sky. I saw the blinking light next to Reg's name on my phone screen. I finally had the courage to hit play.

"I would have said yes," he said. "I wanted——more than anything——to be enough for you. The problem is, I wasn't enough for myself. And that is not your fault. That's no one's fault. It was my destiny."

Except that didn't happen. I looked down at the voicemail I'd refused to hear, I'd refused to delete. And it was alone. And I was alone.

In my sorrow, I'd become a haunted house. A looming amalgamation of memories forced into inconsistencies. Specters filled my vision until they outnumbered the living. Until I became one of them. Stuck in a cycle of reliving every trauma with no means to acknowledge what it was. I became a repetitive ghost, hollowed through until nothing but the evocation remained. I called it a calling forth, a summoning. But inside——the inside that wasn't there——I knew better. I knew my body had long forgotten how to contain me, and I spilled out——oceanic and cold——until I could no longer determine where my thoughts were formed. I emptied until I needed masks to regain my features.

THE HOUSE THAT WASN'T THERE

Gerrie would tell me that Jean-Paul Sartre said, "What is life but an unpleasant interruption to a peaceful nonexistence." That Frederick Nietzsche urged us "to die proudly when it is no longer possible to live proudly." Annie would check in more regularly to make sure I hadn't relapsed. And I would travel through my days in a hollowed haze of remembrance, desperately trying to capture the ghost I wanted to materialize until he was all that was left of me. I would try to hear them until they got too close to my fantasy and my mind would force their exit. I hoped they'd still be there when I returned from my grief, but all I really knew was the leaving.

And then suddenly, on a Tuesday morning, something remarkable finally happened. In the terrorizing face of death, I realized that I had learned to live. That I could want to even as he did not. Reg would forever be a part of me. I could peacefully reside in that knowledge. I could forever lie down with him.

My eyes glazed as they traced along the spiderwebbing of the wrought iron fence, up the robin egg blue siding, passed the cool grey shutters. Reg peered at me from a third story window. His chin quivered, despite his winning smile. Gently, he raised his hand to wave at me. To finally say goodbye.

"Are you ready to go home?" Gerrie asked, slipping her fingers into mine for comfort. "I can help you unpack the new place. If you're ready."

The frog-footed leaves of the ginkgo trees fluttered in the morning breeze, slipping, just so, to reveal the house. The house that would always be there. The house that held his final moments. But those moments weren't mine to know; they were his alone. They belonged to him and the house. Instead, I had his life inside of me. And it was filled with Whats and Ifs.

ACKNOWLEDGMENTS

Where to begin? I suppose where I began.

So much gratitude and heartfelt applause goes to my parents—both birth and married in—for their unwavering support of my artistic and writing pursuits. Ever since I was a child, hiding under the bleachers of my brother's baseball game with a notebook and a pen, you've endorsed and believed in me. So, to Melissa, Michael, Harriet, and Alan: thank you does not begin to cover it.

To my siblings—Evan, Kristy, and Brittany—for showing me the different perspectives which allow my characters to be more than just me.

To Sean. Thank you for putting up with my ramblings, and my edits, and my walk-throughs and re-examinations as I pushed through this work.

To J. Thank you for pushing me, for encouraging me, and for making me believe I could continue to do this.

To Carol: my kindred spirit of struggle and grief. Talking through our processes, how they align and differ, made this work so much richer. I hope it brings you some comfort.

To Mark Booth, Eileen Favorite, Nathanaël, Matthew Goulish, Romi Crawford, and all the other instructors and mentors at SAIC who encouraged me to push myself and my writing, who introduced me to those greats who played with language in a way which made me feel less alone. I can never repay the guidance you've provided.

To Lance Umenhofer, Drew Holden, and the amazing folks at April Gloaming Publishing for believing in this book and guiding it toward realization. I am so honored to be a part of your "southern holler."

And, finally, to Clay. Wherever your energies may be, I hope you understood how important you were, how many lives you'd touched, and just how long your name will continue to sound from those people's lips. You are loved, and you are missed.

If you or someone you know is struggling with depression or thoughts of suicide, there is help.

Please call the 988 Suicide and Crisis Lifeline. Available 24 hours a day. Dial "988" from any US-based phone line.

AUTHOR BIO

Andrew Forrest Baker writes southern gothic lit which explores the edges of queerness, philosophy, faith, and magic. He received a BFA in Writing from the School of the Art Institute of Chicago before returning to his home state of Georgia to allow the mysterious clash of nature and modernity to seep into his bones and his work. He resides in Atlanta with his partner, his garden, and their hound dogs.

9 781953 932136